T0279180

Dashed

Also by Amanda Quain

Accomplished

Ghosted

AMANDA QUAIN

Dashed

A Margaret Dashwood Novel

WEDNESDAY BOOKS
NEW YORK

First published in the United States by Wednesday Books, an imprint of St. Martin's Publishing Group

DASHED. Copyright © 2024 by Amanda Quain. All rights reserved. Printed in the United States of America. For information, address St. Martin's Publishing Group, 120 Broadway, New York, NY 10271.

www.wednesdaybooks.com

Title page art: cruiser © Potapenko/Getty Images; palm trees and dock © VectorUp/Getty Images; landscape © Svetlana Aganina/Getty Images

The Library of Congress Cataloging-in-Publication Data is available upon request.

ISBN 978-1-250-90753-0 (hardcover)
ISBN 978-1-250-90751-6 (ebook)

Our books may be purchased in bulk for promotional, educational, or business use. Please contact your local bookseller or the Macmillan Corporate and Premium Sales Department at 1-800-221-7945, extension 5442, or by email at MacmillanSpecialMarkets@macmillan.com.

First Edition: 2024

1   3   5   7   9   10   8   6   4   2

For Kathleen, and all the books we read over and over again—may this one join their ranks.

I wish, as well as everybody else, to be perfectly happy;
but, like everybody else, it must be in my own way.

—Jane Austen, *Sense and Sensibility*

Dashed

CHAPTER ONE

Before my sister Marianne showed up and threw all of our worlds into a giant tailspin, I'd been on the cusp of having the best summer ever. But my life always went haywire when Marianne showed up, and today was no exception.

In my defense, I didn't think she would follow us onto a *cruise ship*.

"Dashwoods!" I heard my sister before I saw her. Honestly, it kind of felt like I was in a horror movie, the way my hair stood up on the back of my neck, the drop in my stomach that told me *exactly* what I'd see when I turned around. "And Edward, I guess! Hey!"

"Oh my God." Next to me, my oldest sister, Elinor, froze in her place, hands clenched around the passports she was about to distribute to me and her husband, Edward. We were standing just inside the entrance to the Miami cruise terminal, a gigantic mosh pit of security lines and bag scans. It had been stressful enough making our way through the chaos of shouted instructions and ten thousand percent humidity. Now . . . "That's not—"

"Surprise!" Before I could even brace myself, my middlest sister, Marianne, jumped on me and Elinor from behind, pulling us into a gigantic squish of a hug. "I'm in Florida!"

"Marianne. Hi." Elinor got her composure together with a speed I did my best to copy, untangling herself from Marianne's tanned and toned arms and turning around to face her. "What are you doing here?" A great question. Marianne and her boyfriend, Brandon, lived in New Orleans, and I didn't know *that* much about the geography of the South, but I knew that wasn't, like, a super-easy hop, skip, and a jump away. Was she here to see us off or something? Mom had thrown a big bon voyage party for Elinor, Edward, and me back in New Jersey, and Marianne and Brandon were supposed to come up for that, but they'd backed out at the last minute.

If this was some sort of weird last-ditch effort to make up for it, fine. But I hoped it wouldn't take long, because I was one gangway and a set of sliding glass doors away from the best summer of my entire life, and I wanted to get it started as quickly as possible.

"I haven't seen you since Christmas, and *that's* the first thing you ask? Damn, Elinor." Marianne laughed. She had a gigantic suitcase with her, which was weird. And no Brandon, which was even weirder. The two of them were literally always together. Not that I was complaining. These days, Brandon was a lot easier to talk to than my sister. "Are you sure you want to ruin the big surprise that quickly?"

"Surprise?" Edward's eyes were wide behind his horn-rimmed glasses. "What kind of surprise?"

Marianne held her bracelet-clad arms out wide to the side, almost hitting a visored and Hawaiian-shirted tourist in the process. "I'm coming with you!"

And as she grinned at us in the middle of the terminal walkway, I watched my summer crumble away, like a sandcastle that had been hit by a gigantic, unstoppable wave.

"You—you are?" I asked. We just kept repeating ourselves, the three of us, three people who were supposed to be going on the adventure of a lifetime and had just been saddled with the one person who could mess with it. "What about Brandon?"

My sister's face, which had been all bright and smiling, sunshine beaming out of her, fell hard and fast.

"Oh, right." She adjusted her tote bag on her shoulder, pulled her suitcase a little closer. "Brandon and I broke up."

What the *actual* hell?

As we all stared, I realized Marianne was crying behind her sunglasses. She was trying to hide it with a painted-on smile, but tears slipped out past the gigantic heart-shaped frames that still weren't big enough to hide her heartbreak.

Elinor, Edward, and I were frozen in place in front of Marianne, even as our fellow cruisers streamed around us, pushing and shouting to one another. Brandon and Marianne were, in my mind, an immovable force. Theirs was the sort of love that moved mountains, at least according to my sister. And now what—it was just over?

And then I remembered what happened the last time Marianne was heartbroken. Without a great romance to keep her together.

Dread filled my chest, thick and crushing.

⚓

I'D built my life on order and dependence, ever since That Year.

You couldn't get hurt if you knew when things were coming, if they were planned for. But I'd never planned for this. For the end of Marianne and Brandon, for the idea that Brandon might leave our family, even though he had been part of it forever.

As Elinor pulled Marianne into her arms, murmuring into her ear while throwing a panicked look toward Edward over her shoulder, I worried. As Edward struggled to pull Marianne's suitcase behind him as well as his own while on the phone with someone at the ship to figure out our new arrival, I worried. And as we stood in what I hoped would be the last line of the day, waiting to board the ship, I worried.

Because Marianne had one major skill, these days, and it was making my life harder.

She didn't mean to. I assumed she didn't mean to, anyway. But my sister was a tornado of chaos and energy, an actual hurricane of a human. And I'd been super into that once. When I was younger, and I'd prided myself on being just like Marianne.

But then we'd gotten so badly, terribly hurt, and I'd disappeared into Elinor's shadow, where I'd hoped Marianne couldn't follow me. And for the most part, these last five years, she hadn't.

I'd watched a *lot* of horror movies in my day, and I knew one thing to be true—when you were somewhere as enclosed as a ship with the thing you were trying to avoid, you'd run into it at every opportunity.

While my two older sisters were still talking, and Edward was trying to massage some life back into his shoulder after pulling two hundred pounds of suitcase down a super-long hallway, I pulled out my phone, started drafting a text to the guy I'd assumed would be my brother-in-law one day. Who I'd already thought of as a brother.

What happened??? I backspaced, deleting my words. Tried again. Did Marianne—

No, I didn't even know what I was asking, couldn't begin to comprehend what could have caused this. Marianne knew she needed him.

I'd text him later, I decided, once I talked to Elinor. Once she'd caught me up on whatever the hell was happening here. Still, I scrolled up through our messages for a second. Brandon and I had last texted only a couple of days ago. Even though Marianne and I didn't talk much between her sporadic visits home, Brandon always kept me up-to-date on what was going on with their life, sending snapshots of the little herb garden he kept on their balcony and telling me how the different plants were progressing.

Which, yes, I admit sounds wildly boring, but when you compared it to what Marianne was like *without* Brandon . . . I liked boring.

He couldn't be gone.

And, look, normally, I would be great in a crisis like this. I'd been promoted to the head of the lifeguarding team last summer after pulling a little kid out of the deep end; even when her mom was freaking out, I was the one who called 911 and kept the rest of the kids calm. And around the Dashwood residence, I'd learned from Elinor how to keep my head cool in any situation. That time Edward had gotten poison ivy so bad that he looked like the rash-covered version of Violet from Willy Wonka? I'd been the one to talk him down from his panic while Elinor covered him in calamine lotion. When my mom had been wailing about never being able to afford to send me to college, I'd found a school where I could get a swimming scholarship. I *loved* fixing things.

But I never knew how to handle a Marianne crisis. Maybe because deep down, in the places where I shoved the parts of me I didn't want to deal with, we were too alike. Both prone to dramatics and heartbreak. And even though I'd spent the last five years ignoring that side of myself, trying to emulate Elinor in every way I could . . . being around Marianne had a way of bringing it out in me.

But not this time, I thought, tucking my phone back in the pocket of my shorts. In the years since Marianne and Brandon had gotten together, since our lives had calmed down and I'd been able to put myself back into one piece, I'd learned how to act more like Elinor than Marianne. To fill my life with order and plans, not instinct and chaos. I could keep it that way. No matter what was happening with Marianne.

Right?

Right.

CHAPTER TWO

Just ignore her, I told myself, as we inched ever so slowly forward in line. Not that Marianne was an easy person to ignore, but this was my summer. No matter who had showed up unexpectedly. I could handle it.

And even though Elinor was distracted by Marianne, I still had Edward.

"Did you know the ship has Broadway-caliber shows?" I asked him, brushing my red curls back from my forehead as we shuffled forward, as if I could force everything to go back to normal by pretending it still was. "And there's *three* pools." That would have been one for each of us if Marianne hadn't arrived. Maybe she'd share with Elinor.

"Well, did *you* know they have to make the pools on cruise ships smaller because of the weight of the water?" Edward responded, and I held back my grin. No matter how early it was, Edward couldn't help but be a fact-spewing machine. Dressed in a light-blue-striped button-down and a pair of khaki shorts, with a wide-brimmed hat to protect his skin from what he described as *the harsh Florida rays*, he looked like a professor who'd gotten lost on an archaeological dig. "People don't think about it, but the weight of all that water at the very top of the ship could topple the whole thing over if it wasn't carefully designed."

"Horrifying, but good to know." Edward Ferrars was one of my favorite people in the entire world. Maybe it was corny and weird for your brother-in-law to be one of your favorite people in the world, especially since he was ten years older than me, but I wasn't *not* corny and weird, so we'd go with it. Medium height and deeply dorky, with pale skin that made even me look tan and brown hair that stuck up in every direction, he was, according to Elinor, one of the most popular pastors at his church because his sermons were always half as long as everyone else's. "We're assuming this is one of the well-designed ones?"

"They certainly made it sound that way during my new employee orientation Zoom." We could just see the ship rising above us through the glass windows that surrounded us, and Edward eyed it nervously. "Though I suppose they wouldn't say if it wasn't."

"Not if they want to retain any of said new employees," I agreed. Edward's job was the reason we were on this dream cruise in the first place. While the Dashwoods were rarely (never) world travelers, Edward had gotten the sickest gig ever for the summer as a chaplain (aka, boat pastor) on a cruise ship for six weeks. Elinor would be joining him, of course, and as my high school graduation present, they'd taken advantage of Edward's family discount and invited me.

I'd been stoked. An entire summer with *just* my favorite

sister and brother-in-law? Yes please! We'd have the time of our lives, we wouldn't be stuck in Barton, New Jersey, and I'd get to suck up as much family bonding time as I could before I headed off to start my freshman year at UC San Diego in the fall.

It was so typical of Marianne, too, to just show up and ruin everything, just like—

No! No, I refused to dwell on Marianne. So she was coming with us. Fine. I'd deal with the consequences of that later. Because now, as we pushed through the last checkpoint and headed up the gangway, stepping on the wood-paneled deck for the first time and then being ushered into a huge atrium . . .

We were finally on board the *Queen Mab*, and she was absolutely gorgeous.

You know that scene in old movies, musicals especially, where the plucky young heroine has her two packed suitcases and steps off a train platform and into the Big Beautiful World for the first time? That's what this felt like. Like I was an ingenue from a sepia-toned movie with a tilted hat and a big dream, finally leaving the farm (I mean, I guess I was literally leaving our New Jersey farm) to follow my dreams. Even though Marianne had thrown a gigantic wrench into my summer plans, I had the undeniable feeling that finally my life was beginning.

"Wow," I breathed, and even the others seemed impressed, temporarily quieted in awe. Elinor had told me that the *Queen Mab* was considered a modest ship by modern cruising standards: older, without things like waterslides and rock walls and forty decks of wet 'n' wild fun. But if this was small, if this was old, I couldn't even begin to imagine what the newer, bigger ships were like. *Queen Mab* was a floating world, a skyscraper turned on its side and pushed out among the waves.

The whole ship, as far as I could see (not that I could see the whole ship, how could you even begin to see the whole ship?), was designed with an innate elegance that took my breath away. The atrium we'd walked into was open and airy, rising up and up, with walkways crisscrossing over our heads. Branching off the big open space were dozens of hallways, each leading to new and exciting parts unknown, stairs that went up and down onto balconies and over portholes. And way, way above our heads, the pièce de résistance: a stunning chandelier of gold and glass that shimmered and spun over a grand, central staircase.

The rest of the decorations and flourishes were done in royal blues and stately golds, and every inch of the ship gleamed with painstaking attention to detail. It was like I'd stepped into my favorite shows, the best movies, the inside of all the travel books Brandon used to bring me. (Don't think about Brandon, move Brandon to the Do Not Consider List.) Dreams of a future that looked exactly like this one were all that had sustained me when things were at their worst, and now I was finally living life at its very best.

I squealed, louder than I meant to.

"Easy." Elinor laughed, pushing a piece of frizzy auburn hair that had fallen out of her bun back behind her ear. (When I'd suggested she try a more casual hairstyle for our summer at sea, she'd said she'd "used a fun scrunchie!" and I'd let it go.) "She's lovely though, isn't she?"

"Spectacular," Edward agreed, returning the hand sanitizer he'd just used to his fanny pack, and he squeezed Elinor's hand for just a second before dropping it again. The two of them weren't big on PDA, but considering I was going to be on a single boat—ship, Edward kept reminding me that calling it a boat was disrespectful, somehow—with them for a month and a half, I wasn't complaining. Just because I was Team E+E didn't mean I needed to *see* them be all mushy and gross. They could save that sort of thing for their room. Marianne had wandered a little to the side, examining a huge ship's wheel in the center of the atrium that looked like it actually spun.

"Our cabins are just a couple of decks down," Elinor said, pulling over to the side and taking a folder out of her backpack that was stuffed to the brim with documents. We mostly had the atrium to ourselves—I saw a few people on the upper decks, but that was it—and I took the opportunity to move a little farther from my oldest sister, touching every marble column and admiring the intricate pattern of the carpet. When I looked closely, I realized there were tiny anchors woven into the pattern. Adorable. "We should head down and get settled. Edward, you have a crew training at ten, and then I guess the three of us . . ."

I wandered out of earshot, since I didn't really want to hear about all the plans that were supposed to be for just me and Elinor and now had Marianne attached to them. Besides, the ship's wheel Marianne had discovered *was* gorgeous. It was a deep, polished mahogany, and, oh my God, it did spin. What a world.

"It's like one of your pirate books," Marianne said as I lazily moved the wheel beneath my hands. I had to admit, she was right. If I closed my eyes, I could be on a pirate ship somewhere in the Mediterranean, swashbuckling with the best of them. "What are the chances we get boarded by an actual Will Turner lookalike?"

"I wouldn't joke about that." I shot a quick glance back at Edward and Elinor, who were luckily too engrossed in their schedules to hear us. "I mentioned pirates *once* to Elinor, and she sent me articles about hostile takeovers of boats for a week straight. Apparently, it's not as romantic as it seems."

"Devastating." Marianne sighed, spinning the wheel the other way. It was weird to see her without a smile on her face, especially in her brightly pink-patterned Lilly Pulitzer explosion, topped with a wide, floppy-brimmed hat over blond waves. Once she'd gotten together with Brandon, she'd smiled all the time. Now she just looked . . . like she was missing something. Not just a person. But, like, a limb. She looked empty. Usually the problem with Marianne was that she was too much. Now it looked like she wasn't enough. "I could use some dashing in my life."

Right, I thought. That was how Marianne had always preferred her guys. Swashbuckling and just as chaotic as she was. It was how I'd used to prefer them, too. Not that I'd ever really dated, considering I was only thirteen when Marianne tore her whole life apart over a guy. I'd learned that lesson early— romance was only worth pursuing if you knew it would be safe. For example, Edward was safe. I'd thought Brandon was safe, too.

"Why'd you break up with him?" The words slipped out before I could help myself. Before I could think better of it. Marianne's head whipped toward me, so fast that her dangly earrings hit the sides of her face, tiny seashells crashing against each other. I shouldn't have asked. I didn't want to engage. But I had to know. I had to know what self-destructive trait had awoken in Marianne, so I could watch out for it in myself.

Marianne looked at me for a long time. Elinor hadn't seemed to notice we were gone yet, going through one of her many packets with her husband. And then she said—

"I didn't."

"But then—"

"I think we're going to have a great time this summer, Margaret." Marianne reached out and squeezed my shoulder. I barely felt it. I was numb all over. "We never get sister time together anymore, you know? This will be the perfect way to spend your last summer before college. I wouldn't miss this for the world."

I didn't.

In what world would Brandon break up with *her*?

Marianne's boyfriend—or ex-boyfriend, wow, I really hated the sound of that—had come into our lives around the same time Edward had. In an unfortunate series of events I generally referred to as That Year, we lost our dad and our house all at once and had to move in with Mom's cousins, the Middletons (no relation to Kate, no matter what cousin Suzannah said), who had an old cottage on their farmland in middle of nowhere New Jersey. They'd never gotten around to making it into an Airbnb, probably because no one wanted to stay in a musty old cottage on their farmland in middle of nowhere New Jersey, which meant we were the lucky new tenants. We'd moved in, and a lot of it had been terrible, but Edward and Brandon, both family friends of the Middletons, had kind of saved us. Elinor would say that was reductive, probably, but it was how it felt. Edward was the first person who managed to make me laugh after Dad died. Brandon knew exactly how to distract me when things were at their darkest. And I'd figured, even though That Year had shown me that the things you loved were never guaranteed to be permanent, this new family arrangement would be. Elinor and Edward got married and moved into a tiny apartment in town, close enough for near-daily visits. And even though Marianne and Brandon left Barton, I knew my sister was taken care of. When the two of them moved to New Orleans a few years ago, Brandon had promised me he would always look after her.

So what the hell was this?

Do you want to talk about it? I held the question in my mouth, thick enough that I felt like I might choke. It was just that if I asked, I didn't know what I'd unlock. And, sure, five years ago, back when Marianne and I were the ones joined at the hip, she'd have already told me everything. But I had to be more cautious now. Marianne wasn't the only one here who was breakable.

Thankfully, Elinor interrupted us before I could make any uncorrectable mistakes.

"Girls!" she called across the atrium, beckoning us back over to her. "Come on, let's go see our home for the next six weeks!"

With a rush of excitement at the thought of seeing our cabins—maybe I'd have a balcony, maybe I could sit out there every morning and drink tea while I watched the ocean rise and fall, then return to my room, a calming refuge before a day of adventure—I hurried away from Marianne and her sad, lost eyes like the coward I was.

THIRTY minutes later, and my dreams of a clean, calm stateroom had been absolutely demolished.

First of all, I didn't realize that when Marianne announced she was coming with us, she meant that she was going to be sharing my cabin. I'd never actually shared a bedroom before—the benefit of being ten and eight years younger than my sisters, respectively—and I'd wanted to soak up all the space to myself while I could before I got to college. That dream, unfortunately, went out the window as Marianne wedged her suitcase through the front door and Elinor just mouthed *sorry* to me behind her.

Secondly, the cabin was a size that, if you were generous, you might call small. There was definitely no balcony—we didn't even have a window. There was one bed, a slender couch in front of a coffee table that was going to be a real shin buster, and a TV that we quickly discovered was just playing the same spy movie over and over again. A bathroom where you could, if you were so inclined, shower and brush your teeth at the same time; a closet that was half-full already with life jackets and an ironing board. Other than discovering that part of the wall above the couch folded down into a bunk bed, the room was entirely unremarkable.

Worse yet, Marianne took one look at the bed—which I, in a flash of generosity, told her she could have to herself, thinking that since I was younger and not mourning the broken remains of my life, I could handle the bunk—and burst into tears, running for the tiny bathroom and locking herself in.

That was a fun development.

"Marianne?" I gave the door a gentle knock, though I doubted she could hear me over the sobbing. "Everything okay?"

It was a stupid question, one that Marianne didn't bother to answer. So I just sighed and dropped onto the couch, eyeing the piles of clothes I still had all over the floor.

We wouldn't make it through the whole six weeks like this. If nothing else, Marianne didn't have enough hydration in her body to handle this level of daily tears. And selfishly . . . I wanted to enjoy my vacation, hang out with Elinor and Edward, and pretend that all this Dashwood Drama wasn't happening. But without something to keep her occupied, Marianne was probably going to spend her whole summer falling into fits of despair and, most likely, dragging me into them.

I didn't know. Maybe I was being unfair. But I didn't want to spend this summer as collateral damage of Marianne's heartbreak once again.

The exploding smash of glass, showering me all over, a tremendous pain in my arm as I was slammed against the side of the door . . .

Nope. No way. I didn't think about the accident, ever. I wasn't about to start now.

I just needed something to distract Marianne with, an activity that would keep her busy so she wouldn't need to pour all of her chaotic energy into me. For a brief moment, I wished that I could put her into one of the kids' clubs I'd seen advertised in the atrium, where you could drop your kid off for the whole day and pick them up after dinner, exhausted and chill. What I needed was the grown-up version of that.

Holy shit.

I jumped up from the couch, banging my knee on the coffee table and nearly falling over from the force of the impact. Freaking hell, was that table made of marble? I began to pace, or the best I could do with the limited space in the cabin and the throbbing pain racing up and down my shin.

I needed to find a new guy for Marianne.

CHAPTER THREE

This was the greatest idea I'd ever had, and my only regret was that I hadn't thought of it even sooner.

Of course, I was partially distracted by the loud and wailing sobs coming from the bathroom, but even without that, I should have realized the moment she told me that she and Brandon were over that a new romance was the only way to guarantee Marianne—and I—would make it through the summer in one piece.

Look, it may have seemed overly dramatic, but here was the thing—the last time a guy broke up with Marianne, she'd almost *died* and taken me down with her, okay? So no one could blame me for keeping her at an arm's length after that. I'd thrown all of my romantic notions out the window and vowed that Elinor would be my role model sister instead—safe, sensible, and secure. And for the last five years, it had worked, mostly.

But Marianne's energy was as magnetic as it was danger-ous. If I didn't distract her with someone else, she might just suck me back into her chaos again, and I couldn't let that happen.

But a new romance. That would fix everything. She could spend the summer riding on the back of a dolphin with a dream guy or something, and I could read my book with Elinor next to the pool. I was basically doing a good deed here, right? Super Altruistic Margaret, that was me. Not at all motivated by a desire to avoid my sister.

Whatever. I was only human.

The one thing, I thought as I continued to listen to Marianne's wails through the door, was that Elinor wouldn't be into this plan. The Oldest Sister Guilt was strong with that one, and she'd probably say that we needed to *support* Marianne in her time of need, not just throw her back into the dating pool.

But all Elinor ever did was support this family, and I could see in her eyes how exhausted she was by it. I knew from the way she'd looked when Marianne showed up today, from how her shoulders tensed whenever Mom called, from the deep sighs she let out when she thought no one was listening. This was supposed to be her vacation, too.

So maybe . . . I continued my pacing, being more mindful of the table this time. Maybe this was even, like, a thank-you gift to Elinor? Hey, you've been the best sister ever for the last five years, and so to show my appreciation for everything you've done for me, I've taken care of Marianne? Yes! Elinor would *never* turn down a present like that. Even if she didn't think she wanted it, I knew it would be, like, the biggest relief in the world if I took Marianne off her hands.

I was eighteen now, after all. I could handle this.

"Marianne!" I knocked sharply on the bathroom door. "Come out. I need to talk to you."

To my surprise, she opened the door right away, standing by the sink (and by the toilet, and by the shower—this bathroom was minuscule) as she wiped her eyes.

"What?" Even with mascara smeared all over the place, Marianne was still one of the prettiest criers I'd ever seen. It figured. "Sorry. It's just—"

"I know how to fix you," I interrupted, which earned me a raised eyebrow. "How to fix this whole summer."

"Better-lit mirrors?"

"No. Well, that would help," I allowed, "but it's not the plan. We"—I held my hands out to my sides, waggling them around for emphasis like a game show host—"are going to find you summer love."

A beat, and then Marianne burst out laughing, bending over far enough that I had to back away from the bathroom door to make room for her.

"Hilarious, Mags," she said after a second, catching her breath. "That's what I need."

"It is!" I insisted. "Marianne, you're miserable. And what's the best way for you to not be miserable? Being in love!" I pulled her out of the bathroom—because even looking in there too long was making me kind of claustrophobic—and over to the bed. "It's what you're best at. And I bet this ship is full of guys. New guys every week, even! So if you hate one week's batch, boom, next week delivers."

"Won't most of them be, like, eighty?"

"Some of them are traveling with their grandsons!" I countered. "I'm not saying you have to get married, or anything.

I'll even help you find the guys, so you don't end up with more of the assholes you've historically chosen." Although I would have picked Brandon for her, and it turned out he'd been fooling us about being a good guy the whole time, so maybe my judgment wasn't the best, either. Whatever. I'd make up an application form. "You're not completely ancient yet, you know? You can't spend the whole summer being sad about Brandon. You just can't."

"I'm twenty-six, Margaret." Marianne picked at her manicure. "I'm not exactly the Mummy."

"Still." I reached out and grabbed her hand, tried to convey confidence as I squeezed her fingers, just like Elinor would. I'd seen my oldest sister in a crisis plenty of times, had memorized her techniques for getting through them. If you seemed like you knew what you were doing, people usually believed you. "This is the right thing to do."

Marianne looked up at me, watched me for a good long while, like she was trying to figure something out. Then eventually she closed her eyes, sighed, and nodded.

"Yes!" I shouted, punching my fist into the air. This was a *plan*, and, God, I loved a plan. I already felt better, with the promise of a new structure to hang my summer on. "This is going to be so much fun, Marianne. We can send you to singles mixers and set up meet-cutes and—"

"I have one condition." Marianne held up her index finger, pointed it in my direction. I nodded, though I was already thinking of the color-coded schedule I was going to make in my notebook to map out Marianne's summer of romance. Maybe I could even get a *new* notebook from the ship gift shop, or in one of our ports. No, I couldn't wait until we got into port. Gift shop it was. Something with an anchor on it, maybe, or blue and white nautical stripes. "You're doing it with me."

"I—what?" Oh no. *Hell* no. Absolutely no way in the world no. All thoughts of notebooks flew out of my head. I was a planner, thank you very much, *not* a doer. That was for other people, people like Marianne who still wanted things like romance and mystery and all the chaos that came with it. "I don't think that's really necessary."

"Those are my terms." Marianne shrugged, then pulled a compact mirror out of her purse and began to fix her makeup.

I did my best not to collapse under the utter absurdity of her request. Because ever since That Year, I'd turned my back on romance entirely. I wasn't a girl who dated, or even pined after guys. Because to do that would be to open myself up to heartbreak, and I knew that heartbreak, for me, would be an all-over break, just like it had been for Marianne.

And, look, it wasn't as depressing as it sounded. I fully expected to find a nice guy after college, once my life was settled and on track. Someone stable and reliable who I could care for without totally losing myself. Elinor and Edward had a great relationship, after all, and theirs was entirely sensible. I could do that, too.

But I wasn't going to find that guy on a *cruise ship*, and I wasn't even a little bit interested in exploring the possibility of self-destruction in the meantime.

But Marianne looked more determined than ever, her arms crossed over her chest, staring me down. "I'm not doing this by myself. If you want me to do this, to spend my summer dating my way through a cruise ship, you're doing it, too."

"But . . . everyone on board will be way too old for me." I pulled the first objection I could out of the air that wasn't *absolutely not, because I'm freaking terrified of ending up like you. I get too attached to people, like you do, and we all know where that leads.*

"I'm sure they'll have grandchildren." Marianne's smile was perfect, like she knew she'd walked me into a checkmate. And, I mean, she had. Because what was I going to say? *Love is everything* you *need and I've spent years making sure that isn't the case for me?*

Sure, it was true. But it wasn't polite to say it out loud.

"Fine," I said through gritted teeth, holding out my hand to shake my sister's. Not fine, not fine at all, but I didn't have a choice. I'd figure my way out of it somehow. Worst-case scenario, I could always swim for shore. "I'll do it."

"Excellent decision," Marianne said, and I couldn't help but wonder who was the one making big grand plans here, because this one had really gotten away from me. "Now, let's discuss cruise outfits. If you're going to snag a hot grandson, you're going to need to dress the part."

I'd created a monster. But, as Marianne began to flip through my suitcase, shaking her head at most of what she found and, very (very) occasionally, nodding in approval, I couldn't help but feel a sense of relief: this was a monster I understood. I'd spent five years preparing for this, in a way. Putting out small fires to prepare to fight the biggest one of all—my own sister.

And as long as I could find a way to get out of my half of it, this plan could still be perfect.

CHAPTER FOUR

Not long after Marianne and I shook on our summer plans, we met up with Elinor to explore the rest of the ship. I was looking forward to it; I needed the distraction of this whole beautiful ship to take my mind off my impending romantic doom. Maybe if I could pretend I was on an old-school ocean liner or something, smuggled into first class to infiltrate . . . someone—I'd figure out who later—just talking to a few guys on a boat wouldn't seem so scary.

And then Elinor, Marianne, and I walked down to the atrium, which had been so beautifully calm and lovely before, and into absolute and utter chaos.

I mean, it was total mayhem. The space was packed with people, guests and staff alike, all screaming at the top of their lungs—or at least, that was what it seemed like from the way sound echoed through the ship. Children were crying; photography-obsessed dads were panicking that the aperture of their lens was wrong or something; and at one point, an overzealous mom sprayed sunscreen aimed at her child directly into my open mouth. *Yikes*.

"It feels a little different from before!" Elinor offered the understatement of the century as I gagged, trying to get the taste of sunscreen off my tongue. Even Marianne seemed stunned. I'd changed into a floral sundress with a fun tropical pattern, but I didn't realize I'd need a hazmat suit. They'd managed to leave this off the brochures, and I could see why.

"Am I dying? I feel like I'm dying," I said, as my whole mouth started to actively burn. Was sunscreen poisonous? Was I having an allergic reaction to this cruise ship? Maybe I'd made a terrible mistake in coming here. Maybe Mom was right, and we should have all spent the summer in New Jersey, swimming laps at the community pool and chasing down Suzannah's dogs whenever they tried to escape. No amount of planning could have prepared me for this.

But as the sunscreen taste faded, my initial panic did, too. The mass of people crowding the center of the ship started to seem thrilling rather than frightening, pushing and gasping and shrieking with excitement. It was wild and magical and utterly *human*, this gigantic crowd who had all gathered for one thing: to leave their worries behind for a little while, to experience a whole different life from the one they had back home.

I knew that feeling. Even with Marianne's horrifying addition to my plan hanging over my head like the blade of a guillotine, I could chase that feeling.

"Okay, so this is the ship's schedule of activities for embarkation day." I pulled out a large, folded-up brochure that had been waiting in our cabin when we arrived. "We have mandatory muster at two—that's where we go stand by the lifeboats and learn what to do in a *Titanic* situation—and then we *have* to check out the spa giveaway. Then we could go to the pool or we could see the violinist they have in the atrium from five to six, ooh, or there's a preview in the theater of all the shows they'll be doing this week . . ."

"You don't ever slow down, do you?" Elinor chuckled. Marianne headed toward the bar to grab us sodas, which would hopefully help wash the sunscreen out of my mouth.

"Why would I?" I shrugged, folding the brochure back up and tucking it in my bag. "We have to do absolutely everything we can, Elinor. We have to suck this cruise completely dry of fun." *And find a guy for Marianne as quickly as possible so I can actually enjoy it*, I thought, but didn't say out loud. It was weird, to keep my new plan from her. But I'd be at college in a couple of months anyway, and it wasn't like I'd tell Elinor everything that was going on in my life *then*, so this was kind of just like . . . practice.

Oof. I felt nauseous, for a second, at the idea of college, of being on my own, without my sister to guide me.

"That is . . . powerful imagery." Elinor blinked. "I like the idea of the preview of the shows. Marianne?" She called over to the bar, where Marianne was chatting up a bartender with a lot more shoulder shimmying than ordering a drink generally called for. Okay, well, she was jumping into this a lot faster than I expected. And I definitely needed to stop her, because she looked more like she was auditioning for a solo in a show chorus than trying to seduce a man. "Are you coming?"

"I'll meet you later!" she shouted back. Yikes. Was I morally obligated to stop this? Yes, technically, this fulfilled the mission of looking for a guy, but I didn't know if that guy should be a random bartender I hadn't had the chance to vet, you know? I wasn't opposed to Marianne dating the crew or anything, but I wanted the chance to check them out first. He could've been, like, a murderer who had taken a job on a cruise ship specifically to lure people like Marianne into his clutches. My plan only worked if Marianne ended up in a relatively stable relationship while we were on board, not if she ended up on an episode of *Dateline*. But she seemed comfortable enough, and it wasn't like I had an alternative way to find her someone else yet; so until I had a better idea, I couldn't complain or criticize her emphatic use of jazz hands.

And in the meantime . . . it was time to explore, and if Marianne wanted to stay behind, I wasn't going to stop her. I darted toward the stairs, and Elinor had to half jog to keep up with me.

"Ice cream first?" I asked, passing sculptures of mermaids that were tucked into the corners of each stair landing. "I think we have time before muster. They've got machines up on the pool deck open twenty-four hours a day, with signature flavors. Today they've got *lavender*. Can you believe it? All-you-can-eat lavender ice cream? We have to get some."

"Oh, why not." Elinor threw her hands up in the air and laughed, and for a second she looked like she had when she was younger, before the weight of the entire family had landed on her shoulders. "Ice cream first."

No matter what was going on with Marianne—no matter what was going on with *any* of the Dashwoods—I was officially, fully, entirely determined to love it here.

I had officially, fully, entirely broken my oldest sister.

"My God." Elinor was sitting in a deck chair a few rows back from the already-crowded pool, eyes closed as the wind ruffled through her hair, little wisps of red fluttering around her face. Edward had been right. The pools on the ship *were* small, so packed with people that each errant splash seemed to send a new kid into a screaming fit. I longed for the lounge chairs of the ship's brochure, where every seat had an empty space next to it and all the towels were folded perfectly. It was stuffy here, too, the air wet with humidity, a small breeze present only because I'd wrenched open one of the glass windows that partially enclosed this side of the deck. "Is this how you're planning on spending the entire six weeks? You'll die."

"I didn't expect the lines for the elevator to be that long," I said. Elinor had looked like her lungs might explode after the nine flights of stairs we'd had to climb to get here, especially after we'd already looped the ship twice to hit all of the afternoon's activities. "Do you need water? Or an IV drip?"

"I might." She leaned her head back against her chair. The sun beat down on us—partially enclosed deck be damned—and I squinted, glad that Elinor had insisted we wear our matching wide-brimmed hats. I didn't realize how exposed I'd feel, how much stronger the sun felt, even as it slipped into early evening, when there weren't any trees to divert it away. Thank goodness one of Elinor's suitcases had been entirely devoted to sunscreen. I'd seen the prices in the gift shop, when Elinor and I had peeked in earlier, and I'd almost needed to dip into our Dramamine stash from the sticker shock (though

I *had* snagged an amazing notebook, striped teal and white, that I couldn't wait to dig into).

"Think you can make it to the theater?" I glanced down at my phone to check the time. "That show preview thing starts soon. We can pick up some hydration on the way." That had to be less crowded, I reasoned. More the old-school wonderland I was hoping for.

"Only if we can sit in the back in case I fall asleep." Elinor groaned and held out her hands, and I pulled her up to her feet as the ship moved gently beneath us. We'd only just left port, the echo of the ship's horn still ringing in my ears, but I already felt my body getting used to the motion, adjusting for each dip and sway. "Tomorrow, I'm sitting by the pool for the entire day, and I won't allow anyone, not even you, to move me from that spot."

"Won't you get hungry?" We headed back inside the ship—the sliding doors opened automatically with a lovely chiming of bells, a small touch that thrilled me, even as a dad type in a shirt that said *Most Expensive Trip Ever!* almost ran me over—and made our way down the stairs to the theater five decks below. "And thirsty?"

"I'll obviously have a water bottle and a little sister dedicated to bringing me food from the buffet." Elinor smiled, and I rolled my eyes, but, I mean, she was right. "Marianne messaged earlier, by the way. She's going to meet us at the theater."

"That's great." I chose my words carefully. I needed to know if Elinor had her own plans for Marianne this summer, anything that would interfere with what I'd already put into motion. It wouldn't surprise me if she did. I'd learned from the best, after all. "Are you . . . are you worried about her? I don't want things to be the way they were last time."

Vague, but Elinor knew what I meant. She sighed, reached over, and squeezed my shoulder. "I don't want you to worry about that, okay? Marianne is my responsibility."

"I can help, though." Margaret, the little Dashwood girl. Didn't Elinor know I was more than that? She'd been by my side for the last five years, watched me grow and mature and learn from her. She had to know I was capable. A teammate, not another burden. "You don't have to take care of her alone."

"And *you* don't have to take care of her at all." Elinor's voice came out with an edge of sharpness I hadn't expected, and I recoiled. She noticed, sighed. "Sorry. Just—you're here to enjoy your summer. That's it."

"Sure." I knew Elinor saw me as a kid still, but I guess I'd been hoping for . . . I didn't know. Some acknowledgment, maybe, that I was eighteen now, and perfectly capable of pulling my weight in this family. She didn't have to handle everything on her own. She had my help, if she wanted it.

Maybe she didn't want it?

No. That was a ridiculous thought. She just didn't know how much she could use it, that was all. So maybe it even was a good thing Marianne was here (or at least, not a terrible thing). Because if Elinor still saw me this way, as a kid, as part of her burden, then I needed to do something big if I wanted to fix it. And solving Marianne's problems? That was the biggest thing I could do.

When we finally entered the theater—full red velvet opulence, obviously—Marianne waved to us from the back row, holding a frozen red drink with half a dozen umbrellas in it.

"There you are!" She patted the seats next to her, and Elinor and I sidled our way in, offering quiet apologies to the knees we hit along the way. The theater was packed, and I was starting to worry that the brochures had just kind of lied about the number of people that were usually on board. "Quick update, you have to pay for the drinks, but the umbrellas *are* unlimited, so if you just load up on those you get to feel twenty times as tropical for the low, low price of twelve ninety-nine."

"A steal," Elinor said, even though I knew for a fact she didn't like sugary drinks. Marianne nodded happily in agreement. It was amazing how much her mood had turned around just since I'd told her about the plan. *See?* I wanted to grab Elinor and shake her. *I did that. Me, little Margaret.*

"How many umbrellas do you think you can actually take from the bar before you get thrown into the brig?" I asked Marianne as Elinor turned to chat with the older couple sitting on her other side. "I don't want you to take me down with you."

"Please," Marianne whispered as the lights began to dim. The cruise director, a tall Black man a little older than Elinor in a shining white uniform, strode onto the stage to tremendous applause. "If we got boat arrested, you'd get to figure out a whole plan for how to plead our case. You'd love it. Besides," she added, "I bet my new bartender friend would break us out."

"Welcome, everyone!" The man began to speak, so I swallowed down my reply, vowing to go check out this bartender friend for myself before Marianne added him to her emergency contact list. She loved easier than anyone I'd ever met,

Marianne. It would have been endearing if it didn't keep biting her in the ass. "I'm Jono, your director of entertainment for this cruise, and I'm *so* excited to help you kick off your vacations! Are we ready to have a good time?"

"Woo!" The crowd answered, and I joined in, grinning. *Don't worry about Marianne right now*, I told myself, *or Elinor or anything. Take five seconds, enjoy the show. You can relax. It'll be fine.*

"That's right!" Jono nodded along with the applause. I was pretty sure his accent was Australian, and it was frankly awesome. "We've got an amazing preview of this week's entertainment here, so without further ado, allow me to present . . . the performing company of the *Queen Mab*!"

Jono stepped aside, the red velvet curtain rose, and the spectacle began.

First, an elaborate song and dance, dozens of tap-dancing performers twirling and spinning all over the stage as they sang about the wonders of the sea. Then, out of nowhere, a woman lowered from the ceiling on a giant hoop, dressed in a glittering gold dress covered in spangles. As the crowd gasped and applauded, she stood up and waved, then *flipped* off the hoop into the arms of a tuxedoed man waiting below. He spun her around in a circle, pulled a glittering sheet off the stage to cover her, and *poof!* She disappeared entirely, only to reappear in a kick line where she was joined by the rest of the performers, singing a song I vaguely recognized from a musical my high school had put on. I clapped as hard as I could, until Elinor put one hand over my wrist and gave me an indulgent smile.

I didn't care.

This was the summer I'd been looking for. Sitting here, my jaw halfway to the ground, watching these people perform . . . I'd been swept away. Even the technical elements of the show blew my mind, the lights flashing and the music swelling as a crew I could barely see performed wonders of their own from the sound booth. It was like a storybook happening in front of me, in a room where interruptions weren't allowed. It was perfectly planned and marvelously executed magic.

When Jono announced that the performers would be doing a meet and greet before the next performance, I turned to my sisters, eyes wide.

"Can we—"

"Of course." Elinor grinned. "Why don't you finish up here and meet us in the main dining room for dinner? That way you won't have to worry about taking too long, and I can go lie down before I collapse entirely."

"If you think you can make it all the way back to the stateroom, Grandma," I teased, poking her in the side as she yelped and pulled away. "Marianne and I will hang." A sentence I hadn't said in years, but I didn't want my sister to wander off again and find herself in the arms of, I don't know, some sea villain.

Okay, maybe that was a little unlikely. But I'd still feel better if she was with me.

"What? Oh, sure," Marianne said, obviously distracted. Which, I mean, whatever, Marianne. I'm only trying to turn your whole life around for the better—you could at least pay attention. "You can wait in line for both of us, right, Mags? We don't need to clog up the aisles."

"Sure." How much trouble could she get in from her seat? I nodded, then turned to Elinor. "See you at dinner."

"See you then." Elinor gave us each a small hug, and I headed toward the giant mob crowding the aisles of the theater.

As I forced myself into the mass of people, I looked around, trying to see if there was anyone interesting in the crowd. Cruisers, according to all the books I'd ever read, were a rich and mysterious group. Someone here was transporting their family's diamonds across the sea, I assumed, and someone else was harboring a deep secret. Not that you could tell by looking at them. Disappointingly, no one in the theater right now seemed worth watching.

Well, *almost* no one.

Since we were so far back in the theater, we were a few rows behind one of the tech booths, where a guy around my age was leaning back in his chair, messing around on his phone. I'd noticed him during the show—he'd been watching the stage intently, occasionally flipping switches and adjusting sliders up and down. As cool as the performers were—and they were, to reiterate, *amazing*—I'd found myself getting lost in the rhythm of his work, too. Watching him anticipate the next move, the next big crescendo, moving with the music and bobbing his head just a little as the tempo increased.

And, at least from behind, he was, objectively speaking, extremely good-looking. Could you be good-looking from behind? (*That* was a question I definitely didn't want to broach with either of my sisters.) But he was broad shouldered, with strong arms peeking out from his black T-shirt sleeves, his hair thick and dark and wavy. It made me *very* curious about the front.

I might have sworn off romance, but I wasn't a nun. I was still allowed to *look*.

Besides, as mentioned, there wasn't exactly anything more interesting going on right now. Doing my best to keep my glances toward Hottie McTech Guy stealthy, I entertained myself by creating an elaborate backstory for him. Maybe he was a lightboard prodigy, sailing the seas as he perfected his craft. Or maybe he was running from the law? A cruise seemed like a great place to do that. Of course, you had to watch out, or else you'd get thrown into the brig, and what happened at sea . . .

Lost in my daydream, I wasn't paying attention to the line, and we moved forward suddenly, in one big surge. Right at the same time, a wave must have rocked the ship, because I stumbled forward, then sideways, almost falling, saved only by landing in the arms of . . .

"Not used to the chaos just yet, huh?"

"What?" I whipped my head around to see—oh, God— Hottie McTech Guy himself, watching me with a bemused expression, since I had apparently stumbled right into the side of his booth and consequently into his arms. Yeah, that felt about right.

I pulled myself to my feet as quickly as possible, face burning. So much for observing his hotness from a safe distance. And, yes, in case you were wondering, the front *was* just as good as the back. His hair waved in gentle curls away from his face, equally thick eyebrows over deep brown eyes that watched me with curiosity. The muscles I'd observed from behind were just as tanned and pronounced from this angle, and, well, yeah. It was an excellent addition to the show, was all I was saying.

"Oh. No, I guess not." I tried to laugh, but it came out as more of a whimsical choke. Great. Smooth move, Margaret. "There's a lot of people on this ship."

"This is nothing compared to most of the lines." Seeming satisfied that I wasn't going to fall over again, he adjusted a couple more sliders, then switched off the board, swiveling his chair toward me. "This is basically the smallest group of people you'll ever see assembled on a cruise ship."

"That's . . . disconcerting," I muttered, because the group around me had only gotten *bigger* since I'd started talking to McTech, pushing into me from behind with no noticeable forward movement. Giving up for the time being, I stepped to the side, fully into the booth.

"You get used to it." He shrugged, his smile just a gentle flick of the side of his mouth into an upward position. "Biggest ship I was ever on had . . . ten times as many passengers as this? It felt like one of those fancy spaceships you see in sci-fi movies where, like, all of civilization has moved into a single colony."

"You like sci-fi?" A full half of the books I'd dragged along in my suitcase were sci-fi. It felt like science fiction was where all the old-school adventure book energy had gone these days—now that we'd explored all of Earth, the idea of exploring the universe was more intoxicating. And besides, reading about gigantic adventures like that was a lot safer than trying to embark on them on my own.

"Yeah." He shrugged, and I did my best not to stare at the muscles in his shoulders shifting beneath his T-shirt. "I have a lot of time to myself out here, plus rehearsals and everything, so I kind of inhale audiobooks. I got into science fiction because they were the longest."

"And the best?"

"I'm not going to argue with you." There was that subtle half smile again. As someone who lived with the most effusive person in the world (aka my mother), I liked that his emotions weren't written all over his face. It felt like he was letting me in on something. "If you ever need like, recommendations, or anything . . ."

"Good to know." This was starting to get into potential-danger territory. I wasn't having a meet-cute with Hottie McTech Guy or anything, but our rhythm was easy, his expression warm. Back home, this was always where I'd evacuate the situation. The best way to avoid romantic entanglement was to avoid people with whom you could romantically entangle, after all. And, sure, technically this was what I was *supposed* to be doing this summer to go along with Marianne, but I still planned on finding my way out of that.

I glanced around for a good excuse to leave. The line to get to the stage hadn't shortened, but when my eyes darted over the back of the theater, I saw Marianne, waving her phone around and pointing at her wrist.

That was my cue.

"I should go." I almost fell over again, stepping back, but I caught myself at the last moment, grabbing a nearby chair for support. "Dinner calls, and all that. Thanks for saving me, though. Next time I'll wear my life jacket."

"You can never be too careful." He didn't smile, but the words felt kind anyway.

Then again, Brandon had seemed kind, too.

CHAPTER FIVE

Marianne spent the whole walk to the dining room inter-rogating me about Hottie McTech Guy, but I brushed her off, said that I really needed to pay attention to the ship's map on my phone so that we didn't end up wandering over-board. And once we got there, of course, she didn't mention it again—we hadn't talked about it, but I suspected Marianne also knew telling Elinor about our romantic quest wasn't a great idea. On the one hand, I was relieved to be on the same page. On the other hand, it made it feel extra weird to keep a secret from my oldest sister when my middlest sister was in on it with me. To be bound together with Marianne, like we always used to be.

I excused myself after dinner and headed up to the run-ning track laid out on deck eight. I needed time alone, time to think, to figure out how the hell I was supposed to pull all of this off while still keeping my heart safe. I picked up my pace when I emerged onto the deck, the wind whipping at the skirt of my dress, just a step below running as I tried to sprint away from my feelings. If I stayed still too long, if I thought about all the ways this summer had already gone off the rails, I'd never start moving again.

This deck was mercifully, finally, empty, save for the occasional couple talking in low whispers on the loungers that had been set up to observe the moon-dark sea. And what was with all the couples on this ship, anyway? Did everyone see coupling up as, like, the great purpose of human existence? Because I was totally fine on my own. *Just* fine.

I was walking with so much purpose that I didn't notice the person in front of me until—surprise, surprise—I ran straight into him.

Great.

"Oh my God!" I shouted, stumbling out of the way of whoever I had just barreled into. "I'm so sorry, I—oh. Hi?"

"Hi," Hottie McTech Guy answered dryly, which was ironic, considering I'd run into him at top speed and spilled the drink he was holding all over his sleeve. "You know, I get not having your sea legs yet, but if you're going to bump into people this much, you should probably come with a warning sign."

"I promise, I'm not trying to make a habit out of it." I was glad it was so dark out here—hopefully that meant he wouldn't see the full extent of my flush. "Can I get you anything? A new drink? Or a new shirt? I can also just chuck myself into the ocean, if that would be easier."

"Legally, as a crew member of the *Queen Mab,* I can't let you joke about jumping overboard." His expression was serious, but I thought I heard the hint of something like humor in his voice. "It's fine. You mostly got my sleeve. It'll dry. Or it won't. Whatever." He shrugged. "Stuff's always getting wet around here."

Oh, God. Flush, meet entire body. He seemed to realize what he'd said at the last second, too, since he coughed and turned his attention to the ocean, which became a pitch-black expanse of nothing once you looked past the lights of the ship. It was wild, really, how dark it got out there. Anything could be lurking just beyond the ship's lights, and we'd have no idea.

I probably needed to stop reading so many horror novels.

"Right." I coughed, trying to salvage whatever remnants of this conversation that I could. "Anyway. Sorry, again. I'll get out of your way."

"Yeah. Sure." Tech Guy looked down at his feet—he was wearing athletic sneakers, and when you combined that with his basketball shorts, T-shirt, and vaguely disheveled appearance, I realized he must have been working out—and back up at me. "Unless you want to grab some ice cream? The machine on the top deck is basically abandoned this time of night. It's, like, the only time you can get close to it without a line."

"Oh." Part of me wanted to leave, to head back to my cabin and avoid any extra time spent in the moonlight with this *extremely* hot guy who wanted to keep hanging out with me. But it was just ice cream. Just casual, super-chill ice cream. No flirtatious strings attached. "Um. Okay. Yeah, that would be cool."

"Cool," Tech Guy echoed, a smile playing across his face, the first I'd seen from him. "I'm Gabe, by the way. Gabe Monteiro. Do you have a name? So that I don't have to keep just thinking of you as Falling Over Show Girl?"

"I promise I don't normally fall over this much. You bring it out in me." He'd been thinking of me. Holy shit. He'd been thinking about me? It had only been a couple of hours. Had I been thinking about him?

Aaaand we were shutting that train of thought right on down now, thanks! Because that was Marianne-style thinking and I was not here for it!

I followed Tech Guy—Gabe—back through the sliding doors, turning toward the winding staircases and making our way up. "I'm Margaret." I managed to say it in a totally normal voice, too, so he'd have no idea my internal monologue sounded like an audiobook sped up two and a half times.

"Nice to officially meet you, Margaret. Welcome to the *Mab*." We stepped out onto the top deck, and the view made me gasp. *This* was the completely empty, glittering-in-the-moonlight deck of my dreams I'd been hoping for since this morning. Gabe looked over at me, but didn't say anything as he led me to the ice cream machines I'd seen earlier and had, in fact, been unable to get close to. "Flavor of choice?"

"Has to be the lavender." Not that I'd ever eaten lavender ice cream, but it was the most outlandish flavor on offer, which meant I was obligated to try it. "I can get it, though. I watched a bunch of YouTube videos on how to get the perfect swirl in anticipation of this trip."

"They have videos for that?"

"Please," I said, pulling my curls back into a quick ponytail before stepping up to the machine, my flip-flops slapping on the wooden deck beneath me. "They have videos on everything. What kind of child of the internet are you?"

Gabe stepped obligingly out of the way, hands up. "All right, Madam Expert." Again, no smile, but his eyes twinkled, and I was beginning to suspect that was, for him, equivalent. "Go for it."

That sounded like a challenge, but I wasn't worried. According to one of the cruise vloggers I'd watched before coming out here—shout out to Cruise Baby—it was all about the twist in the wrist. She'd repeated it over and over again, in a rhyming singsong, so I felt confident that it had gotten fully ingrained in my brain. I stepped up to the machine, grabbed a cone, positioned it under the spout, pulled down on the lever, and—

I managed a twist and a half before my paltry tower of ice cream toppled over entirely.

"Shit!" I yelped, grabbing at the pale purple ice cream as it spilled onto my wrist. All about the twist, my ass. This was way harder than it looked. Gabe, next to me, was barely holding back a laugh—rude—but handed me a pile of napkins to wipe myself clean. "All right, clearly this machine is broken. We should tell someone."

"Right." Gabe nodded. Luckily, the ice cream had missed my clothing, especially since I had only packed so many outfits and I didn't really want to start the trip by staining them purple. "That's probably it. But maybe I should give it a try first. Just in case."

"Be my guest," I muttered, then gasped as Gabe proceeded to create the tallest, most gorgeous cone of chocolate and vanilla swirl I ever saw. "Are you kidding me? That looks like an emoji."

"High praise." He licked at the top of his cone, and I

turned away quickly so I wouldn't be staring weirdly at his tongue. "Are you going to eat yours? Or just let the rest of it melt all over you?"

"Ha." Begrudgingly, I raised the cone to my mouth; though it was, indeed, a gigantic mess, the ice cream was tasty, smooth and floral. "Is this what the rest of the crew does in their off hours? Roam the ship and make fun of guests' ice cream techniques?"

"Not usually. I made an exception for you." He licked at his cone again, and I felt a shiver go through my chest. Absolutely not. Yes, Gabe the Tech Guy was unfairly hot, and, yes, our rapport was as snappy as an old-timey tap dance, but I was *not* going to fall for him. I had more important things to do. Like protecting my heart from this exact scenario.

But some casual conversation never hurt anyone, right? As long as I was vigilant, I could keep myself in the friend zone. "I'm honored."

"Good." Gabe cocked his head to the side, indicating I should follow. "So, Margaret from the show. What brings you onto our floating island of misfit toys?"

"Vacation?" I gave the side of my cone a quick lick, trying to avoid both going to town on this ice cream in front of Gabe and letting it drip even further all over my hand. "Kind of. My brother-in-law is the ship's chaplain for the summer, so I got to tag along."

"I think I saw him at one of the all-hands meetings." Gabe led me to a tucked-away area I hadn't found before in my limited exploring. All the while, he managed to make eating an ice cream cone look way cooler than I did, perfectly at ease in this environment. I envied it. I'd never looked at ease anywhere. "He's filling in for someone, right? Are you on for his full contract? Or just visiting?"

"Full contract," I confirmed, and Gabe lifted one eyebrow in surprise. "What?"

"Nothing." He shrugged, kept eating his ice cream. "You just seem superexcited for someone who's going to be trapped on a floating cesspit for the next six weeks, that's all."

Okay, that was *not* what I'd expected.

"That's a bold indictment of your place of employment." Our little corner was protected from the wind, and we leaned against the tall smokestack that took up a large portion of the deck. It towered up above us, making it feel like we were in a playground's secret spire. "I was told cruising would be the best experience of my life."

"Ha!" This time, Gabe's laugh barked out, echoing across the deck. "Yeah, not exactly."

"Really?" I was surprised. Gabe's job seemed like the absolute coolest in the world to me. Making magic for the shows, living on the ship, your days perfectly planned out so that they went exactly as you expected. "I'll admit the crowds have been a little . . . untenable." Not to mention that my family was in a crisis, but I didn't need to bring that up. "But it's still exciting, you know? Underneath all the chaos, cruises are like . . . old-school glamour. If I wait it out long enough, it'll be what I need it to be."

"Right." Gabe looked at me sideways. "I'm not trying to ruin your vacation or whatever. But life on a cruise ship isn't exactly what they tell you in the brochures."

"Oh yeah? What is it, then?"

"A manufactured attempt at selling an adventurous life to

people who would never have a chance at one otherwise?" he offered, and I almost spat out my ice cream. Okay, so maybe he didn't think of it as a super-cool life of adventure. *He's just cynical,* I told myself, swallowing the remains of my dessert. *He doesn't know what he's talking about.* Because if I was already giving up a huge chunk of my summertime adventure playing matchmaker for my sister, I for sure wasn't going to *also* give up my dreams of what this cruise could be.

"Why are you here, then?" I could just leave, I reminded myself. Go back to my cabin and get out of this weird bubble of a guy I didn't know and a sky full of stars. "If you hate it so much?"

"I don't—I don't hate it. Not really. Sorry. I'm being an asshole, aren't I? My aunt says I need to work on that." He did look apologetic, his dark brows knit together, so serious. "I spend a lot of time in the tech booth. Not so much with other people. I mean, I'm with other people all the time, but I don't usually . . . talk to them."

"Lucky me, to be the exception."

"Probably not so lucky." He shrugged, a breeze picking up his thick, dark hair. "I've just been around these ships my whole life. Tia Luisa and Tio Peter, my aunt and uncle—you saw them in the preview. The magic act."

"That was your aunt and uncle?" The spangled woman and the man in the tux, who had absolutely blown my mind. "They're amazing."

"Yeah, they are." He nodded. "But it means I've been on ships like this forever. It's maybe made me a little jaded."

"A little?" I teased, and he had the decency to look chagrined.

"Okay, I'm basically made of jade. But you have to be to get through a whole season here, I promise."

"So is this your standard move, then?" My ice cream was finished, and Gabe's nearly gone, so we moved back toward the ship's railing, leaning against it while the wind whipped through the curls that had come loose from my ponytail. "Linger on the track and try to alienate the first person who comes along?"

"I don't know that I have 'standard moves.'" Gabe leaned forward on his elbows, eyes trained on the ocean. "Just occasionally decent luck."

The silence that fell over us was weighted, heavy. Pulsing with meaning. A meaning I'd only experienced a couple of times in my life before shutting it way down. Which was why, as nice as it was to banter with a boy on the deck of a ship in the evening air, a scene straight out of a romantic movie, I loudly announced, "Just so you know, I don't date. Or do anything that, like, resembles dating. Or hooking up. Or anything."

Smooth, Margaret. So incredibly smooth.

The outburst clearly took Gabe by surprise, too, because he choked mid-bite of ice cream, and from the look on his face and the coughing fit that ensued, half of it went down the wrong pipe.

"Sorry!" I clapped him on the back. "You probably weren't— God, this is embarrassing. I didn't think you were, like, coming on to me or whatever. But it's just something I try to tell people right away, if it seems like we might hang out? Because I don't want anyone to get the wrong idea. It's not anything personal," I continued, because rambling or not,

I'd made this speech before, and I'd learned that it was a lot easier when I just powered through it, without letting anyone get a word in edgewise. Edgewise was where things got messy. "It's just a matter of principle."

"Okay." Gabe nodded, still looking a little stunned, though it did at least seem like the ice cream had cleared from his esophagus. I didn't blame him. People usually looked stunned at first, when I gave them this speech. Then they'd try to argue with me, tell me that I was wrong, or they'd just storm off in a huff of embarrassment. "Just for the record, I wasn't like . . . hitting on you."

"Oh yeah, of course, I know." God, embarrass me even further, why don't you. I braced myself for the inevitable, the part where he left, because it was totally fair, but I'd liked talking to him. Liked the way it felt to be around him. It was a lot more relaxing than being around my family. "Anyway. Sorry."

"It's okay." Another rare Gabe smile, then he wiped his hands on a napkin he pulled out of his pocket and tilted his head back in the direction we'd come from. "I should probably go, anyway. Early show tomorrow for some sort of kids' entertainment thing."

"Right." I was never going to see Gabe again, I decided. It would be easier that way. "Well. Thanks for the hang. Sorry again for . . . you know."

"Nothing to be sorry about." He shrugged, ran a hand through his thick, dark hair. "If you ever want to do it again . . . you know where I work."

"For sure." I was definitely not going to do that, but I raised my hand in a wave anyway as Gabe nodded and left, heading for the sliding doors that would take him back inside. I settled back against the railing, watching the ocean rise and fall, and thought about what a weird interaction that had been.

And then I had another light bulb of an idea, the kind that meant I had to immediately book it inside the ship, where Gabe was luckily still waiting for an elevator.

"Hi!" I said, skidding to a halt in front of him, managing not to run into him for once. "Weird question. But do you know any guys?"

CHAPTER SIX

Gabe blinked at me slowly.

"Um. I guess?" He tilted his head to the side. "Do you want to find more people to announce your anti-love crusade to?"

"The opposite, actually. I need to find a boyfriend."

"Didn't you just say . . ."

"Not for me," I clarified quickly. Not yet, anyway. "It's for my sister. Marianne—that's my other sister, not the one married to the chaplain—she just went through this horrific breakup and she's one of those people who doesn't do well without a guy, you know? So I told her I'd help her find one. And I want to make sure that all of her options are good guys and not just, like, cruise jerks, and so I thought maybe you could help me find them."

"Cruise jerks," Gabe repeated.

"Is there a more official term?" I shook my head. "Whatever. She's dated some real losers and I just want her to go out with someone nice who won't emotionally destroy her, which means I need to vet whoever she's going out with first."

"And this has to do with me . . . how?"

"Gabe." I was practically bouncing back and forth, my flip-flops squeaking against the floor. "You work on the ship. You know everybody, probably. You can help me run background checks. That way we guarantee none of them are terrible people who will ruin Marianne's life even further, and she can have her grand shipboard romance in a safe, controlled environment."

"That's . . ." Gabe leaned back onto the wall dividing the two gilded elevators. "That's so much."

Self-doubt washed over me, but I stayed strong. "It's the best idea I've got. You're the one who said you were dreading spending the whole summer on board, right? You're clearly in need of a project."

"I am, am I?" He wasn't saying no. He was skeptical, but he wasn't saying no. I could work with that. "And what would my involvement be in this project, exactly?"

"Just help me find the guys." Obviously, I wasn't asking him to like . . . date me. I'd need to find *someone* for me, someone I could hang out with for the summer so Marianne didn't think I was shirking my end of the deal, but I was taking Gabe *off* that list, because the way his dark eyes looked at me and the way my heart kept racing whenever he leaned close meant that I had to keep him in as firmly a friend capacity as possible. Marianne's heart wasn't the only one I needed to worry about. I flashed him my best, most dazzling smile. "Come on. Please?"

I held my breath, hoping he'd say yes. I didn't know why, but this suddenly felt incredibly important. Like the success of my plan was entirely dependent on this relative stranger being a part of it. And it *definitely* didn't have anything to do with wanting to spend more time with Gabe, because I had rules and boundaries, and they included avoiding any guys who I had even the slightest chance of falling for. But I'd laid out the rules for him, and he was still here, so what was the harm in taking him up on that?

"Okay," he said finally, and I jumped up into the air in excitement, throwing my arms out wide. He sighed. "Not because I think this is a good idea. But because if I don't help you, who knows who you'll recruit to join you on this absolutely bonkers task, and I feel like you need someone who can keep you from, like, committing fraud."

"What part of this says 'fraud' to you?" This was the most excited I'd been since I'd found out about the cruise in the first place. My summer had been taken out of my hands when Marianne showed up, and finally I was reclaiming it.

"You just seem like the sort of person who escalates things quickly." Gabe pressed the button for the elevator. "Give me a couple of days to get some guys together. I have Monday afternoon off; we can reconvene then."

"Amazing." This could work. This could actually work. "Well, I should probably go." It was getting late, and my sisters were going to be looking for me. "This was . . . kind of a great time."

"That's the *Queen Mab* way." Gabe shrugged. "Always here to raise your spirits."

We said our goodbyes, and I practically skipped down

the stairs back to our stateroom, letting the adrenaline of a plan well made push me forward as I pictured the end of the summer, when probably everyone in the family would gather around me and offer me a round of applause for a job well done.

Which obviously wasn't the validation I was looking for. I was just fine with my own self-validation, thanks. But if they *offered* me an applause circle, I wasn't about to turn it down.

When I let myself into the stateroom, Marianne was still awake, sitting up in bed and reading a Rupi Kaur poetry collection she'd packed.

"Big night?" she asked as I collapsed on the sofa below my bunk bed, suddenly exhausted from the world's longest day. "You were out late."

"Just happy." I couldn't hide my smile, and I didn't try. "I think we may just have an excellent summer, Marianne."

"Yeah." Marianne's laugh was hollow, but I was too excited to let it worry me. "We'll see."

CHAPTER SEVEN

———

Two days later, to my astonishment, Gabe had pulled together a roster of eligible guys, ready for me to audition in the weirdest version of *The Bachelor* ever created. (Well, probably not. That show was a mess.) But nevertheless, it still felt entirely surreal to be standing in the theater on Monday morning, preparing to pick out my sister's summer fling while the rest of the family checked out the port at Nassau.

And maybe mine, too. But I was trying not to think about that.

"Don't worry, sweetheart." Luisa, Gabe's aunt, came up behind me, startling me out of my reverie. Gabe had filled her in on my scheme, and she'd been wildly enthusiastic— apparently binge-watching downloaded reality dating shows was a favorite pastime of the crew, so she was all-in from the get-go. "This is going to be a blast."

"I'm not worried," I lied, straightening my shoulders with a smile. We were both sitting in the front of the theater, just a few rows from the stage, where our eligible bachelors would soon be lining up for judgment. I'd aimed for professional chic today, with one of Elinor's blazers over my sundress, both to emulate the calm, no-nonsense attitude of my oldest sister and so that I'd appear older than eighteen. "Our plan is basically foolproof." Our plan was, in fact, not at all proofed against fools, but I was channeling confidence.

"All right." Gabe stepped out from the wings of the stage, dressed in his usual tech uniform of black jeans and a black T-shirt. Out on the ship, mixed in with the tropical prints and Hawaiian shirts, it was one of the things that made him stand out; but here, of course, he fit in perfectly. I glanced down at the flowers all over my sundress, hoped they didn't scream *I'm a tourist and I don't know what I'm doing!* "Got 'em lined up backstage. I tried to bring them out all at once, but there were . . . protests." He grimaced. "You ready, Margaret?"

"As I'll ever be," I said. I fingered the lapel of my blazer. It was good that Elinor wasn't here, good that she was out wandering Nassau with Edward, because of *course* I could do this on my own. Could do anything on my own, because I'd learned how to do that from her. But it still felt like I was taking the training wheels off my life a lot faster than I'd expected, you know?

At least I had Gabe. He hopped off the stage and settled down beside me, Luisa leaping up to replace him and help bring out the guys as I leaned toward him. "Is this what it feels like to be a judge on *American Idol*?"

"Is this what it feels like when someone mentions *American Idol*, the world's oldest pop culture reference?" Gabe shot back, and I laughed, grateful for the break in the tension. My shoulders relaxed, my arms settled down beside me. This was fine. I could do this. I'd wanted to prepare for life on my own this summer, and that meant doing things without the protection of Elinor's guidance. "That show's, like, twice as old as you are."

"Baby sister problems," I said, as Luisa ushered out our first guy: a tall, redheaded man with freckles covering his skin and the worst sunglasses tan line I'd ever seen. "It does *not* hold up."

"I believe it," Gabe said, as the guy onstage coughed loudly, and both of us whipped our heads forward. Right. Because we were here to find a guy to distract Marianne for the summer, not for me and Gabe to hang out. I elbowed Gabe, and he elbowed me, and then the guy started to cough again so we actually did get our acts together and turn to face him.

"My name is Leonardo da Vinci Carpenter," he announced grandly, and my eyebrows shot all the way up into my hairline. I didn't dare look at Gabe, too afraid of his expression. "When I was in the womb, my mother felt as though I was painting the stars in her stomach, and so when I was born, she gave me a name to match my ambitions." His strong Minnesota accent took away from the grandiosity of his words, but I did my best to smile with encouragement, even though inside, I was dying. "Since then, I have become accomplished in *all* manners of art, from painting to dance. Luisa"—he turned in a wide circle toward Luisa, who was keeping her face mercifully neutral—"my music, if you will." Luisa nodded, bending down and pressing play on a small portable speaker that I was pretty sure contained an *actual* CD.

As dramatic orchestral music burst through the theater, Leonardo began a series of leaps across the stage, which might have been impressive if his ankles weren't so wobbly and his arms didn't flail as much every time he spun. I leaned over to Gabe.

"This guy is a performer?"

"Leo? God, no." Gabe shook his head. "He's a lifeguard. Auditioned for the dance company a few years in a row and didn't make it, so he took this job. I guess he's just hoping he'll improve by proximity."

"If this is him improved, I hate to think of what he was like before." I shuddered. Yeah, this wasn't going to work. Marianne liked them romantic, but if she saw Leo's twirls, she'd twirl herself right into the arms of the first sleazeball she met on board. "Thank you so much!" I called out. Luisa stopped the music, and Leo almost toppled over midair. "We'll be in touch."

"Gabe said you'd let us know at the end of the audition, though?"

"We'll be in touch," I repeated, and out of the corner of my eye, I saw Gabe holding back a smirk.

I was pretty sure that, over the next hour, I witnessed the full range of humanity's worst talents. I didn't know why everyone had gotten it into their head that this was a variety show audition, since Gabe had explicitly told them what this was for, but there was juggling (terrible), Irish step dancing (worse), and even a fire-swallowing demonstration from one of the ship's magicians (supercool, but he was old enough to be my father, so it was a hard pass).

By the end, I'd narrowed it down, with the help of Luisa and Gabe, to a few possibilities. Torden, a tall Norwegian with light blond hair and blue eyes that I knew Marianne would go crazy for, was a performer in the Broadway variety show, and Luisa assured me that he was a good guy. (It also helped that his performance, where he played the ukulele, wasn't actively grating.) Our next candidate, Tomas, was from Brazil like Luisa and Peter, which I had to assume was why she was pushing for him. He had a killer smile, with dark skin and short hair. He worked in the kids' club, too, and Marianne would definitely be into his accent—especially if I could convince him to memorize some poetry ahead of time. Plus, he spent a *lot* of his audition talking about how much he missed his family, which had to be a good sign that he was a down-to-earth person who could keep Marianne from spinning out into further chaos, right? And finally, Xander, a Filipino guy with a deep tan and a shaggy haircut whose stories of taking care of his mother would hopefully enchant my sister.

The problem—besides the aspiring ventriloquist who kept trying to audition a second time, like that would make his act any less horrifying—was that there wasn't anyone here who would work as *my* date. This was probably since I still hadn't told Gabe I needed to find a guy for me, too, because it felt embarrassing to bring up after my whole "I don't date" explosion Saturday. But the fact of the matter was that everyone here was way too old for me, and although I could always try my luck out in the real world . . . God, I didn't want to.

Luisa, Gabe, and I were huddled in our seats, keeping our voices low so that the guys gathered onstage wouldn't hear our conversation. I took a deep breath and decided to broach the topic, hoping that Luisa would help act as an emotional barrier.

"I forgot to mention . . ." I glanced up at the stage, where a dozen guys who wanted to date my sister were all watching us with anticipation. "I told Marianne that I'd also try dating this summer."

"What?" Gabe's eyebrows went way, way up.

"I know." Update, Luisa's presence wasn't helping; this was still majorly embarrassing. "I don't date at all, like, ever," I added for Luisa's sake, "and I don't really want to try now, either, but I had to agree so Marianne would go along with my plan in the first place."

"Oh." Luisa nodded, her brow furrowing just like her nephew's. Then she shrugged. "Why not just date Gabriel, then?"

"*What?*" Gabe repeated, louder this time, as I sucked in a breath. The two of us looked at each other, horrified. Okay, "horrified" maybe wasn't the best word to describe how *I* was feeling, even though it was clearly how Gabe felt about the proposal. (Which, rude.) But I couldn't—Gabe was a terrible choice because he was dangerous. Because we got along so easily, because he already knew how to make me laugh, because even when my foot had nudged against the denim of his jeans a moment ago, I'd felt energy shoot up my leg like a live wire.

I kept myself far, far away from boys like Gabe. The fact that we were hanging out at all was a sign of my desperation and, I supposed, my weak willpower. Probably from dehydration.

"Come now, what's the problem?" she asked, looking between the two of us. "You two get along, yes?"

"I don't know," I began, trying to figure out how to shut this down, because *obviously I'm attracted to your nephew and dating him would be a disaster of epic proportions* wasn't an option here.

Unless.

"What if we just pretended to date?" I said, forgetting to whisper for a second, and the heads of all the potential suitors whipped over to me. I waved at them in apology, then lowered my voice. "You and me, I mean." I turned to Gabe. "We can tell Marianne we met at the show preview, or whatever, and then just, like . . . pretend we're together. And then I won't have to find anyone else."

"I don't know, Margaret." Gabe had gone kind of pale; maybe he was getting seasick. "That seems like a lot."

"And a lie," Luisa added, which, yeah, thanks, Luisa, I was fully aware, but some of us had to work proactively to protect ourselves around here. "Is that the best thing for your sister?"

"Trust me, the best thing for my sister is getting her coupled up as soon as possible," I said, running my hands over the velvet armrests of my chair. "Once she finds someone she likes, she won't even worry about me. I just need to hold her off until that happens, and a fake boyfriend means I can fully concentrate on making her happy. Please?" I clasped my hands in front of my chest, looking at Gabe with what I hoped were big, puppy-dog eyes. "I swear it'll be super low-key. Just a few double dates, at most. And this way you can help me supervise Marianne and whichever guy we pick out."

I paused, waiting for Gabe to, most likely, laugh in my face and leave. Because this was a ridiculous proposition. I mean, fake dating? What were we, a Netflix movie?

"Fine," Gabe said, with absolutely zero enthusiasm, and I pumped my fist into the air, even though part of me wished he'd seemed a little more excited. "I guess it's the best option." Thanks, Gabe, way to make a girl feel wanted.

Not that I *wanted* to feel wanted. I just wanted—

Nothing!

I was in way, *way* over my head.

CHAPTER EIGHT

A mere few hours later, Marianne and I were at the *Queen Mab*'s official singles mixer, and I was trying to pretend that I had confidence in my plan. But standing outside the entrance to one of the *Mab*'s many lounge spaces, which were tucked in around the ship like comb in a beehive, all I could think about were the ways that this could all go wrong. Torden— whom we'd selected as our first official Marianne Option— could turn out to be a serial killer. Marianne could decide she hated Torden *and* me and run off with some rich old guy she met in the casino, abandoning us forever. Gabe could decide he was tired of the chaos I'd brought into his life and push me overboard.

In the moment, though, just the idea of pretending to date at all was enough to make me sweat.

At least I didn't feel as nervous as Marianne.

"You said this guy was nice?" she asked, tugging at her skirt. I'd never seen Marianne uncomfortable like this. Tragic wailing heroine, sure, but awkward in social situations? No way. Usually it was Brandon who was this uncomfortable. Besides her obvious nerves, though, she looked perfect as always, draped in an off-the-shoulder dress in purple and white florals that fluttered down her legs, her sky-high wedges putting her half a head above me. "Where did you meet him, again?"

"Just up on the deck." Yes, I was adding an *additional* lie to my plan. But come on. Marianne didn't want to know that I'd auditioned guys for her like I was casting an a cappella group in a fourth *Pitch Perfect* movie. She wanted romance. Spontaneity. "He—um—saw a kid having trouble in the water and totally saved her."

"Really?" Marianne raised her eyebrows. "Impressive."

"And real." God, I was a terrible liar. How, exactly, had I gotten myself into this level of chaos again? It didn't matter now. I was in too deep. "He should be just inside."

"Okay." Marianne took a deep breath, straightened her shoulders, and stepped forward. "Let's do this."

In the couple of days we'd been on the ship so far, you'd think I'd have become accustomed to waves of sound, but no. It still took me by surprise when we walked into the lounge; the combined force of pulsing music and a hundred shouted conversations almost knocked me over. I didn't even know how all these people *fit* in here. But I couldn't waste too much time wondering about that; I had to be alert, make sure the plan went off perfectly.

Torden was going to swoop in quickly, dazzle Marianne, and sweep her off her feet. Luisa was running point for us, minimizing interference by intercepting any other guys headed Marianne's way. (Not that I thought Marianne was *that* easily distracted, but I didn't want to take any chances.) Gabe would follow soon after, both guys would charm us (well, Torden would; I was more than a little worried about how Gabe would do in this department) and then ask us to join them on a port excursion later in the week. Marianne would be thrilled, and we'd have a safe, low-key double date with absolutely no chance for disaster. With any luck, she and Torden would hit it off, she'd be set for the entire summer, and I could go back to my original, way-more-independent-from-my-sister plans.

Except there was the whole matter of *now I need to hang out with my sister one-on-one* that I still wasn't quite ready for.

Look, I loved Marianne. Obviously. But except for a few moments here and there, we hadn't really hung out on our own much since she and Brandon had moved away. Even on this cruise, we hadn't been alone together that often so far, and when we were, we were getting ready, or doing something else with a specific task.

But my only task now was *chat with Marianne until Torden gets here*, and that didn't have nearly the structure I so desperately craved.

"So." I poured myself a cup of water from a pitcher on a table near the entrance to the lounge, one of those fancy spa waters with cucumbers and oranges floating in it. "How's work been going?" Oh my God, was that the best I could do? Was I *that* boring? From the look Marianne gave me, she thought so, especially since she had used up all of her vacation for this trip and probably didn't want to even think about work. Which was honestly so unfair, because if I *was* boring, it was only because I had to be, to balance her out.

A memory slipped into my mind, unbidden, from my

freshman year of high school. It was the last day of school before winter break, and she and Brandon had just arrived from New Orleans to spend part of the holidays with us. And even though I'd been nervous, seeing her for the first time in so long, part of me had been thrilled, too. Because maybe we'd just needed a little time away from each other to get back to how we were. To heal the real and metaphorical hurts and be Marianne and Margaret again.

And when they got in, at first, it was like nothing had changed. Sure, we were all a little more cautious since the accident, especially Elinor, but it was still Marianne. Still the missing piece of our family.

But then I told her that we had a dance at school that night. That I was just going with some friends. And she couldn't understand it.

"You're young, you're gorgeous, you've got your whole life to play it safe!" she'd said, borrowing my phone to look at my Instagram, scroll through my friends and classmates. "You have to take someone to this dance. Come on, just ask them. What could go wrong?"

Everything? My arm still ached from where I'd broken it the year before. I still heard Elinor's screams from when she'd seen us, seen the smashed-up car in some of my dreams. I'd tried to push back.

"I'm good with how things are, Marianne." Good with the stasis I'd found for myself, after she'd left. Good with how I'd absorbed Elinor's penchant for safety and security, wrapped it around myself like a blanket. "Why mess with something that's working?"

"Why—because all the big rewards come with risks, Mags!"

She'd flopped onto her stomach on my bed, still scrolling. "And you'll never get the highs if you don't chance a couple of lows."

I'd still protested. Pushed back, albeit weakly, because pushing back against my sister was never my strong point. But after a while, she wore me down, and had me message one of them, a guy in my biology class. And then another. And then another. And none of them even responded.

When she left a week later, Elinor had taken me aside, asked if I was okay.

"I just don't know how she forgot what it feels like." I watched out the window, watched Mom back her car out of the driveway to take Marianne and Brandon to Newark. "To get hurt."

"Brandon makes her forget." Elinor sighed, put her hand on my shoulder, and squeezed. "I know it's easy to get swept up in everything when she's here. I should have kept a better eye on things. Taken care of you."

"I can take care of myself." I didn't mean it. I wanted Elinor with me, to be tucked thoroughly under her wing, so I didn't have to feel this way ever again, watching my messages go unanswered.

"The whole point of a big sister is having someone to take care of you," Elinor said. "That's what I'm here for."

The same thing happened every time Marianne visited. *Tell me about boys; that guy on the swim team I've seen you talking to is cute; why don't I come up and take you into the city for the weekend—we'll have so much fun! Just blow off swim practice, there'll always be another practice; let me do something fun for you, Elinor won't mind; I'm your sister, don't you trust me?*

But I learned to avoid it. To make excuses, to claim swim meets and midterms and not answer the phone enough times that she just stopped calling. I stuck with Elinor and rejected Marianne's wild ideas and schemes. And Elinor, in turn, always made sure I was okay. Helped me make excuses when I needed them. Showed me that a life lived without risk could still be perfectly fine.

I'd memorized the blueprint, over the last five years, of how to be an Elinor. And I was stronger than I used to be. Could be around my middle sister without immediately getting pulled in. I could do this. Could trust my own brain to keep itself safe.

"Okay." I poured a second cup of water and handed it to Marianne as I went straight for the big guns. "Kiss, marry, kill." We'd played this game all the time growing up, even though Elinor hated it, which made it a perfect recipe for instant, careful closeness. I needed Marianne to feel like I was opening up to her to get this to work, even if inside, I was keeping my heart carefully protected. "To get us warmed up for mixing, singles style."

"Really?" Marianne wrinkled her nose, sweeping her eyes over the other attendees. "I feel like it'll set the bar too high. Like, in what universe would I kill Hugh Grant but then chat up Daiquiri Joe over there?" She nodded toward the bar, where some guy—not Torden, thank God—was holding a frozen red drink in each hand, insisting that the bartender pile them up with even more cherries. Yes, he was horrifying. You're welcome for my careful audition process, Marianne.

"First of all, there's no world in which you'd ever kill Hugh Grant, which is ridiculous, because he's ten thousand years old." The words slipped out of me, easy. Maybe pretending Marianne and I were close again wouldn't be as hard as I'd thought. "And second, come on. You love this game."

"I do." Marianne grinned, bright and lovely, just like she'd always been. "Fine. Kiss, marry, kill . . . God, I don't even know what celebrities you're into these days. Do you still like JoJo Siwa?"

"I mean, obviously." I'd been captivated by JoJo's ponytail at a very young age, much like everyone else I knew. "It's fine. I'll go first and pull out some of your favorite olds. How about—Tom Holland, Bowen Yang, and Chris Pine?"

"Unfair list!" Marianne gasped, and I snorted, sending orange-and-cucumber-flavored water up my nose. *Ouch.* I threw my hand up over my face to try and cover it, but she obviously saw, because she burst out laughing, too. "Serves you right, smart-ass. You know it's against the rules to put that many certified saints into one round. And Tom Holland isn't *old.*"

"Fine." I giggled, wiping water off my face. If Elinor had been here, she'd be horrified by my lack of decorum. But it was kind of fun to let loose a little. "We'll call it a draw."

"I'll allow it." Marianne laughed, too, taking my cup from me. "I better hold on to this, just in case."

What had I been so afraid of? I could totally do this. I was having a fun time with my sister, which I hadn't pulled off in approximately forever, and my plan was falling perfectly into place. I saw Torden take his position at the bar, drinking what I knew was water disguised as a cocktail (Torden had gotten very into the idea of subterfuge, even when I reminded him that Marianne *knew* he was going to be there), with Luisa hovering off to the side. I didn't have anything to worry about.

Or at least, I didn't until I saw Gabe making a beeline toward me, eyes wide.

"Hey." He stopped in front of me, and Marianne immediately turned toward him with an eyebrow raised. I didn't blame her; he'd approached us at a super-high velocity. "You're— I'm—hi. Um. Do you want—could we—do you—"

"Are you asking her if she wants to dance?" Marianne supplied helpfully, full-on grinning, though she tried to hide it behind her hand.

"I—yes." Gabe's face had turned bright red, and if I wasn't so concerned about him breaking from the plan by coming over to us before Torden did, I'd have been grinning, too. This was a far cry from the confident, aloof Gabe I'd gotten to know. "Let's."

Before I could even say yes, he'd grabbed my hand and pulled me into the cluster of madness that was the dance floor, pushing us toward the middle until I couldn't see Marianne at all.

"Hey! What the hell?" I said. What was the point of a plan if people were going to go around changing it? Gabe dropped my hand and took a few deep breaths. He looked like he needed them. "What are you doing? I'm supposed to hang out with Marianne until Torden sweeps her off her feet."

"Yeah, well, you may want to adjust that plan." Away from Marianne and no longer pretending to be into me, he had reverted to confident, self-assured Gabe, which made me feel . . . disappointed? Which I had no right to be. If he found the idea of asking me to dance so abhorrent that it nearly sent him into a panic attack, that was just fine, because we *weren't* going down that road. He and I both knew that. "Because Torden has developed an accent."

"Like . . . his Norwegian accent got stronger?" I asked, holding my ground as an overly enthusiastic couple behind me threatened to drag me into their grinding. "I don't think Marianne will care. She'll probably think it's mysterious."

"No, like *he's using a British accent*," Gabe clarified, and okay, yeah, that was bad. "He said he was watching *The Crown* last night and got inspired, and now he's developed a full backstory about how he's a lord or something and was friends with Eugenie at Oxford."

"Oh my God." I turned in a circle, trying to see Torden, but I couldn't through the crowds. "We need to stop him. See if Tomas is free tonight. Can we send Torden to the brig?"

"Absolutely not. Come on." He grabbed me by the wrist— not the hand, I noticed, which had to be purposeful—and pulled me toward the bar. "You can talk him out of it."

Gabe sure sounded confident considering that Torden was already leaning over my sister, speaking in a low voice, when we made it over to them. She brightened when she saw me, her cheeks flushed the same color pink as the wine in her hand.

"Margaret!" She touched Torden on the arm, giggling. "You didn't tell me that Torden was a viscount. And did you know that his family personally protected the Queen's corgis during World War Two?"

Well, damn it.

⚓

BY the time we settled into bed that night, Marianne still couldn't stop gushing.

"He's tall, isn't he?" She hummed to herself as she plumped her pillow into the correct shape, stacking three on top of one another for maximum support. "Torden. And can you believe what he told us about his dad? I didn't realize they still banished people. Seems a little extreme."

"Almost made-up," I agreed, glad I was in my bunk already and Marianne couldn't see my face. Now that Torden had started his fake royalty routine, there was no turning back, even if it would have been way easier if he'd just been himself, like we'd agreed. "Do you like him?"

"Sure," Marianne said, though the effusiveness had dropped out of her voice. That was weird. If anything, I'd expect Marianne's affections to only grow for Torden the more she talked about him. Marianne could always talk her way into love. "He's excited to see Key West with us."

"Do you *not* like him?" I wanted Marianne head over heels for this guy. If she wasn't, I'd rather cut my losses early, head back to the Boyfriend Drawing Board (patent pending), and not waste anyone's time. "Because we don't have to hang out with him again if you don't want to."

"What? No, he's fine. It's just weird." She sighed, dropping back onto the stack of pillows. "Dating again."

Oh. This was . . . not a road I'd expected to go down.

"I guess it's been a while." I remembered the first time Brandon had taken her out on an actual date. He'd brought flowers for all of us—me and Mom and Elinor, too. I'd thought it was so exciting, so romantic, that I'd gotten swept up in the high of it, just like Marianne had. "But I'm sure it'll be great."

"I hope so." Marianne's voice was earnest, and I realized, maybe for the first time, how much she needed this. She looked lost, lying there in the bed. Loveless. *Well, you can fix that*, I thought. *You're fixing that.* "What are we going to tell Elinor?"

"No idea." Elinor wasn't going to be thrilled about us going into port with some guys we'd just met. "Maybe we tell her that Torden and Gabe are tour guides."

"Or maybe . . . we don't tell her at all?" Marianne sat up again, and I felt my heart drop into my stomach. "I know. I don't like it, either. But it seems easier. You know how she gets."

You know how she gets. How many times had Elinor said that to me about Marianne? How many times had I thought it? But it wasn't like Marianne was wrong. The idea of us going off with a couple of guys we had just met would send Elinor into a tailspin. *The last time you went off with Marianne without Elinor knowing, she almost killed you both*, my brain reminded me; and, okay, yeah, that was true, but I wasn't thirteen anymore, and I'd be the one behind the metaphorical wheel of this excursion. Elinor would just have to learn that I could take care of the family just as well as she could.

"We'll tell her we want to spend our first day in Key West together. Just the two of us," I said, as Marianne turned off the lights. The ship rocked gently beneath us, making me sleepy. This would work. And maybe we'd still have enough time after the date for Elinor and Edward to come out and meet us. I could still get in some of the E+E quality time I'd come on this cruise for in the first place.

"Yeah. Good night, Mags," Marianne said, turning over. I closed my eyes, trying not to think about what it would feel like to outright lie to Elinor.

It wasn't like anyone was asking me to choose one sister over the other. This was going to be fine.

CHAPTER NINE

As it turned out, lying to Elinor wasn't that hard.

"Who's ready to see the Florida Keys?" Edward announced on Friday when he and Elinor met me and Marianne at the entrance to the dining room, his eyes shining with excitement behind his glasses. Although Edward tended toward the serious, each new port on our trip brought out this puppy-dog excitement in him as he'd marched off to Nassau and Nighthawk Cay, the ship's small island where we'd docked midweek, with the enthusiasm of an eight-month-old Labrador. "Come on—we got a table with a view!"

The *Mab* had a few different options for dining—a humongous buffet laid out practically twenty-four hours a day, a taco stand by the pool, a coffee shop up on one of the top decks—but we kept coming back to the dining room, partially because it was a lot less crowded than the other options and partially because the space's elegance thrilled me every time. The room was dressed in light green wallpaper, patterned with small cameos and scenes of ships, a piece of art that always surrounded you. The chairs were high-backed and gilded, the chandeliers elaborate, the servers immaculately polite. One of the servers we'd gotten to know over the last few days, Ramon, led us to our table, nodding and smiling as Edward filled him on whatever specific historical fact he was excited about today and doing an amazing job of looking interested.

"The Conch Republic!" Edward exclaimed as Ramon pulled chairs out for us before leaving to grab coffee. "Did you know that Key West briefly formed its own country? The Conch Republic? And to defend their fortress, they threw stale Cuban bread at the American military? Fascinating."

"Edward accidentally stayed up all night reading the guidebook," Elinor said, as Edward accepted coffee and grinned sheepishly. They were, I realized with some horror, wearing matching button-down shirts, each emblazoned with leaping dolphins on a light blue background. With Elinor's tight bun and bright red hair, she looked like Ms. Frizzle had gone back to school to become a nautical librarian; Edward just looked like he'd wandered into the bargain bin at a Jimmy Buffett concert. I couldn't help but compare their looks to Marianne's. She was wearing a cutout white maxi dress that she'd decked out with a bright pink flamingo belt and about a thousand jangly bracelets. One of these women seemed way more primed to have fun than the other, and a wave of guilt passed over me at the thought of who I'd rather hang out with today. "And he's been in contact with one of the guides at the Hemingway Home and Museum so we can all go and meet up with her to learn some behind-the-scenes facts. There's fifty-four cats on the property, did you know that? And most of them have six toes on each front paw. One of them even has *seven* toes on two of his paws."

"Um." I turned to Marianne for support, and she nodded back, encouraging. "Marianne and I are actually—we're booked on a different excursion today." Although it was a shame to miss all the cats. I'd have to make time for that the next time we were in port.

"You are?" Elinor glanced up from the menu, where I assumed she was deciding between one or two egg whites. "Why?"

"We thought we could get some sister time in." Marianne smiled wide. Any hesitation I'd heard last night was fully gone now; her enthusiasm served as a reminder that my plan was a great idea. "Just the two of us, you know?"

"What?" Elinor looked stunned, and I didn't blame her. It had been years since I'd willingly gone off with Marianne alone, and the last time that I had . . . "I don't know if that's a good idea."

"El, chill." Marianne tossed her hair back over her shoulder, and Elinor bristled, probably because she'd never been chill in her entire life. "I just want to show Margaret some fun. It's been forever."

"I'm expanding my horizons," I added, which was technically true, if you counted conducting an elaborate ruse involving your older sister's love life as horizon expanding. I did. "It's one island. How much trouble can we get into?"

And, yeah, I understood why Elinor was staring at me like I'd grown a third head. But I'd been thirteen when the accident happened. Marianne's passenger. This time, I thought, trying to send a secret, sisterly message into Elinor's brain, I was the one in charge.

The message didn't seem to reach her, because she stood up from the table, fast, and looked me straight in the eye.

"Margaret, can I chat with you for a second? Alone?"

"Sure." I gulped. Oh God, she knew somehow, I could just tell. Elinor always knew everything.

I followed her just outside the dining room, where she sat on one of the benches at the base of the *Mab*'s portholes.

"I don't think this is a good idea."

"Why not?" I hadn't expected this level of pushback. Some, sure, but it was like she didn't trust me at all. "I'm responsible. I'll make sure we don't get into any trouble."

"And how, exactly, will you make sure of that?" She tapped her fingers against the bench, drumming out a nervous beat. "You know what she's like."

"Yeah, but I can handle it, Elinor." Thank God I hadn't told her about the double date. "Trust me."

Elinor watched me for a long, long time. Then, finally she nodded.

"All right. But be careful."

"Always," I said, as we made our way back to the dining room. As if I ever wasn't. As if the past five years of my life hadn't been built around that very principle.

A hint of resentment blossomed in my chest, reaching toward my oldest sister.

"RIGHT this way, right this way. Watch your step as you enter the train. Please, everyone, watch your step!" Our tour guide for the day, a short woman named Carla with tanned skin and a no-nonsense attitude, was holding a large, closed umbrella over her head so that we could see her in the mass of people. Marianne was by my side, her arm linked through mine in a gesture that felt more familiar than I was used to; just behind us, Gabe and Torden (sorry, *Viscount* Torden) did their best to stick close as we climbed onto the orange and yellow open-air train that would take us through my very first tropical island of the trip.

"This is amazing." I was doing my best to seem like a cool woman of the world in front of Gabe and Torden, who were *actually* well traveled and didn't need to hear me geeking out, but I could only restrain myself so much. I'd waited until Key West to get off the ship, wanting to get the lay of the land on board before I disembarked at any ports, and that meant that I was *filled* with new-adventure adrenaline. And when I'd first heard about the Conch Tour Train ("Key West's Number One Destination!" according to the cruise website), I'd envisioned, you know, train tracks. But this train drove through the streets instead, designed to look like an old-fashioned steam engine that pulled all of us behind it. We sat down on wooden benches, Marianne in front of me with Torden (who had promised Gabe he wasn't going to pull any more stunts like last night's) and Gabe beside me. He was, inexplicably, still wearing a black T-shirt, even though it was approximately ten thousand degrees outside and I was already sweating through my sundress. Gabe didn't seem like he was ever impacted by his environment, though. "It smells—I know it's weird to say it smells tropical, because that's not a smell, but it must be, because it does. You know?"

"I think that's sunscreen." Gabe looked down at the map Carla had handed him, unfolding it so it covered both of our laps. In front of us, Torden was doing his best to charm Marianne—they'd entered into a lively conversation about various royals of England. (They were both team Harry and Meghan.) "So what's the plan? Are we taking this to Duval Street? Mallory Square? I assume you want to hit all the big tourist sites."

"I mean, we'll see them from the train. That's why it's open-air, right?" I pushed my sunglasses down from my hair and over my eyes, squinting into the bright sun. The *Mab* had docked on the west side of the island, a short walk from the main attractions, and since Key West was tiny, it wouldn't take us long to see everything. "I figured we'd do a full loop first, and then for the second time through, I made a ranked list of which stop we should get off at first." I tapped on my cross-body bag, where my notebook was carefully tucked away. After my chat with Elinor at breakfast, I was determined to keep today as safe and carefully planned as possible. If even *one* thing went wrong, Elinor would shoot into helicopter mode, and I couldn't afford to let that happen, not with Operation: Marianne at stake.

Gabe quirked the side of his mouth down into the beginning of a frown as the train started to pull away. Palm trees lined either side of the road, swaying in a gentle breeze. "That's a long time to be on the train."

"Yeah, but we'll get the lay of the land that way." I ran my hand over the map, following the route with my finger. "Plus, we can pick out which of these coupons we want to use and cross-reference them to the stops that look the best. 'Discounted key lime pie' is my middle name."

"This is how you like to do things, huh?" Gabe leaned his

head out the open side of the train, the breeze ruffling his hair. He ran his hand through it, sending it even further into disarray. "Orderly?"

"We live in a chaotic world, Gabriel." I folded the map back up, though I kept it in my lap, where I could check it again with ease. "You can't blame me for trying to assign order to it."

"Mm," he said in response. It sounded like he wanted to say more, but he didn't elaborate and I didn't ask him to as we pulled away from the cruise terminal and made our way into the heart of the island.

⚓

MARIANNE hated my plan.

"Come on!" she said, standing up before the train came to a full and complete stop—which earned her a dirty look from Carla, who was in the middle of a long series of jokes about why the various chickens of Key West crossed the road—and grabbing the back of her bench for balance. We'd been on the train for maybe ten minutes, just long enough for Carla to tell us about the history of the island and take us to our first stop, Mallory Square. "Let's explore."

"Marianne." A few other folks started to get off the train, but I stayed firmly put. "There's a bunch more stops. If we get off here, we won't learn anything about the rest of them."

"Please," she said, grabbing me by the wrist and pulling me from my bench. I yelped, doing my best to hold my bag as she started walking forward. "It's a hop on, hop off situation, isn't it? You're supposed to hop off. Later, if we want, we can hop on."

"But we paid for the whole—"

"We're in Key West!" With a wave to Carla, Marianne hopped down onto the sidewalk, still pulling me along. Torden and Gabe had followed us, Gabe watching me and Marianne with confusion while Torden started greeting passersby with calls of *Chip, cheerio!* "We don't need plans. We can wing it."

Ah, yes, my least favorite sentence.

"I just . . ." I watched longingly as the train pulled away, Carla leading a new batch of tourists through the tour I'd envisioned for myself. "I didn't even hear the punch line for the last joke."

"We'll google it. Let's go!" She dove into the crowds that were filling the sidewalks, moving slowly up and down like molasses—or maybe hermit crabs would be a more apt tropical simile—as Torden followed her with a shrug. I stood still, stuck in place like I'd grown roots. Behind me, I heard Gabe cough.

"You okay?"

"She always does this." Every visit back to New Jersey, where she pulled me along into her chaos with no regard for how it would affect me. The time she'd taken me to get my hair cut and convinced the hairdresser to give me bangs without telling me because she thought they would look *just so cute, Margaret!* Moving to New Orleans with Brandon just a few months after they started dating, saying, *I'll bring you out to visit so much, you won't even notice I'm gone!* The sounds of the hospital, the beeps of all the monitors they'd hooked her up to after the accident. Waiting for the results from the surgery to see if she would make it. To find out if I'd been the last one to see my sister alive. "She just gets *ideas* and follows them without thinking about the consequences." This was what Elinor had been worried about. She knew what Marianne was like without boundaries. Why had I been so convinced she'd respect mine?

"We don't have to go with them, if you don't want to," Gabe suggested, and I almost laughed. No matter how bad I felt now, anxiety clawing up from inside me, I'd feel a hell of a lot worse if I wasn't keeping an eye on my sister.

"Yes, we do." I sighed, watching Marianne chatter animatedly to a woman selling little critters made out of shells. "Someone has to."

Gabe didn't say anything else. Just nodded as we pushed our way into the crowds, too. And as we did, I realized that my map had been abandoned on the train in Marianne's rush to make us leave. My hands crumpled at my side, longing for the smooth feel of the paper beneath my fingers, tracing a path I understood.

CHAPTER TEN

The island was overwhelming. Over the next few hours, we all followed Marianne wherever she decided we should go next, like ducklings behind their mother, if ducklings spent a *lot* of time asking the mother duck if they could please just get back on the Conch Tour Train that they'd already paid for in full. And, sure, I was charmed by Key West's narrow streets, the chickens that roamed everywhere (chickens! on a tropical island!), and the cats that peered at us with curiosity from Ernest Hemingway's house. (We didn't get close enough to count toes, unfortunately.) We'd seen the southernmost point of the United States, places you could buy conch fritters and sponges (like, from the sea, not from Costco), drag performers in tall headdresses dancing in the streets, and hunched-over old men smiling as they ate slices of cream-colored pie bigger than my head.

And every time I saw something that interested me, something that *I* wanted to pay more attention to, Marianne would pull us in a different direction.

At first, it was annoying. Now, hours in, I was just about ready to try and swim back to the ship. Marianne didn't want to stay in one place longer than five minutes, I was exhausted, and Torden's accent was falling apart. If this was what travel was like, it was the opposite of exciting. I had never been so drained.

We'd ended up in front of the Hemingway house again, not because Marianne had any particular attachment to Ernest Hemingway, but because she'd chatted up a group of women on tour bikes who *looked like they knew how to find something fun* and ending up following their terrible directions back here, instead of to the *totally picturesque and perfect little garden* they'd promised her. Seeing the breezy, two-story white house was cool the first time, but now? Now I was ready to let the cats eat me so that this day would be over. I slid down against the fence to sit cross-legged on the sidewalk, utterly exhausted from my day trying to keep up with the Energizer Bunny. When she'd been with Brandon, he'd kept her on track. Made her a less frantic version of herself. I wished Torden had the same power.

"Huh. Didn't mean to end up here again." Marianne tutted, looking at the house with disappointment. "Oh, shoot, and we probably need to run, right? We're getting close to all-aboard time."

"What?" I tried to scramble to my feet, but my legs were exhausted from all the walking we'd done, so it was less of a scramble and more of a slow stagger. How had I lost track of the time like that? Elinor would have never. "We were going to get pie. There was a coupon in the map."

"Didn't we leave the map on the train?" Torden asked,

putting so many trills in the word "train" I thought his tongue was going to end up tied into a knot. "So we don't have the coupon. And I wouldn't risk it, love." Torden's accent had morphed from posh British into Cockney as exhaustion crept over him, which would have been hilarious if I wasn't so tired. "They don't mess around with all-aboard time."

I knew, objectively, that he was right. That I should be pushing us back to the ship, anyway. If the goal for today was to give Marianne a great time with a nice guy, mission accomplished. We'd be back next week—we'd be back once a week for the next five weeks—and I could get pie then. I could get it five more times, if I wanted it. Today had been Marianne's day, that was all.

But a tiny part of me had hoped it could be my day, too.

Elinor would have known how to handle this. I was suddenly worried that I couldn't.

That was probably why my eyes welled up with tears, which I quickly tried to cover by pushing my sunglasses up to cover them. Unfortunately, Gabe noticed.

"Hey." He moved in closer, so that Marianne and Torden wouldn't hear. "You okay?"

"Fine." My voice was sharp, I knew, but if it came to a choice between sharp and vulnerable, I'd choose sharp every time. "Let's get back to the ship. It's just pie. Who even cares."

"You do?" Gabe's brows furrowed.

"This doesn't have anything to do with the plan, Gabe." I jerked my head toward Marianne and Torden. Framed against the backdrop of the house, she was like a postcard for cruising: hair down and gently curled against her shoulders, the blond shining in the sun; big sunglasses and flower earrings made of clay that she'd found in *the cutest little boutique in New Orleans, I'll take you there sometime*. She looked like what she was—the fun one. The whimsical, jet-setting, hopeless romantic. The sister who was meant for exploring new places like this, who could let go of the agenda and just float wherever life took her. And I'd been more like her once, but now I was all bent in on myself, crying because I hadn't gotten a piece of pie that I'd planned on. Pathetic. Plans were supposed to *protect* me from feeling this way, not make the feeling worse. "We're good."

I doubted he believed me, but he stepped back anyway.

But as we sped toward the ship, the terrible feeling didn't leave. It was just this deep and undeniable dread. The sort of dread that forced its way down inside of you, crept through your veins, and froze your fingers and your toes. Paralyzing.

Marianne and Torden were in front of me, and they were having the time of their lives, laughing and joking and running hand in hand. *Good.* That should have made me feel better. Today's plan had fallen to pieces, but I was still on track when it came to the big picture.

Was Torden even the right guy for Marianne, though, when he hadn't balanced her out the way I'd hoped? Because Brandon would have kept Marianne to the plan. He would have kept our family running smoothly. Helped me relax. Bridged the gap between my sister and me.

God, maybe Elinor was right. Maybe I was in way, way over my head.

"You want to talk about it?" Gabe asked finally, as we turned down Duval Street, already nighttime raucous, despite it being mid-afternoon. The sights and sounds pressed in on me, a steel drum playing against screams and whoops, and I felt buried. "Or just keep walking in silence until we get back to the ship? I could go either way."

"Funny." As we cut behind Duval, the sound quieted down a little—more rustling palm trees and bird calls than screams of "Shots, shots, shots!" and bachelor parties. "I'm fine. I promise."

"Because new places can be overwhelming." Gabe kept talking, like he hadn't heard me. "Especially when you're already putting a lot on your plate, what with, you know, your master plans and all." He darted his eyes toward Marianne and Torden, like I wouldn't know which plan he was talking about. "It's okay to have feelings about it."

"I promise, Gabe, there are no feelings to worry about here." I needed to get myself together. I was just hot, I was just tired, there was no reason I couldn't keep the situation under control. I'd never prove my worth to Elinor if I fell apart the very first time I tried to help Marianne. I just needed practice, that was all. It would get easier. It had to get easier. "I just got too much sun."

"Right."

"I mean it," I said, pulling at a loose thread at the bottom of my dress. This outfit had seemed perfect when I'd picked it out this morning, something that felt easy and breezy while everything I planned fell into place perfectly. Now it was stained from the day, with patches of sweat under my arms and a small tear in the hem where I'd gotten it snagged on a bush. "I don't—I just like to be in control. That's all." Strong meant keeping it together, always. And I had to be strong, because my sister needed me.

I didn't want to just shut Gabe down, though, not after he'd given up his day off to help me, so I did my best to conjure up an explanation.

"And I really wanted key lime pie." Yeah, when I said it out loud, it sounded even more pathetic than it had in my head.

"We'll be back next week. You can go without Marianne." Gabe nodded, confident, like he knew for sure that next week I'd be able to get off the ship and do my own thing without needing to keep an eye on my sister at every turn, like I didn't need to play the ever-present puppet master to guide her into making the right decisions.

Today, it had felt like she was the one pulling the strings.

But I put on a brave face for Gabe, nodded, and did my best to smile, because at the end of the day, I barely knew him. And he barely knew me.

And that was how I'd said I wanted it.

I must have fallen asleep when I made it back to the stateroom, because I dreamed about the accident.

It was blurry, of course. My memories of that day—of that week—always were. Mostly what I remembered was how dark the house was. Marianne had been in bed for a week, ever since the guy she'd been seeing had broken up with her via text message. Marianne came home wailing and Mom had wailed with her, tucking her into bed and pulling all the blinds closed, with strict instructions to me and Elinor *not* to open them.

It gave the whole week a foggy feeling, even before everything else that happened.

Because Marianne left the house one day, finally, and we all thought it was a good thing. A sign that she was moving on. She'd even let me come with her, when I'd asked. I didn't know she was going to confront her ex. That she'd find him with his newly pregnant, newly married bride. And she'd been so distraught on the drive home. Couldn't navigate through the tears. And she'd gotten cut off, spun out in a panic, and then—the tree. The impact. The way I'd screamed from the pain and then screamed even more when Marianne wasn't responding.

In my dream, I mostly saw the ambulance lights. But I heard Elinor's voice, too, cutting through the sirens. *We shouldn't have let her go. She can't be trusted to make good decisions right now.* At first it had seemed unfair, but she was right, wasn't she? Marianne needed someone to guide her. Someone to take care of her.

Brandon had been so good at that. Had he spared a thought for what would happen to Marianne, once they'd broken up? Spared a thought for me, for Elinor, who would inevitably be forced to pick up the pieces of what he'd broken?

I woke up in a cold sweat, sheets twisted around me. I'd slept through the start of dinner—Elinor would be worried, but I'd check in with her later. Make sure I wasn't another sibling she had to worry about.

But still, I needed to get some food. I didn't want to deal with going into the main dining room halfway through the meal, so that left the buffet, where I could grab a sandwich or something easy. Something to eat quickly and then fall back asleep until I'd shaken off as much of this day as I could.

But when I made it to our door, I saw a tray with a silver

dome on it, room-service style, sitting in the hallway. Weird—maybe Ramon had noticed my absence at dinner and sent something down?

When I carried it inside and pulled the lid off, though, I knew it hadn't been Ramon, or anyone in my family.

There, on a gleaming white plate, was a small slice of key lime pie.

CHAPTER ELEVEN

The next morning, changeover day, my stomach was full of pie and the rest of me was full of optimism. Sure, yesterday had gone wildly off the rails, but that just meant I needed to make a stronger plan, one that had less room for error. But I could do that! I was basically the plan captain. Did I need a captain hat from the gift shop to make it official? Maybe. One step at a time.

I managed a quick breakfast with the fam, where Edward spent the whole time talking about a wedding he was officiating that afternoon, whose bride was, in his words, "alarmingly anti-seagull."

"Are most brides pro-seagull?" I asked around a mouthful of chocolate croissant. "Or do they tend to lean neutral?"

"Trust me, Margaret," Edward said, as Elinor chuckled, in on a joke I didn't understand. "When it comes to weddings, no one is neutral on anything."

Elinor invited me to try morning trivia with the two of them, but I passed. As much as Elinor and Edward would probably be a calming presence for me, a port in the metaphorical storm that was Operation: Marianne, after what Marianne had told me this morning, I needed to find Gabe.

"He just spends a lot of time talking about the aristocracy, you know?" Marianne had said back in our cabin, applying sunscreen to her face as she explained why she wasn't going to see Torden again. "I love Meghan and everything, but there comes a point where enough is enough."

Which meant it was back to the drawing board for me and Gabe. So as the ship welcomed new guests and said goodbye to old ones, I headed down to the theater, where Gabe was working the rehearsal for tonight's welcome show preview.

I slipped into the back of the theater unnoticed, pulling the door closed softly behind me so I wouldn't disturb the performers onstage. This was the first time I'd seen the theater in rehearsal mode, and I was struck by how grand it still felt, even though everyone was in shorts and T-shirts and leggings instead of their elaborate sparkles and spangles. They were practicing the big kick line, thirty dancers lined up across the stage with the variety show performers, like Gabe's aunt and uncle, interspersed between them. The curtain was pulled halfway up; the stage was bare; and the whole thing had a magical, liminal quality to it. Like this space existed outside of time, because in here, the only thing that mattered was the show, the performance. A single-minded pursuit, executed with perfect control.

I liked that.

I slid into the tech booth beside Gabe. He nodded without breaking his concentration on the stage, where the kick line was moving into the big rousing finale, and Gabe was lowering sliders and adjusting levels like he was the one doing magic tricks. I liked watching it. Watching him.

When the performers hit their final pose and the director called for a break, Gabe lowered his headset down around his neck and turned to me, tapping a rhythm out on the board in front of him.

"Good breakfast today?"

"Yeah. High proportion of blueberry to pancake, which is always ideal." I reached into my bag and pulled out a cheese Danish wrapped in a napkin to hand to Gabe. He'd mentioned he liked them. "Brought you a snack."

"Aw, hell yeah." He grabbed the Danish from me, glancing around furtively before biting into the pastry (though he made sure to do it over his lap, and not over the soundboard). Crinkles of flaky pastry scattered down, and he did his best to catch them as he swallowed and made an appreciative noise. It was weird, I thought suddenly, that I'd only known Gabe for a week. It felt like a million times longer than that. But maybe that was just what happened when you were on a ship, when your world was reduced to the same people around you every moment for days on end; it made time different.

"Speaking of pastry." I took a deep breath, shaking my hair out of its ponytail before I pulled it back again. The sea air wreaked havoc on my curls, so up and out of the way was the only style I'd managed to stick with. "That pie was from you, right?"

"Maybe." To my surprise, Gabe flushed, a definitive red hue appearing underneath his tanned cheeks. "Key lime is a top pie choice. You wanted to try it."

"It wasn't even on the menu last night." Obviously I had

checked. "Did you have the chef make an entire pie just for me? And if so, what happened to the rest of the pie?"

"Please don't make a big deal out of this." He looked pained, which I kind of enjoyed. "It's just pie. The kitchen makes, like, ten thousand a day."

"Well, it was sweet. And I'm going to remember you were nice to me." I waggled my eyebrows at him, and he groaned, leaning back in his chair, which squeaked beneath him.

"When am I ever not nice to you?"

"You won't let me play with the sliders, for one," I said, and Gabe scoffed. "I just think the background vocals deserve their chance to shine, that's all."

"You'll play with these sliders over my dead body." Up ahead, the director was calling the actors back to places, but Gabe kept his gaze locked on me. "You feeling better?"

"Definitely. Here's the thing . . ." It would have been easier to not talk about this, to just let the summer keep going the way it had been. But for better or for worse, Gabe had become my partner in Operation: Marianne, and he deserved to know what was going on. "Marianne doesn't want to see Torden anymore. Which is super annoying, but whatever—that's why we have Tomas and Xander lined up. So we need to figure out what the next step is; and this time, I need to make a *way* stricter plan for it. Like, maybe we do an escape room where we literally can't leave?" Not that I was any good at escape rooms. We'd done one for Edward's birthday last year, and I'd gotten my hand stuck in the body of a guitar because Elinor was convinced there was a clue inside. "What do you think?"

"I don't know." Gabe picked a pastry flake off his jeans. "That doesn't seem like your sister's thing."

"My sister's 'thing' is throwing herself headfirst into everything and hoping that she doesn't land on something sharp." I handed Gabe a napkin. "She's all into, like, carefree spontaneity. If we were doing this the Marianne way, there would be no plan at all."

"Which wouldn't work."

"Exactly." I ran my hand over the bottom of the soundboard, far enough away from the actual controls that Gabe couldn't get mad at me. "Because we need to account for all the variables."

"Oh. I mean, I guess that, too," Gabe said. "I just meant because you're like, allergic to carefree spontaneity."

Excuse me?

"What do you mean?" I must have misunderstood him. "I'll have you know I have an *extremely* spontaneous side, thank you very much."

As I spoke, I realized something weird.

Gabe was *smiling*.

It was small, and he was trying to hide it. But he was smiling.

"What?" I asked, shifting toward him to try and get a better look at his mouth, scooting my chair in his direction even as he pushed me away. "Are you laughing?"

"No!" Gabe gasped, in what was definitely an undisguised laugh. He straightened up, facing me head-on. Some of his hair had fallen in front of his eyes, disguising his thick eyebrows, and he pushed it back before continuing. "I'm not trying to offend you. And I know we haven't known each other long. But you're probably the least carefree and spontaneous person I've ever met."

Yeah, I was a thousand percent offended.

"What's that supposed to mean?" We'd been whispering before, but I spoke at full volume, completely forgetting my theater decorum.

"Shush." He darted his eyes over twenty rows of red-velvet stairs to the bare wooden stage, where the director had turned to look at us with concern. "No, no problem, sorry," he said into his headset, closing his eyes briefly. "Yeah, five would be great. Thanks, Jamila." He turned back toward me, forehead furrowed. "Come on," he said, reaching out a hand to pull me up from my seat and not so gently guide me up the aisle and out of the theater. I didn't protest, just let him push me, too stunned by what he'd said to do anything else. I mean, sure, I liked plans, but I could be carefree! I could be go with the flow! I hadn't even preplanned my breakfast choices this morning!

Once we were out the doors and in the small, carpeted lobby lined with posters advertising the different performances and flanked by a bar that sold everything from frozen cocktails to elaborately flavored popcorns, he finally spoke again.

"Can you try not to get me fired if you're going to hang out in the booth, please?" He ran a hand through his hair, which I was starting to suspect was perpetually ruffled. "Just because I'm related to Luisa and Peter doesn't mean they won't terminate my contract early and make me stay in Miami."

"That seems dramatic, even for a bunch of performers."

"You have no idea." He leaned back against the wall outside the theater, letting out a deep sigh. "I guess if they tried to fire me, I could rewrite all the show cues so that they played the

Grease soundtrack during the ballet number. That would show them."

"The perfect revenge," I said. "Can we forgive my drama queen moment and go back to where you told me I wasn't spontaneous? Because I totally am. I'm on this cruise, right? And I'm moving to California for college in the fall. That's like, the capital of carefree living."

"Sure." Gabe kicked his sneaker against the carpet, scuffing it. "But a cruise is all structure, Margaret. So is college, no matter where you put it. And structure isn't bad, but *everything* you do lives in that structure. And that's why you had so much trouble yesterday, right? Because Marianne was ignoring all the structure you'd built for yourself."

"Maybe." He had a point, even though I hated to admit it. "I used to be different, though. Before . . . well. A lot of stuff went down." Not opening myself up *that* much to Gabe. Not here. "I could be that way again."

"Oh yeah?" Gabe came as close as he ever did to smiling. "So you're actually going to chill out about this thing with your sister? Because that might involve actually—gasp, I know— relaxing into it. Take your sister—and you, I guess—on a date with more flexibility than 'follow a carefully planned-out map with a guy who sounds like he was kicked off the set of *Bridgerton*.'"

"You asking me out, Gabe?" I shot back, shoving my hands into the pockets of my romper. "Because that's not the kind of date I know how to plan."

"We both know that me asking you out is against the rules, Margaret," he replied, and I swore I could feel the words through my entire body.

"Maybe I can lift the rules, just this once." I was playing with fire. But no one could accuse me of not going with the flow. "You're my fake boyfriend for the summer, after all. Plan a date for us. Teach me your ways. Show me the true meaning of spontaneity."

"You think you can handle it?" When had Gabe moved closer to me? I didn't know, but I didn't mind it. And maybe this was being carefree. Not caring that I liked it. "You trust me?"

One week. That was how long I'd known Gabe. One week. Which, out in the real world, wouldn't even *begin* to qualify him as someone I trusted. Hell, most people I'd known my entire life didn't qualify as someone I trusted. And yet for whatever reason, the answer was still a firm, total, and unde-niable—

"Yes."

I would have to unpack that one later.

"Great." He glanced over his shoulder. "I need to get back inside before I *do* lose my job. But I'll see you later. And, Margaret?" he added, just as he was about to slip back into the theater, leaving me out here to reckon with what, exactly, I'd just agreed to.

"Yeah?" The word hung between us, containing a lot more than one syllable could let on.

He tapped out a beat on the side of the door, the same rat-a-tat-tat that he'd done against the soundboard earlier. "Try to loosen your shoulders, will you? You're on vacation."

CHAPTER TWELVE

For the rest of the day, I did my best to exude *carefree*, if only to prove to myself that I could. No plans? No problem! Let's just dawdle in the atrium and see what looks interesting. No idea what to get for lunch? Just stop in the first place you walk past and get whatever's listed first on the menu! It would be easy, I told myself. I was adaptable. I could turn into a go-with-the-flow person overnight, if I had to.

Except that I lasted maybe two hours before overwhelming anxiety pushed its way into me.

It was just that there were so many things going on in the atrium, and how was I supposed to just pick one without doing thorough research into what all my options were? The first thing that caught my eye seemed like a cool jewelry raffle, but it ended up being the cruise equivalent of an infomercial where we were very heavily encouraged to buy gold by the inch. Who needed gold by the inch?

They almost got me, too, but I faked a coughing fit and escaped out a side entrance.

After my near miss with the gold thing, I choked down the dry hot dog I'd grabbed by the pool and considered my next move. Clearly, I was going to need help with my full personality shift, and Gabe was working for the rest of the day. Not that I wanted to ask him, anyway. I couldn't believe I'd flirted with him so blatantly—and worse, that he'd given it right back. *He knows the rules*, I reminded myself, but it still made me nervous. No, I needed to give him some space. Besides, it would be way more powerful to show up to our next excursion already fully chill-ified.

Which meant I needed a different teacher. And there was only one available solution.

"Mags!" Marianne called when I found her at the pool deck, sipping something frozen and neon-colored as she waved her book in my direction. "There you are."

"In the vaguely sunburned flesh." We used to be so alike, Marianne and me. We were always swooning over the same movies and sighing over the same poems, stuff that Marianne would read me off her Instagram feed, since Elinor was still insisting that I was too young to have an account of my own. That was why I'd gone with her, the day of the accident. Because a big confrontation like the one she was planning had seemed romantic. Exciting.

And the results had been the opposite.

Afterward, I'd prided myself on getting as far away from her as possible, on being like my more sensible older sister. I'd made myself into a copy of Elinor in every way I could. But Elinor wasn't the one I was seeking out now, was she?

I was clinging to my plans, but maybe they were holding me back more than they were helping me.

"Don't let Elinor see you sunburned." Marianne patted the chair next to her, mercifully empty, and I plopped down into it. "You'll be up to your neck in aloe vera."

"Ha. Yeah." I rubbed my hand over my neck, trying to seem casual. "What are you up to?"

Marianne gave me a weird look, which was valid, because her activity *was* pretty obvious. "Lounging, Mags. Why? You're not trying to re-hook me up with Torden, are you? Because I think I have a new no-royalty rule. And also"—she leaned in conspiratorially—"I have an admittedly wild idea. What's been missing from the guys I've dated?"

Lifelong commitment to you? I thought, but didn't say out loud.

She raised her book in the air again, waving it around in excitement. "Athleticism! So I was thinking, what if we found a couple of jocks to hang out with?"

"You want to date . . . a jock?" Was this some weird grieving step I didn't know about? Like, after your supposedly lifelong partner breaks up with you, you go through denial, anger, bargaining, acceptance, and then you skip depression and hop straight into dating athletes. Taylor Swift could get a whole album out of that, if true. "Marianne. You *hate* sports. You made us change the channel during the Super Bowl." And also, it was weird that she'd been so chipper since ending it with Torden. I'd expected her to go right back into full-on Brandon depression mode, but instead she'd seemed . . . fine.

"I made you change the channel to the Puppy Bowl!" she protested, which, fair. It was objectively a better use of our time. Shake it off, Margaret. If Marianne could let go of Brandon, so could I. "And whatever. The guys I've been going for clearly didn't work out." Something flashed across her face, a moment that almost looked like grief, and I was reminded that she maybe wasn't as okay as she kept claiming. "Maybe it's time to try something new."

Something new. That wasn't something I'd done in . . . forever. Since the accident, it was all about plans and goals and sticking to what I'd set out to do, zero deviations.

And it hadn't worked, had it? I mean, it had worked for *me*, but it wasn't working for Marianne. She definitely wasn't going to go along with an even firmer plan. I remembered Gabe's face when he told me I wasn't spontaneous. Well, yeah, that made sense. I was trying to be Elinor.

But maybe I needed to play by Marianne's rules for a while. And it wasn't like I was *only* like Elinor. There was still plenty of Marianne in me, too. And even though I'd spent the last five years pushing it down, maybe it was time to embrace it.

Gently embrace it. Baby steps.

"And how are you going to find these athletic specimens?" I asked, making a mental note to tell Gabe about Marianne's new athlete goal. Everyone we'd picked for her lived firmly in the looked-like-poets realm. Or maybe being like Marianne meant not planning out her boyfriends. Maybe we'd just find someone in a meet-cute, like I'd done with Gabe. Not that Gabe was a meet-cute. Or a boyfriend. "Host a cannonball contest?"

"Please." Marianne pulled out her phone, scrolled through her cruise app until she found what she was searching for. "We're going to find our future boyfriends in America's favorite pastime."

"Baseball?"

"Maybe in 1952, Margaret." She held up her phone in my direction, sunlight glinting off the screen, and my stomach dropped into my knees, because while I would definitely consider myself an athlete, my hand-eye coordination was zero. "*Pickleball.*"

If this wasn't going with the flow, I didn't know what was.

OPEN pickleball play started in an hour, so we had just enough time to pop back to our stateroom and change into something Marianne deemed "pickleball appropriate." For her, that involved a short white dress with a swishy skirt, and a scoop-neck top showing off a necklace with an actual pickleball paddle charm hanging off it. Where she'd managed to find that with such short notice, I had no idea; I had to imagine her side of the closet was one of those magical trunks that contained an endless supply of accessories.

Devastatingly, I didn't look nearly as cute. Not having realized that "clothes that you could exercise in while looking hot" was part of the dress code for a cruise, I was forced to pull together the best outfit I could out of my regular gym clothes: black bike shorts and a tank with *Women love me, fish fear me* printed on the front. (Marianne had given it to Edward for Christmas a couple of years ago; as soon as her back was turned, he'd passed it over to me and I'd cut off the sleeves to maximize its dorkiness.) I looked like I was going to lift weights in a garage somewhere; Marianne looked like she was heading for the US Open.

No one was surprised.

What *was* surprising was that we'd managed to pick up Elinor and Edward along the way.

Elinor had poked her head out of her stateroom just as we were coming back to change, her eyes lighting up when she saw us. It made me feel kind of guilty, if I was being honest. We'd come on this cruise with the intention of spending time together, but I'd basically ditched her at every turn to hang out with Marianne or Gabe. And, sure, it would be worth it when she realized that I'd nobly used my summer to save Marianne's love life, but still. I owed her some of my time, too.

It was just that when they looked at me, both of my sisters, I felt stretched in two wildly different directions, and when I tried to split my time between them, I was afraid that I might snap before I ever figured out who *I* was.

"What are you two up to?" she'd asked, leaning out the doorframe of her cabin. She'd started decorating her door with magnets, inexpensive trinkets I recognized from the gift shop. It made me smile, the way Elinor could turn any place into a home. "I feel like I've barely seen you."

"We were just heading up to the pickleball courts," Marianne said, and I stifled a laugh. The only person I knew who was less athletic than Marianne was Elinor. "Going to try our hand at it."

"Did someone say pickleball?" Edward appeared from inside the cabin, poking his head out. "Mind if we join you?"

"Really?" I tried to hide my skepticism, but it was a challenge. I'd once seen Edward trip getting off a Ferris wheel. "You know it's, like, a game, right? Not a pickle-based activity?"

"Trust me." Edward and Elinor exchanged one of those looks I'd come to recognize in their marriage, the kind that said they knew something we didn't know, a look that I assumed only came around when you'd known someone so well that they'd become a part of you. "We know pickleball."

CHAPTER THIRTEEN

Elinor and Edward were absolutely whupping our asses on the court.

I had never played pickleball before, but I had played tennis, which I assumed was basically the same thing. Plus, I considered myself a reasonably athletic person, and had already been recruited to be on my college's swim team next year, which had to count for something, right?

Famous last words.

"Seven–one one!" Elinor called, dropping the yellow plastic ball on her paddle and hitting it square into the middle of Marianne's side of the court. Marianne dove, catching the edge of the ball with her paddle and barely getting it over the net again. Which could have been a great move, if Edward hadn't gotten there like lightning, smashing the ball—how did you even smash a ball as light as this one? It was basically a worse version of a Wiffle ball—back to us, firmly in the line but too far for either of us to reach in time.

"That's how you do it!" Elinor shouted, tapping her paddle

against Edward's as they both jogged backward and I ran, breathless, to get the ball before it rolled overboard. (Hadn't happened yet, but the threat added an extra dimension of fear to the game.)

I had never seen my oldest sister like this; and it was something to behold, even if it *was* terrifying. Ten minutes after we'd agreed to let them join us, she and Edward had appeared on the top deck, both dressed in matching floral shorts and tank tops that said *Hate the Pickle, Love the Ball.* This was so out of character to begin with that I'd walked straight into the basketball hoop still set up on the court; it was going to leave a nasty bruise later. I would have bet money that Edward barely knew what a tank top *was*, let alone owned one; his arms were so pale it looked like they'd never seen the light of day.

But, damn, the two of them moved like they were extensions of the same body. When Edward shifted forward, Elinor shifted back; they knew who would go for the ball without ever having to call it out, whereas Marianne and I had run straight into each other on several occasions. I'd managed to get a single point only when a guest had greeted Edward just as I hit the ball into his corner of what Elinor kept calling the kitchen; otherwise, we were getting completely and totally creamed.

After the game mercifully ended 11–1, and Elinor and Edward had performed a choreographed dance to celebrate, the four of us collapsed on the benches next to the court.

"Not bad for your first time!" Edward said, sipping from his water bottle. If it had been anyone but Edward, this would have been condescending; but even in victory, Edward didn't have a condescending bone in his body. "Marianne, are you feeling all right?"

"No," she groaned from beneath the bench, where she'd lain down to seek out the barest hint of shade and poured the contents of an entire water bottle over her head. "I'm dying. I might already be dead. Edward, you're a church guy. If I was already dead, would I still feel like I was dying?"

"Nope," Elinor said quickly, before Edward could respond. "The pickleball court is a theology-free zone. House rule."

"You heard her." Edward leaned over and kissed Elinor on the cheek. "If we don't obey the house rules, the whole world descends into chaos."

"Amen," Elinor said with solemnity, and then the two of them laughed, leaning into each other like they were sharing a secret Marianne and I would never be part of.

It was weird to see them together like this, in what I was quickly realizing was their natural habitat. The way they moved perfectly in sync with each other. And when I looked down at Marianne, I saw something in her eyes that I didn't expect. She was watching Elinor and Edward, too, and she was absolutely grief-stricken. It could have been from losing our pickleball game so badly. But I knew instinctively that she was thinking of Brandon. So much for using pickleball to avoid the stages of her mourning. All it had done was remind her of what she had lost.

And, listen, did I feel a pang of something when I looked at Elinor and Edward? Of course I did. But I figured I'd find it eventually. Elinor hadn't lost herself in some big romantic love affair to end up with Edward. They'd just sort of . . . come together, rather sensibly. So after college, probably, once

I'd gotten myself firmly established in the real world, I could work on that. To look for it now—it just didn't make sense.

Marianne didn't care if love made sense. She just wanted it.

But maybe in the meantime, fun, easygoing Margaret could help her, in a way that rules-loving Margaret had failed.

"I think," I said, reaching down and offering her a hand to pull her up to her feet, "that we need to take an ice cream break and regroup, and then we're going to kick your butts. Especially once I hop into the internet café and learn what dinking is."

"You're sure?" Marianne asked, sitting up. "You don't need to run off for the afternoon?"

"And admit defeat?" This might have been a terrible idea. But what did I have to lose? "Absolutely not."

CHAPTER FOURTEEN

After that, I made it my mission to stay glued to my middle sister's side.

At first, it had felt like a chore. Following her up and down the ship, letting her whims dictate wherever we went . . . my poor, plan-loving brain could barely handle it.

But after a while I started to have . . . fun? There was something to be said for hanging out with Marianne. We went dancing after dinner, jumping in the air and screaming when Marianne's favorite vintage nineties hits blasted through the club. We spent an entire day trying to sample every dessert offered on the ship, starting when the buffet first opened at six in the morning and shutting it down at midnight. (Admittedly, my body did its best to shut that expedition down *way* before then.) We even teamed up for a synchronized cannonball contest, splashing into the water with such force and enthusiasm that Jono, the cruise director, called us the Cannonball Twins every time he saw us over the next few days.

And even though she was still dateless—Xander and Tomas

kept flaking—Marianne didn't seem nearly as torn up about it as I'd anticipated. I kept expecting her to bring up Brandon, to have to deal with emotional outbursts and breakdowns, but my sister seemed perfectly content to flit through our cruise in pursuit only of fun. It turned out that chill, easygoing Margaret was the perfect match for this stage of Marianne's life.

I'd seen Gabe a few times, too, tried to weasel clues about our next excursion out of him, but he wouldn't crack, just told me that it was going to "blow my mind." So that was a little nerve-racking, but I didn't push back on it, because in my new go-with-the-flow state, that sort of thing was totally cool.

The only person who seemed less on board with our carefree days was Elinor.

The more time I spent with Marianne, the more Elinor seemed extra uptight by comparison. And while I'd always valued that, admired it, out here it seemed . . . unnecessary, maybe? All I knew was that I was gravitating to Marianne more and more.

"Leaving so soon?" Elinor had asked that Sunday at dinner, as Marianne and I scarfed down our entrées and told Ramon that we'd be skipping dessert. "We've barely seen you today."

"They've got a miniature golf course set up in the atrium, and Margaret and I want to be the first ones on it," Marianne explained, gulping the last of her iced tea. "Otherwise, all the good clubs will be gone."

"Can't miss out on those good clubs," I agreed, and steeled myself against the hurt on Elinor's face. If she'd just trusted me to help take care of Marianne in the first place, we could be doing this together. If she felt isolated, that wasn't on me. Besides, she had Edward. What did she need us for?

That dinner seemed to be the last straw, though, since Elinor decided that I *had* to get off in Nassau with her and Edward, our first port of the week.

Immediately, I panicked. I'd been doing a great job embracing my chill side. Hanging out with Elinor and Edward could send me right back into my world of lists and rules and careful planning, and then what would have been the point of all this learning-to-be-spontaneous stuff?

Not that it was for me. I was doing that for Marianne. To be more like Marianne. Well, to help her. Because of course I was more like Elinor. Except for the parts of me that were starting to feel more and more like Marianne again.

God. No wonder I was wound so tightly.

So when I was finally walking down the gangplank off the *Mab*, dragging behind Edward and Elinor as they walked with more purpose than I thought was necessary for a supposed day of leisure, I was feeling frankly overwhelmed. Marianne wasn't even with us, because she'd made a spa appointment before Elinor told us her plans; and while a week ago that would have been the best news I'd heard all day, now I just felt kind of weird and lost without the purpose of entertaining my middle sister.

I'd make it through. This was just another test of my ability to adapt. Maybe it would be easy. Maybe it would be great. I'd spent the last five years doing everything I could to hang on to Elinor. My rock. After all, wasn't this why I'd joined them on the cruise in the first place?

I had met my sister and brother-in-law in the lobby, then

followed them down to the end of the gangplank, where a crew member was waiting to scan our key cards. I handed mine over and followed Elinor and Edward through a turnstile into, officially, Nassau.

"All right!" Elinor paused just beyond the checkpoint, rummaging in her bag to make sure we had everything. "I've got a full day planned, but, Margaret, do you want to look it over? Is there anything you want to do?"

"What?" No one had asked me that in days. Marianne just bounced from location to location, assuming (correctly) that I'd follow her. "No. Whatever you want is fine."

"Are you sure?" Elinor smiled, but I could read the confusion in her eyes, even though they were well shaded under her straw hat. "I know you did a ton of research of your own going into this trip."

"Nope! I'm completely open!" I had, in fact, done the aforementioned ton of research, but I wasn't going to undo all my careful chillness by jumping into it now. Even if, on the inside, I was itching to check out some of the town's pastel-colored government buildings, which all the guide sites said were a can't-miss stop. "Whatever you planned is fine."

"Oh. All right." Elinor shrugged. As she started walking us through our itinerary, I did my best to look around, to soak up just being in the Bahamas. We were on a covered pier, with a huge market just in front of us, full of Bahamians selling everything from elaborate creations made of straw to T-shirts with sayings and pictures I was glad Elinor hadn't seen yet. Our fellow cruisers were piling off the ship behind us, streaming toward the market and the city of Nassau beyond it without a care in the world; I envied them.

"It's a bit of a tourist mecca more than anything else, but this is where your mother requested we get her a souvenir," Edward explained as Elinor led us to our first destination, the straw market, falling back beside me so that we weren't walking three across on the crowded sidewalk. "Are you're sure you're feeling all right, Margaret? It's not like you not to have an opinion on what we're doing."

"I'm just trying to be more spontaneous," I explained, figuring I could go into the vague vibes of my plan with Edward without revealing the whole Marianne part. Besides, if there was anyone in the world I could talk to about, well, anything, it was Edward. "Planning too much takes the fun out of things sometimes, you know?"

"Does it?" He tilted his head to the side, considered my statement. Edward had sunglass lenses clipped on over his regular glasses, which took away from his usual air of seriousness. "I suppose you could think of it that way. But I've always found that planning can be the best way to guarantee you'll do the things you most enjoy."

Unless your plans are absolutely and totally torn apart by life and the people in them, I thought, then reared back, blinking. Where had that come from? That wasn't why I was avoiding plans. This was just the easiest way to handle Marianne. It wasn't anything deeper than that.

But it was kind of true, wasn't it? Because I'd had a plan for what my life would look like before Dad died. We all did. And then Marianne had a plan, probably, for what her life looked like with Brandon, and he'd torn that into pieces. Maybe it wasn't just that plans could hold you back. Maybe, sometimes, it was that they could actively hurt you.

"We should wait and give this to you in May." Brandon smiled over at Marianne, who was sitting next to him on their green velvet couch, squished together in their New Orleans apartment. "But we thought it might be better to have more time to get ready."

"And you couldn't wait that long," Marianne said, her voice teasing as she knocked her forehead into her boyfriend's shoulder.

"That, too," Brandon admitted, and they both laughed. I was visiting the two of them in New Orleans, my first time ever. Their apartment was small, but utterly romantic, with a little balcony and magnolia trees that draped all over it.

"What is it?" I shifted in my chair, nervous. This life seemed perfect for them, but it was also clear that I didn't fit in it, that it had been built for two, an enclosed unit. I'd be back in New Jersey soon, though, back with Mom and Elinor and Edward. I could handle a surprise.

"Here." Brandon passed me an envelope, thick and cream colored, and I opened it quickly, my hands shaky as I revealed a brochure for the University of Lisbon. I looked up.

"What is this?"

"It's your graduation present." Marianne squeezed Brandon's arm, talking fast, while I looked to him instead. Brandon was the centering calm to Marianne's hurricane. He centered the whole family, really. "Brandon's lecturing there as a visiting professor next December, during your winter break. He'll be there for a week, and we thought you could go with him."

It was like the Earth had stopped moving.

"What?" I asked, my eyes immediately filling with tears. "That's—really?"

"We've been saving up our frequent flyer points, and no one

will appreciate the trip like you, Mags." Brandon smiled, and I knew that he realized what this meant to me. *I'd always wanted to see the world, and his travels were the first thing we'd bonded over when he met us. "It's the perfect plan."*

There'd be no trip to Portugal now, of course.

Edward placed his hand on my shoulder, gentle.

"Margaret?"

"All good!" I kept my voice chipper.

Plans were for people who trusted the universe. My mom had planned to spend her whole life with my dad. Marianne had planned to be with Brandon. I'd planned to keep my family intact.

What was it they said, about the best-laid plans? Brandon had quoted a super-old poem about it once. *The best laid schemes o' mice an' men / Gang aft a-gley.* He said it meant that they went astray.

Mine had gone further than astray. They'd jumped ship entirely.

And maybe Elinor could still find her plans comforting, but I was starting to realize I didn't. Not anymore.

I spent a dutiful day with Elinor and Edward, following them from shop to shop and doing my best to absorb everything Elinor read out loud from the guidebook. But I kept missing Marianne, too, hearing the echoes of her laugh around every corner, picturing the way she would liven up our visit.

Which, again, weird! Wasn't Elinor the sister I was supposed to feel safe around? Marianne was the one I was actively puppeteering, and yet I wished she were here with us.

Brains. They were complicated little monsters.

When we met up with Marianne for dinner that night, though, she was bursting with excitement, and I welcomed it.

"I had *such* a nice day." Marianne was eating chilled fruit soup with a vigor I'd never seen from someone consuming what was, basically, a smoothie with a weirder name. "My massage was to *die* for, and then I ended up in this napkin-folding class that sounded super dorky but turned out to be great. I'll have to show off my creations after we eat." I should have been grateful that she didn't have a Brandon breakdown or convince the ship's captain to marry her to the bartender, but instead I just felt . . . envious, maybe. I bet *she'd* never had an existential crisis about plans, or lack thereof.

Down in the theater with Gabe after dinner, sitting on the stage between shows with our feet swinging beneath us, I brought the problem up to him.

"It's weird." My voice echoed in the empty space, bouncing back at me no matter how quietly I spoke. "I started this summer determined to be a full-on Elinor. Now I'm wondering if I've been modeling my behavior on the wrong sister."

"I don't know." Gabe shrugged, his hand deep in a box of popcorn I'd brought for us to snack on. "Isn't Marianne, like, deep in the throes of heartbreak? How much of how she's acting right now is, like, a post-breakup reaction?"

"That's the weird thing." I snatched the popcorn back, and Gabe let out a groan that made me feel things I wasn't going to think about right now. "She should be devastated. The whole reason I came up with this dating plan was to hold off said devastation. But she seems . . . mostly fine. Like, sometimes she'll get sad looks when she sees Elinor and Edward together, but otherwise it's just hashtag cruise life fun."

"Guess she's just figured out a good way to cope with it." Gabe leaned back against the stage, propped up by his wrists. "People change."

Not like this, I thought. "Well, either way, I think she's excited to go out with Tomas. You're sure you're not going to tell me what the big date is?"

"Margaret Dashwood, you have no sense of romance." He shook his head, and I got the sense he was laughing at me. "Let me surprise you."

"That would only apply if this was a real romance."

"Which it's not."

"No." It felt like we were reminding ourselves, repeating the words back to each other. "It's not." Silence hung heavy between us for a few seconds, before I hastily changed the subject. "I did a good job being chill today, though. I just followed along with Elinor's plan for everything."

"Congratulations?"

"I know how it sounds." I sighed. I let myself fall backward, onto the stage, and Gabe leaned back the rest of the way to lie beside me as we both stared up at the ceiling. All the harshest stage lights had been switched off—and a good thing, too, or else we'd be literally blinded—but the remaining lights scattered over the theater's ceiling sparkled down on us like stars. "But I think for me that's progress. And Elinor isn't the type to just, like, jump on top of the nearest bar and start dancing. Following her from place to place without inserting myself into her itinerary officially counts as being carefree."

"See anything cool?" Gabe shifted onto his side, propping his head up on his hand to look at me. He'd swapped his usual uniform of a short-sleeve black T-shirt and black jeans for a long-sleeve black T-shirt and black jeans, but his expression was always the same when he looked at me like this. Serious. Intense. "Or did you just stay in Bahamian Disney World?"

"What do you mean?" I mirrored his pose, suddenly aware of how close we'd become and shifting back slightly, scooting my hips across the stage with approximately zero dignity. "I took a picture of a city sign. I can show it to you if you don't believe me. That was, legally and officially, Nassau."

"Thanks, *Guinness Book of World Records*." He rolled his eyes, scoffing. Rude. "Yes, that was *legally* Nassau. And, sure, it's all that most tourists will ever see of it. But if you go, like, half a mile off the souvenir strip, you can see the parts of it that are at least a little realer. Like, the Government House has really amazing architecture." Damn it, I'd known that! I'd looked it up! "And the beaches that are further than ten feet from the cruise ships are way less busy, so you can actually, you know, enjoy the beach, not just be packed in like sardines with the same people you've been trapped on board with all week."

"Once again, you have a knack for making vacation sound like a prison sentence, so great work." I flopped onto my back again, my heart sinking. What the hell was the answer, then? Go with the flow, end up on a super-standard tourist expedition; or make a plan, freak out when it didn't go well. It was starting to feel like I just couldn't win.

"Look." Gabe must have realized he'd sent me further into an existential crisis. He kicked gently at my ankle, and I tried to ignore the tingly way it made me feel. "I work Wednesday, but if you meet me in the morning when we're docking at Nighthawk Cay, I can point out my favorite place on the island. Somewhere passengers hardly ever go. Going off the beaten path like that feels very in line with the vibe you're trying to curate." Nighthawk Cay was a private island owned by the cruise company, and on our port day there, it was mostly populated by passengers of the cruise and whatever crew members were working on the island.

"Yeah." I felt kind of funny, a quick beating in my chest, and I wanted to believe it was excitement about seeing something new. But if I was being honest with myself, I knew that it was about Gabe. Thinking of me. Working to help me. "Maybe."

"Good." Gabe sat up, sweeping loose popcorn kernels off the stage back into the box, like we'd never been here. "It's a date."

And the way he said that . . . I hated it and liked it, all at the same time.

I didn't expect Gabe to take me up on a *helipad*.

"You're sure we're allowed to be here?" I asked for the thousandth time. We were standing in the middle of the giant white *H* that marked the ship's designated helicopter landing spot, a coffee in one hand and a plate of pastries I'd taken from the buffet in the other. I'd met Gabe at the theater a little before sunrise, still blinking sleep out of my eyes, so it took me a minute to realize where he was taking me. When we'd climbed up the last set of stairs onto the giant green-and-white platform, I'd gasped.

"Positive. Crew privilege." Gabe was standing right at the railing, pointing toward the island that was rising out of the sea before us. "I thought you'd like the quiet. Most guests don't get to come up here unless there's a special reception or they're being medically evacuated."

"Would you call this quiet?" Sure, there weren't any people, but the wind was whipping around my ears loudly enough that it was hard to even hear Gabe. He smirked.

"You know what I mean. Come on." He tilted his head, and after a moment of hesitation, I walked toward him, swallowing when I made it to the railing. I had to give it to Gabe—this felt like we were on a different ship entirely. I had to resist the urge to do a *Titanic* king-of-the-world moment.

"Okay," I admitted, once I'd put down my breakfast plate so I could cling to the railing and adjust to the roar of the wind. Gabe's arm was pressed against mine, which didn't hurt, either. "This is pretty cool."

"Told you. And look. There's the lighthouse." Gabe pointed off the port side of the ship. (Port, I knew now, was the left-hand side of the ship when you were facing forward. It was one of *several* nautical terms I'd picked up in the last couple weeks on board.) "See it sticking up at the very point of the island?"

I peered forward, squinting. It was a hazy day, with choppy water—I was staggering more than usual, guarding the top of my coffee cup like it was precious cargo—but I could just barely make out the glint of a lighthouse through the fog that enveloped the island. From the way Gabe looked at it, it was the most special thing he'd ever seen.

"I think I see it." Rays of pink and orange coated the water, the sunrise making its way toward us. "So that's your favorite place on the island?" I was skeptical, and Gabe noticed.

"I mean, sure, if you were expecting a Diamonds International . . ." he deadpanned, and I rolled my eyes. I'd seen about half a dozen of the tourist-geared jewelry shops in Nassau, and Gabe had told me they were in almost every cruise port in the world. "It's just nice, you know? I'm not trying to get you into cliff diving here. But I've been going there since I was a little kid."

"Wow. They let you in the tech booth young."

"Ha." Gabe kept watching the water, like he was searching for something. "I used to visit Peter and Luisa every summer. My avó—that's my grandmother, she's the one who raised me—would send me down for a couple of weeks so she could get a break and I'd basically have the run of the ship. It was awesome."

"Gabriel Monteiro." I placed the hand that wasn't clinging to my cup of coffee over my heart, shocked. "Did you just express a positive memory related to this cruise ship?"

"Shut up." This time he did grin, just a little. "I was young and didn't know any better." The grin faded and he turned back out toward the island, which was coming more into focus as we got closer, piercing our way through the fog. "It really was great, though. The crew has a lot of faults but it's still kind of . . . a big family. I know, that's unbelievably dorky." He sighed as I snickered. "But I didn't have that much. Anyway." He looked at me sideways and I wondered what the deal with his family was. If he'd been raised by his grandmother, did that mean he didn't have parents around? He clearly cared for Luisa and Peter, and vice versa, but I never saw them act parental toward him.

I wondered if he was lonely. I wondered if he was lonely in a different way than I was.

But Gabe didn't like talking about himself, so I didn't pry, just looked back out toward the lighthouse. It was a faded white, with a black top and a light that flashed from within every few seconds.

"You can go up there." He pointed to the top, and I followed his gaze, the strong curve of his arm. "So that's what I would do. Go up to the top and see the whole island. Think you can manage that?"

"Oh, for sure." Maybe. "If Baby Gabe can do it, I'm pretty sure I can, too."

"I'll have you know Baby Gabe was a stone-cold killer, thank you very much." We had pulled all the way up to the island now, and way down below us, members of the crew were securing the ship to the dock. Gabe turned away from the railing, grabbing a croissant. "You should go today. Check it out."

"Marianne is meeting Tomas today," I reminded him. Since Gabe was working, it wouldn't be a proper double date, but I'd still arranged to get brunch with Marianne and her newest beau so I could nip any British-royalty-related role-play in the bud. After Torden, I couldn't be too careful. "I don't know that I'll make it ashore."

"You could just let her do this by herself," Gabe said, and I didn't know why, but something about that felt completely and totally . . . wrong, a wave of fear crashing over me. Gabe didn't notice. "Tomas is a good guy. And we screened him.

You don't exactly need to be there for every moment of their dates."

"I guess." But I did, was the thing. And a week ago, I would have said it was because Marianne couldn't be trusted to be on her own, but now . . . I didn't know. Maybe it was that I didn't trust *myself* on my own, without a sister to mimic. "I don't know."

"Right." Gabe didn't comment any further. Gabe was great at not commenting any further—it was one of the things I liked best about him (in a *friendly* way, obviously). "I should get down to the theater. There's a pirate party for the kids' clubs tonight and the tech is kind of absurd."

"Sounds right up your alley." I tucked a loose curl behind my ear, doing my best to secure it against the wind. "Are there costumes involved?"

"I might have a puffy shirt," Gabe said, and I almost choked at the image. Did they let non-children into those parties? Probably not, if they were just going to undress the tech guys with their eyes.

Whoa. Slow down there, Margaret. God, I was up way too early, if I was having thoughts like that about my purely platonic friend. I needed a nap before brunch. I grabbed one of the pastries, if only to have something to do with my hands. "Okay, well, I'm going to need a picture of that."

"Absolutely not." Gabe bumped his shoulder into mine, biting into a croissant. "Good luck today, okay? Be the Margaret Dashwood you wish to see in the world or whatever."

"Mags." The word came out of my mouth before I could think about it. "That's what my family calls me. You can, too, if you want. Or not. It doesn't matter."

"Mags." He said it slowly, testing it out in his mouth. "It suits you. My family just calls me Gabe, for what it's worth. Or Gabriel, I guess, but I stick with Gabe."

"Yeah, that feels right." I laughed, filled with a relief I didn't quite understand. "See you later, Gabe."

"See you, Mags." He waved, and I liked the way my name sounded when he said it. Like a promise.

I tried not to think about what he was promising.

CHAPTER FIFTEEN

Let it be known I fully intended to get off the ship right away and go have a carefree, spontaneous adventure at the lighthouse. (Sure, I'd technically planned it out with Gabe, but I didn't want to get caught up in technicalities.) At least, after I went to brunch with Marianne and made sure Tomas hadn't been disguising his serial killer intentions this whole time.

But I fell asleep for *way* longer than I meant to when I made it back to our cabin, only waking up to a harsh pounding on our door. I jolted up in my bunk bed, just barely missed hitting my head on the ceiling, and half jumped, half fell to the floor in my race to stop the knocking. I almost expected to find one of the crew in the hallway, telling me we were going under, but when I flung the door open it was just Elinor, extra chipper in a huge sun hat with a beach bag slung over her shoulder.

"What's happening?" I gasped, still not fully emerged into the land of the living. "Is the ship on fire or something?"

"What? No." Elinor's brow furrowed in concern. She was

dressed for island adventure today, or at least, Elinor's version of it: the aforementioned hat (one of the ones that had a hole in the back for her ponytail to stick out of), an oversized button-down, and a pair of khaki shorts that stopped just above her knees. The whole vibe was very OG *Jurassic Park*. "You just didn't come out the first few times I knocked. Were you asleep? It's after ten."

"Yeah, well, I'm not anymore." I held the door open for her to come in as I yawned, moving groggily through the room toward Marianne's bed, which I threw myself down on. "Where's Marianne, anyway?" She'd still been asleep when I got back to the cabin, and I was surprised to see her bed empty. The light coming in from the hallway was bright, and I blinked against its harshness. "She could have woken me up." And she should have, I realized with a sinking feeling—we were supposed to meet Tomas for brunch at ten. Apparently she'd gone on without me.

"I ran into her in the gym earlier—she said she had plans and that she'd catch up with you later." Elinor tried to smile through the words as she sat down beside me, but when I looked over, I could see the tension in her face. Join the club. I didn't love the idea of Marianne doing brunch on her own, to be honest. Not that I didn't trust her. It was just—*let go, be chill, trust the process.* I took a deep breath, tried to believe it when I told myself everything would be fine. "But Edward's doing another wedding today, so I thought you and I could spend the day together. Explore Nighthawk. How does that sound?"

"That sounds—great." With Operation: Marianne still a secret from Elinor, I didn't have any excuse to go running after my middle sister. *She probably just forgot you were coming,*

I thought, which, yikes, I hated the idea of Marianne just forgetting about me like that. But she was in mourning, right? If her behavior was erratic, it was justified. It might not have been that she forgot about me. She just—decided she didn't need me.

Yeah, that didn't sound any better.

Half an hour later, I'd showered and changed into my two-piece, pulling denim cutoffs and a baggy T-shirt over it and slipping my feet into sandals. With an Elinor-approved level of sunscreen applied everywhere, and more tucked into my bag along with my book and hat, I met Elinor down in the atrium. She'd grabbed me a breakfast sandwich from the buffet—the kind I'd grown to love, where the egg yolk was still mostly soft and squishy in the middle and the cheese was perfectly melted—so my annoyance with my wake-up call had faded a little as we headed to Nighthawk Cay.

"Wow," I breathed, once we'd stepped off the gangplank. Nighthawk Cay had been completely undeveloped before the cruise line had taken it over, and parts of it still looked like an unexplored jungle. A shiver went through me as I peered just off the sandy walking trail and into a tangle of trees, low and scrubby, that seemed to go on forever. Even though I kept thinking about Tomas and Marianne at brunch, wondering if they were getting along, if he was as good of a guy as he'd seemed at his audition . . . it was hard to feel too worried, now that we were on the island. It was hot today, humid, and the air felt like it was pressing down all around me, almost like a weighted blanket. It forced me to slow down, to take deep breaths, letting the sticky humidity fill my lungs. *This is good*, I told myself. *This is different.*

"Margaret? Did you hear me?" Crap. Elinor was looking at me funny, her sunglasses dropped down on her nose; I must have zoned out entirely on her. And now I was feeling that suffocation again, the squeezing I'd felt a few times on this trip, and I was picturing all the ways that Marianne's date with Tomas could be going wrong as we spoke. He could be married, for all we knew. He could be the kind of guy who seemed great for weeks and then turned out to be an asshole, or the kind of guy who seemed great for *years* and then turned out to be the worst thing that had ever happened to you. I just wanted Marianne to be happy. I wanted her to be safe. I didn't know how to keep her that way.

Focus, Margaret.

"Sorry. What did you say?" *Just look at Elinor. Look at Elinor and don't think about anything else but what was happening right now. Take in the rounded shape of her sunglasses, their tortoiseshell pattern. Breathe in through my nose and smell the ocean, salty and stinging, picked up in the light breeze that did little to push back against the heat.* The vague scent of coconut, more likely from someone's sunscreen than the actual fruit. Seagulls, cawing overhead. We had seagulls in New Jersey. They may have been the same ones I knew, migrated south for the—the summer? I'd work on the theory.

The feeling wasn't gone, but it was subdued. Managed.

"I asked if you wanted to check out some of the activities, or head straight to the beach?" Elinor pushed her sunglasses back up on her face, tutting with concern. "Are you dehydrated already? We've been out in the sun for five minutes. Did you not drink water when you woke up this morning? I told you that it was important—"

"I did. Sorry. I'm fine." God, Elinor could go on. I knew it was because she cared about me, but I missed Marianne's carefree attitude. "Let's beach." This would have been a great time to check out the lighthouse, but I wasn't in the mood to be adventurous right now. If anything, I wanted to go back to the ship and lie down in my cabin, go back to sleep, and exist entirely in that space between making plans and plans breaking, where nothing could hurt me. Wait there until Marianne came back, then let her take me around the ship and mold me into whoever she wanted me to be.

But I couldn't leave Elinor.

I'd never wanted to leave Elinor before.

AFTER that, the beach day was kind of a bust. We snagged a couple of chairs in the shade, and both Elinor and I settled in with paperbacks and smoothies, but it all just felt . . . off. Sitting quietly with Elinor, which had always been the most natural thing in the world to me, suddenly felt stilted. Uncomfortable. Like I was constantly trying to read her for cues on what she was thinking in a way I never had to with Marianne.

I hated it. I didn't want to gain one sister at the expense of the other. But maybe I didn't have a choice. I even suggested we check out the lighthouse, just to have something to do, something to break the impenetrable silence.

"It's not far." I pointed over toward the palm trees behind us, the scrub that overtook the island just behind the main path. You could just see the top of the lighthouse jutting above the greenery, beckoning us. "The views are supposed to be spectacular. The best vantage point on the island."

"I'm comfortable," Elinor said, which seemed impossible to me, because how she could be comfortable when I was so thoroughly not? "Maybe we can check it out later? Or you can head over there, if you want. I'll hold down the fort."

"It's okay." Elinor kept asking me to make decisions, to *choose*. Marianne never did. "I'll go a different day."

Later, I ran into the ocean to cool off, and it was the best I'd felt in the hours since we'd arrived. Plunged beneath the surface, sound distorted, light coming in as twisted rays from above me, the world was both reduced to just my own thoughts and broadened way beyond them, all at the same time. I'd felt hopeful, under there, that I could change. That I could do better.

Then I'd run out of breath and burst, gasping, from the surface, and Elinor had made me reapply sunscreen again, and I'd gone right back where I'd started. How much of life was like that? A constant series of nearly finding what you were looking for, just for it to slide out of your grasp?

Whatever it was, it was frustrating. By the time we got back to the ship and I discovered Marianne, lounging on the pool deck with a frozen drink in one hand and a thick romance novel in the other, I was ready to get away from do-you-want-me-to-get-you-another-water? did-you-put-on-more-sunscreen? are-you-totally-sure-about-that-water? Elinor, and be around someone happy to make all the decisions for me. I threw myself down into the chair next to my sister.

"Mags!" She reached over and squeezed my hand, folding

down a page in her book before tucking it into her bag. "I had the *best* morning. Tomas was a great find."

"You liked him?" I'd half expected an apology for ditching me at brunch, but she was smiling so much that it was hard to feel annoyed. Besides, this was what I'd wanted all day. To just lie here and let Marianne run the show. And it wasn't like this was a totally one-sided relationship, either. It had been barely two weeks since she'd been sobbing in the bathroom of our stateroom, but in that time, I'd fixed her.

It felt like it used to, when I was a kid. Marianne and Margaret, two sides of the same coin.

"Oh, yeah," she said, flipping her hair back. She'd kept it down today, and somehow still looked like she'd stepped out of a salon, despite the humidity. "He's just like, really cool and down-to-earth, you know? I think it's from being around kids all the time." Tomas worked in one of the kids' clubs, which I'd thought was just a recipe for constantly having a cold, but I guessed Marianne was into it. "We hung out all morning. It was nice."

"Romantic?" I scooted closer to Marianne on my chair. "Dreamy?"

"Something like that." Marianne's smile flickered. "I thought the four of us could go out on Friday? Have another shot at a double date?"

Friday's date. Right.

"I kind of told Gabe he could plan it? He thinks it'll help me relax or something," I added fast, feeling myself flush as Marianne cocked her head to the side. Crap. Hopefully she'd just think it was sunburn. "I know it's stupid."

"I don't know." Marianne shrugged, a smile playing around

her lips. "Sounds kind of . . . romantic. You like this guy, don't you, Margaret?"

"I—um—" I was torn, because honestly, I wanted to tell her the truth. That maybe I did, maybe a little, though I was totally in control of it and anyway, nothing could ever happen between us because I was way too scared of all the ways it could go wrong. But Marianne had made it through all these years of everything in her romances going wrong and she still kept trying, so would she even understand?

Ultimately, I knew that this plan was one I needed to stick to. "Yeah. I do." There. It wasn't even a lie.

"Precious!" Marianne crowed, throwing her arms around me and pulling me into a hug. I only half resisted. "My baby sister! Falling for a boy!"

"You're suffocating me," I said, my face muffled into her shoulder. But the thing was, even though it was built on a lie— even though so much of this summer was built on lies—it felt good to have Marianne hug me. To have her be proud of me.

And even though I'd started off the summer missing Brandon, or at least the person I'd thought Brandon was, in that moment, I was almost glad he'd broken up with her. Because for a second, I had my sister back.

CHAPTER SIXTEEN

The closer we got to Friday, the more I was jumping out of my metaphorical seat with nerves, trying to get Gabe to tell me what we were doing.

"Are we working as volunteer cat groomers at the Hemingway house?" I asked on Thursday afternoon, following him around backstage as he laid out mic packs for the performers to grab later.

"There's no way they let people volunteer for that. Do you know how protective those Hemingway people are about their cats?" Gabe shook his head. His hair was reaching what I had to assume was peak shagginess, falling over his eyes every time he moved his head too emphatically. "Sorry. I know that's your dream."

"It was, and now I'm devastated." I smoothed down the edge of a piece of tape stuck to the backstage table. "Are we setting up in front of the Southernmost Point marker and charging tourists to let us take their picture?"

"Do you think I'd tell you even if you guessed it correctly?" Gabe turned to face me, taking me by surprise. I stepped back, hitting the edge of the red velvet curtain. "What's the fun in that?"

"I think we'd still find a way to make it fun." Now that I'd run out of room to back up, I realized how close Gabe and I were standing. I was aware of every breath he took, the way his T-shirt rose and fell with his chest. Felt my hands tingle, like they had a mind of their own and wanted to reach for him. *Shut up, hands!*

Gabe stepped back, and I should have been relieved.

"You're not going to weasel this one out of me, Mags." He gave me a small push away from the mic table, and I did my best to pretend that his fingers on the bare skin around the straps of my tank top did nothing to me. "Come on. I have to work."

Later that night, he sent me a message on the ship's app, telling me to wear a swimsuit. Other than that . . . nothing.

"The one thing I won't do is swim with sharks," Marianne said on Friday morning as we shoved towels and sunscreen into our beach bags. "Everyone has to draw a line somewhere, and that's mine."

"I can respect that," I said, tossing my bag over my shoulder. No matter what we were doing, though, I was excited to spend the day with Marianne and Gabe. And Tomas, I guessed.

Still, as we headed down the gangway into Key West, Gabe hung back with me, while Marianne and Tomas barged ahead.

"You sure you're good on all of this?" he asked as we showed our cruise cards to the crew members stationed at the bottom of the gangplank. "The last time we were here . . ."

"Was a whole week ago." I tucked my card back into my backpack. "And I've become a whole new person in that week."

"Have you?" Gabe raised an eyebrow as we stepped onto the pier and into the blazing Florida sun. I blinked hard as I pulled my sunglasses over my eyes; I still hadn't gotten used to the harshness of the rays down here, and squinting would *not* help the confident image I wanted to exude.

And what did I have to *not* be confident about? I was in a tropical paradise with my sister, whom I'd successfully paired off with a guy who was under strict instructions not to break her heart. We were on a double date, which normally went against everything I stood for, but my date was a friend who explicitly knew that there couldn't be anything romantic between us. I even had on a super-cute bathing suit I'd stolen from Marianne's closet, a pink-and-green two-piece that showed off my shoulders. It was a gorgeous day—probably in the low eighties, sunny, the kind of warmth that bathed your skin like sliding into a steaming tub. I was thriving, and there was absolutely nothing to worry about.

"I have." I pulled my baseball cap down firmly on my head, then nodded. "Bring it on, Monteiro."

OKAY, maybe there were *some* things to worry about.

The main one being that Gabe had led us to a not-nearly-secure-enough hut by the beach, with a crookedly painted sign that read *Conch-Tastic Parasailing!* hanging over the entrance.

Talk about throwing me into the deep end.

"Absolutely not." I shook my head vehemently as Marianne let out an excited whoop, her eyes sparkling. "This can't possibly be safe."

"I know the company looks sketch, but they've got, like, a thousand reviews on Tripadvisor." Gabe stayed close to me as he spoke, like he knew I needed the extra level of protection. Which, weirdly, did make me feel kind of better. "Figured we'd go big or go home, right?"

"Is going home an option?" Because even with the Tripadvisor stamp of approval, heights had never been my favorite thing. I was a swimmer, after all; I preferred depths. Tomas, for the record, also looked kind of pale, staring at the boat docked behind the hut. "Because I would be willing to consider that."

"Come on, Mags." Marianne cut in before Gabe could say anything else, grabbing my wrist and pulling me toward the hut. "What are you scared of?"

I didn't say anything. I didn't have anything to say, because I certainly wasn't about to reveal my vulnerabilities to the very sister I was bending over backward to protect.

And then, running to keep up with Marianne and me, Gabe grabbed my hand.

I wasn't going to pretend that, wow, a guy touched my hand and suddenly all my anxieties and fears went away! One, because if that was a real thing, that meant Gabe was superhuman and I'd have to report him to Nick Fury, or something, so that he could be recruited into the Very Specific Superpowers division of the Avengers. But also because it was just Gabe. He wasn't some anti-anxiety superhero here to save me. This fear was something I needed to work out myself, like I always did.

But I had to admit his hand was grounding. A connection to something besides the whirring panic in my head.

Marianne dropped my wrist and strode up to the hut, apparently deciding that I was as good as in. Tomas took the opportunity to go sit on a nearby bench with his head in his hands. But Gabe stayed next to me, holding on.

"We don't have to do this." His voice was low and soft, a breeze against my ear. "We can turn around and go back to the ship right now, if you need to."

"I know." And I could have, and it would have been fine. If I didn't want to do this, I didn't have to.

But Elinor would have turned around, and I could see Marianne charging forward, which meant that I had to, too.

No matter how much it freaked me out.

"Let's do it." I squared my shoulders, tried to sound as brave as I wanted to feel. Across from me, a chicken wandered over Tomas's foot, and he shouted loudly enough that the chicken seemed shocked, too. A good omen.

THE wind was whipping something fierce around me, my life jacket felt *way* too tight, Marianne was screaming encouragement to me at a level that didn't actually feel very encouraging, and I was being hooked into a parasail, once again holding Gabe's hand for dear life.

"You're going to be fine, love!" The parasail instructor,

who was inexplicably British and paler than I was, patted me on the shoulder. "Just close your eyes and think of England, yeah?"

"Is that advice relevant here?" I shouted, trying to be heard over the roar of the boat zooming through the water, but he just chuckled and stepped back, ready to let me and Gabe, seated next to me in what felt like rope swings attached to a giant parachute, get pulled up, up, up into the sky.

Gabe squeezed my hand again. I hadn't let go of it the entire time we'd been out on the water.

"You've got this, Mags!" When I looked over at him, he was grinning like I'd never seen him, and that loosened something inside of me. If Gabe could be this free . . . then I could be, too.

And in one fluid motion, just as the rope let out and we were pulled back and up into the air, I let go of Gabe and threw my hands above my head.

I screamed as our parachute pulled us away from the boat, Marianne and Tomas and the instructor getting smaller and smaller as we went, until they were far enough away that I couldn't hear them anymore. I couldn't hear much of anything, just the wind rushing through my ears. Below us, the sea spread out in a sparkling wonderland, a quilt of waves and fish and birds and boats, and I was a part of this, I was a part of something, and I was doing it, actually doing it, just like I always said I would.

Wow.

We were up there for about ten minutes, all told. The instructor lowered us so that our feet skated across the surface of the water, and Gabe laughed like a little kid, and I was right there with him. When we finally made it back onto the boat, half running the last few feet as we came to a stop, the instructor released us from our harnesses and the first thing I did was turn, arms out wide, toward Gabe.

Marianne intercepted me, though.

"What a ride!" She hugged me tight, and I only stiffened for a second before relaxing into it. "Okay, Tomas, we're up."

"Yeah. Sure." Tomas had been full of debonair swagger back when Gabe and I had auditioned him, but he was way less confident now. Marianne didn't seem to notice. "Let's parasail. Just to check." He turned to the instructor. "Can I make sure you have my emergency contact information correct? And where is the nearest hospital, exactly? Would I be medevaced by a seaplane out here if something went wrong, or do we have to wait for the coast guard?"

So at least I was more chill than *one* other person on the planet.

Unable to assist with any of Tomas's questions, Gabe and I sat down inside the boat, a smooth, thin slip of a thing that looked like something you'd escape on in a James Bond movie. His hair was an absolute disaster, blown everywhere by the wind, and I laughed as I reached over to smooth it down. He leaned back against the side of the boat, propping his long, tanned legs up on the seats across from us. He'd gone casual today—a black *tank top* instead of a regular T-shirt, the whole world was shocked—and as he stretched his arms out behind him, I couldn't help but notice the muscles shifting. I gulped.

Gabe glanced over at me, propped his sunglasses up on top of his head.

"So how did it feel to be out of control for a while?" He nodded toward the instructor, who was clipping in Marianne and Tomas. This was made extra challenging by how much Tomas was shaking. "You put yourself in someone else's hands up there. Not like you."

"I didn't have much of a choice." I pulled my own sunglasses back down over my eyes, so Gabe couldn't read them. "But I managed."

I didn't tell him how free I'd felt, letting go. Letting *myself* go. Because if I did that, what would I let go of next?

We didn't discuss how I'd held on to his hand like a lifeline for most of the day. *I don't date*, I'd told him the first night we'd met, and I was sticking to it. It was one thing to fly above the ocean. It was another thing entirely to place my heart in the hands of another person. I had to protect myself. And that meant keeping things strictly friend-based with Gabe, no matter how much I wanted to know what questions his eyes were asking.

No. This was the way it had to be. Being friends with Gabe was great—being more than friends with Gabe was dangerous.

Still, we were supposed to be dating in front of Marianne, right? So it probably wouldn't hurt if I scooted a little closer to him. Tucked myself under his arm. And when he turned to me in alarm, I explained, "You know, in case Marianne can see us. This is a double date, after all."

"Right." Gabe nodded, his voice serious. "Wouldn't want to mess with the plan."

I couldn't tell if he was being sarcastic or not, but his arm tightened around my shoulder, so it didn't matter. All that mattered was that I was in Gabe's arms, rushing across the ocean like the girl I'd always wanted to be. And even if most of it was just pretend, I was fine pretending for a while longer.

CHAPTER SEVENTEEN

Tomas passed out in the air.

At first, I was horrified, but once we confirmed he was fine, I mostly found it kind of funny. Tomas did his best to laugh it off, too, but as soon as we made it back on land, he politely told Marianne that he'd have to bail on their dinner date to go sleep off his trauma.

But, hey, that didn't mean this wasn't a love match, right? Marianne had fallen for Brandon while he was nursing her back to health post-accident; maybe she'd be into the role reversal. Sure, she didn't seem too concerned about him once we'd parted ways with Gabe and headed back to our stateroom to get ready for dinner, but that didn't mean she didn't care.

Back on the ship, at dinner, Elinor was shocked when we told her what we'd done (leaving out the guys, of course), digging into Friday night's customary lobster tails and filet. (I was going to have a hard time adjusting to dorm food once I got off the ship, I knew that much.) But then the shock transformed into something I didn't expect.

"That's great, Mags," Elinor said. Ramon had convinced her to get a glass of champagne, and she was sipping it slowly, making it count. "I'm proud of you."

"Really?" I asked, using a piece of bread to soak up the juices left from my lobster. And by juices, I meant butter. "I didn't, like, steer the boat or anything."

"It's just the sort of thing you would have been really excited about when you were younger, that's all." Another sip, a knowing smile. "Glad to see you channeling that side of yourself again."

"I guess." I glanced over at Marianne, who was full-on beaming. Maybe she was thinking the same thing as me—that I was channeling the *Marianne* side of myself. But if Elinor had realized that, she'd be a lot less thrilled.

OVER the next week, though, our fourth at sea (and it felt a million times longer than that, like I'd lived on this ship forever), I tried to keep channeling that Marianne side. After all, I'd been happy, back when we were attached at the hip, before That Year. When I was too young to make my own plans and naïve enough to not be so afraid.

Marianne was busier than I'd liked, hanging out with Tomas; but every morning, I asked her what looked like fun on that day's list of activities, and I tried to do whatever appealed to her. I went to all of the shows the ship offered, not just the ones Gabe was running sound for. I ordered every menu item Ramon recommended. Highlight: brown butter scallops with blistered tomatoes; lowlight: a cheese soufflé that roasted the roof of my mouth because I didn't realize how hot it was going to be.

I even took an excursion of my own, riding a glass-bottomed boat in the Bahamas that went right over a sunken ship turned into a reef. It was amazing, and I was so glad to have seen it, but it was weirdly lonely, being out there by myself. I kept wishing Gabe were there, kept looking to the side like I expected him to be next to me, ready to make a snarky comment or offer me some unexpected insight. Doing stuff without him felt wrong, and, yeah, that made me nervous. But I chalked it up to dehydration and pretended it wasn't an issue.

Overall, though, I was having fun. I even went along with Edward to one of the lectures he wanted to attend, about the history of cigar making in the Caribbean, and it was—well, it wasn't thrilling, but it was nice, being with him while we did something he was interested in.

The problem was, at the beginning of our fifth week, my mother decided to join us.

Not for the rest of the cruise, thank God. But she'd called Elinor back in Key West and arranged to use all the credit card points at her disposal to come visit us on our changeover day, which meant the full force of Mama Dashwood, in all its nightmarish glory, was going to rain down on the *Mab*.

I loved my mother. Obviously. But when she was around my sisters (*especially* when she was around Marianne), she could be . . . a lot. And I didn't love who I was when I was with her. Baby Margaret Dashwood, the littlest and least useful Dashwood girl. That was the person I was trying to leave behind in New Jersey, not cart all over the world.

But you can't just tell your mom you don't want to see her because it gets in the way of your self-actualization. So here I was, standing in the atrium in my best Mom-approved sundress, early Saturday morning—a thrifted Lilly Pulitzer shift that totally clashed with my hair, thanks, Mom—waiting with Edward and my sisters for Mrs. Dashwood to arrive.

"What's the plan again?" I asked Elinor, shifting from foot to foot in my sandals. She'd been up for hours, and judging from the dark circles under Edward's eyes, she hadn't been the only one. It should have been reassuring that I wasn't the only person thrown by Mom's presence, but instead, it just made me more uncomfortable. If Elinor didn't feel confident about today, how would I manage to?

Marianne was the only one who seemed well rested. She'd gone to bed weirdly early the night before, humming to herself as she finished up a romance novel (with a *very* dashing pirate type on the cover; I'd have to borrow it from her) and was taking advantage of being in port in Miami to spend the whole morning texting, although she kept hiding her screen whenever I leaned over to look at it, as was my little-sister-given right. Hopefully, she was texting Tomas, and even more hopefully, she'd tell me all about it later.

It was ten a.m., which meant that the first wave of guests would be boarding any second now. Elinor was watching the gangway from one of the giant portholes that lined the atrium, each with a bench seat at the base so you felt like you were sitting in a giant fishbowl. I stood behind her, watching the highest level of VIP and concierge guests begin their boarding—probably the last time I'd ever see them, since they tended to stay in their private, exclusive areas of the ship. Women with giant hats, more men in polo shirts than had ever been gathered at once, including at an actual polo match, the occasional kids in matching outfits, and then . . .

"There she is." Elinor couldn't hide the resignation in her voice. I was surprised, honestly; Mom loved Elinor, counted on her for everything. Maybe she'd been enjoying the break from that?

Mom saw us the same moment we saw her, throwing both hands up in the air and waving them wildly, almost hitting the person behind her with her giant tote bag in the process. She was only going to be on board for about five hours before we set sail again and she headed back to the deeply discounted hotel room she'd snagged for the weekend, but judging from the size of her bag, she was prepared for anything that might happen during that time. She wore a white mesh cover-up over a brightly colored tankini, her straw hat so wide that it was a wonder she fit through the gangplank at all. Her sunglasses took up half of her face, and her smile at seeing us took up the other half. The whole vibe was *very* Jennifer Coolidge at the White Lotus.

She made it up the gangway, rushing toward us and throwing herself into—who else—Marianne's arms as she burst into tears.

"Oh, Mom." Marianne patted her on the back, rocking back and forth. "Come on. I'm fine, really."

"But you've been *grieving*," Mom wailed, and, oh no, was she going to talk about Brandon the whole time? I glanced over at Elinor, who looked suitably alarmed. But Mom shook her head, pulling back from Marianne. "I'm sorry! We won't talk about it. I'm just glad to see you. Come here, the rest of you." She hugged us in a predictable order, Elinor and then me, with a quick pat on the shoulder for Edward, which was more for his comfort than for Mom's. "Have you been having the most fabulous time?"

"It's been nice." Elinor moved us out of the way of the other arriving guests, helping Mom onto one of the atrium's many couches. "Lots of relaxing."

"Relaxing! Pishposh. You can relax when you're old like me." Mom sniffed, as though she was crumbling into dust and not barely fifty. "I want to hear about the trouble you've gotten into. Marianne tells me you've been getting into *quite* a few romantic shenanigans."

Marianne said *what?*

"Um," Marianne said as I turned sharply to stare daggers in her direction. "I don't know that I phrased it like that."

"You told me," Mom went on, completely unaware of the way I was staring at Marianne and Elinor was staring at both of us, "that you and Margaret were trying out your hands at new romantic liaisons this summer! So, no, I suppose we don't have to call them shenanigans, but I think it still . . ."

"Margaret?" Elinor had sidled up beside me and spoke low into my ear. I gulped. Edward, lucky bastard, wandered a few feet away as discreetly as possible. "Want to tell me what she's talking about?"

"It's possible . . ." Oh, God. This was *not* how I wanted to tell Elinor about this. To be fair, there wasn't *any* way I wanted to tell her about this, but still, this seemed particularly bad. But there was nothing to be done about it now. Marianne was still standing next to Mom, nodding as she rambled on, but sending quick glances over my way. "That Marianne and I have spent a good chunk of the last few weeks going on dates with boys."

It was hard to leave a Dashwood speechless. Even Elinor, by far the least loquacious of the three of us, would still be considered chatty by normal human standards. But from the way she gaped at me, it was clear she didn't know how to respond to that particular confession.

I didn't blame her.

"Look." I grabbed her by the wrist and pulled her away from Mom and Marianne. "I know it's stupid. But Marianne needs this. She was in such a shitty place, and I thought setting her up with someone would help. And it totally has, right? She's way happier now."

"Uh-huh." Elinor didn't seem like she believed me. "And you're . . . also dating?"

"Oh. Yeah." I rolled my eyes. The more casually I treated all of this, the more casually I hoped Elinor would think about it. "Marianne wouldn't do it unless I did, too, so . . . here we are."

"You've been dating," Elinor said again, her voice skeptical; and, okay, she didn't need to keep repeating it like that—it wasn't that out of the question. Sure, I'd spent the last few years swearing off dating like I was allergic to it, but people could change. I could change.

And, well, I really hadn't, because I wasn't *actually* dating Gabe, but I wanted Elinor to believe that I *could*.

"I have been." I didn't hold back the hint of defiance that crept into my voice. That's right, me, the littlest Dashwood girl, was grown-up enough to join her older sister in romantic shenanigans! Let the polo-shirt-wearing crowds surrounding us hear and bow before me in my dating prowess! "This guy Gabe. He runs sound for the shows. And he's a nice guy, he's not a serial killer," I added quickly, just to cut off Elinor's next line of questioning. "He knows the crew really well, so he helped me make sure that I could find good guys for Marianne to go out with." There, that part wasn't even a lie.

"If he was a serial killer, I don't think he'd announce it." Elinor sighed, rubbing her thumb and forefinger over the bridge of her nose like I was giving her a migraine. But then, to my surprise, she reached out and put her arm around my shoulders, pulling me into a side hug. "But that's . . . that's great, Mags. I'm proud of you for stepping out of your comfort zone. I just wish you'd felt like you could tell me."

"Sorry." I wasn't about to tell her that I'd liked having this little secret between Marianne and me. No way would that end well for anybody. "I didn't want you to worry."

"What are you two whispering about over there?" Mom waved us back in her direction, arms jangling with bangles above her head. "Marianne was just telling me more about these boys. Margaret, dearest, they sound positively yummy."

"Please don't say yummy. Especially about people." I followed Elinor back toward our mother and the corner of the atrium she had commandeered as her own; Edward wandered back over, too, albeit slowly.

"I'm just so glad you're getting involved with romance." Mom fanned herself, as if she expected to swoon. "I've been so *worried* about you, Margaret. All through high school, whenever I tried to introduce you to a nice young man, you completely ignored them in favor of . . . swim times. I'm glad that Marianne is finally taking you under her wing." Mom nodded with satisfaction.

Great. First of all, Mom had no idea what made a "nice young man," and everyone she'd ever tried to introduce me to at, like, a church potluck had been absolute garbage. Second, yes, maybe I'd leaned on Marianne a lot more recently, but the initial dating idea had been all mine. I'd been able to take charge, and, sure, I had stepped back recently but it wasn't because I was incapable or a baby or . . .

I didn't even realize I was breathing heavily until I felt a hand on my shoulder, bringing me back down to earth (or, rather, to sea). I looked back, expecting Elinor, and was surprised to see Edward instead, resting his hand lightly against my skin with his head cocked to one side.

"All right?" he asked. Elinor had taken control of the conversation, filling Mom in on the plan for the day and promising that she'd get a tour right away, of course.

"Yeah." I nodded, and Edward offered me a small, comforting smile. "Thanks."

"You got it." He tilted his head toward Mom, who was loudly exclaiming over how beautiful the carpets were. "After you, Mags."

"I want to get back to this dating extravaganza you two are participating in." Mom sipped her piña colada, and I suppressed a groan. For the past hour, she seemed to have forgotten the subject, too busy oohing and aahing over the *Mab*. But now that she'd settled in, lounging on the side of the pool deck, romance was back in the forefront of her mind. Figured.

It hadn't always been like this. After Dad died, though, during That Year, it seemed like Mom retreated too far into her romances and her stories. She didn't have any interest in me outside of that, outside of when I would find someone to, as she put it, "take care of me."

Brandon had been the first one to talk to me about it, actually. When I'd skipped my sophomore year homecoming dance because I had a swim meet that weekend and wanted to make sure I was rested, Mom had called Marianne to cry about how I would never find love. (Thanks, Mom, just what a fourteen-year-old needs to overhear!) But while they were on the phone, Brandon had called me. It was like he'd known I was listening in, needed the distraction.

"She just doesn't get it," I'd said, pacing back and forth in my attic bedroom. "Why does it matter if I get all dressed up and go hang out with a bunch of idiot boys?"

"I think she wants to live that part of her life again through you, Margaret." Brandon's voice was quiet, as always; I had to put him on speaker just to get him to a normal volume. "She's lonely without your father."

"I know." I'd felt ashamed, like I'd done something wrong. "I miss him, too."

"But that doesn't mean you have to live for her," he'd continued, and I'd stood up straight. "Live for yourself. Just know how she might react."

Brandon could always do that. Distill hard situations into a single sentence. I knew Edward talked to him constantly for that very reason; more than once, I'd been listening to one of Edward's sermons and picked up a Brandonism that had snuck its way in.

I could have used him this summer. Except that all the confusion this summer was entirely his fault.

But whatever. The point was that, for Mom, hearing that I was dating was officially the greatest news of her entire life.

"Margaret's doing a lot better at it than I am." Marianne was sharing my deck chair, sitting next to me so that we both faced our lounging mother, and she nudged her shoulder into mine. "Or rather, I suppose I'm going for quantity, and she's going for quality."

"Oh?" Mom said, sitting up straight, so fast that she splashed frozen piña colada mush over the side of her glass. "That *is* interesting."

"That's not true." I didn't like the direction this conversation was going. "Marianne's been seeing the same guy for a little while, too. His name is Tomas, and he—"

"His name's Gabe," Marianne continued. I didn't know if she was purposely trying to up my embarrassment level or if she really didn't realize how much I hated talking about this. "They've been hanging out *all* the time."

"Marianne." I rolled my eyes. "Come on."

"What? Do you not like him?" She cocked her head to the side. She was drinking the same thing as Mom, another fruity cocktail that smelled more like sunscreen than anything I'd want to consume. "Then why does he keep coming out with us? If this guy isn't boyfriend material . . ."

Crap.

"That's not what I meant," I said hastily, praying that perhaps this would be the moment the ship got hit with a giant wave and we all got *Poseidon Adventure*d. It would be better to try and deal with that than to continue this conversation. "Of course I like him." I didn't know where the truth stopped and the lies started anymore. Or even worse, I knew exactly how much of what I was saying was true, and I just didn't want to face it. "He's . . . he's great. Totally dreamy."

I was pretty sure I heard Edward disguise a laugh with a cough, but Mom was too busy shrieking with excitement to notice.

"Oh, Margaret!" She reached over and pulled me into a hug. "I'm so happy for you. I have to meet this young man." Oh, God. No. No thank you. "If Marianne says things are that serious, he should absolutely meet your mother. Bring him to lunch. I insist."

Nightmare, meet daytime. I looked at Elinor in a panic, but she just offered a sympathetic smile. I knew what she thought I was thinking—that I didn't want to subject a guy I liked to Mom—and even though she was only half right, because I didn't even like Gabe in that way, the result was the same. And the *end* result was that she wasn't going to do anything about it.

I should have just signed up for summer school or something.

"That sounds . . . great," I managed, and Mom clapped her hands together. "I'll have him meet us at the dining room?"

"Do." Mom giggled, swishing her straw through her drink. "And tell him I have a *lot* of questions for him."

Yeah, the whole ship toppling over was definitely my best-case scenario.

CHAPTER EIGHTEEN

Mom was on her third course already, and as our server (not Ramon, unfortunately, although even Ramon couldn't save me from this) removed her lobster tail from its shell with perfect technique, she continued to pepper Gabe with questions.

"Tell me what it is you *do*, again," she asked for the millionth time, cutting into her lobster. I felt my shoulders tense, like they'd done every time Mom had interacted with Gabe. But Gabe, sitting on my right, was holding it together remarkably well. Almost *too* well. This smiling, overly polite guy barely felt like the Gabe I knew.

"I run the sound for the shows on board." He hadn't touched his own lunch, which was my only indicator that he was uncomfortable, too. "I only come on contract during the summer, though. I'm still in school the rest of the year."

"Where do you go to school?" Edward was enjoying his spaghetti carbonara with gusto, unaware of the high level of awkward I was feeling. Next to him, Elinor's smile was indulgent—she liked Gabe, that much I could tell. And

Marianne was acting like a proud mother, like it was entirely because of her that I'd found myself a Gabe in the first place.

"I just finished my freshman year at Carnegie Mellon," Gabe said, giving his best attempt at a smile as he poked at his food. "Electrical engineering."

"That's a great school," Elinor said, and Gabe shrugged, modest.

I was deeply, incredibly confused.

Which didn't make any sense. Because Gabe was doing exactly what I'd asked of him, when I'd frantically messaged him from the pool deck and begged him to come to lunch and keep the illusion going that we were, if not deeply in love, at least interested enough in each other to hang out constantly. He'd agreed—especially when he'd heard we were eating in one of the specialty dining rooms that Edward had gotten us into in honor of Mom's visit—and met us at the entrance fifteen minutes later in, of all things, a pair of khakis. I'd never seen him wear anything that wasn't black before, so that was jarring enough, but it turned out to be just the tip of the iceberg.

He was unfailingly polite. Not charming, exactly—I could still see his discomfort, and I suspected my family did, too, though it didn't stop Mom from giving him the third degree. But he was giving off every impression of a guy who was super into a girl and trying to impress her family. He'd even, at one point, looked over at me and squeezed my hand, just once, under the table, which was confusing in its own way, because why bother doing something like that where no one in my family would see? (Although I suspected Marianne saw it, from the way she smirked.)

And I didn't hate any of that. I'd asked for it. What I

hated was the way it made me feel. Because when I watched Gabe with my family, watched him work to fit like a puzzle piece we'd always been missing, I felt something pang deep in my chest. Something like—*this* is what you need. *This* is what you want.

And that simply wasn't true. I didn't need Gabe. I didn't want Gabe. Not like that. I didn't want him like something you needed.

"How did you two meet?" Gabe asked Elinor, gesturing between her and Edward. "If you don't mind me asking."

"Oh." Elinor laughed, sipping her iced tea. Edward put his arm around her, his smile indulgent. "It's a long story. But Edward found his way into our life when we all needed him, I suppose."

"You make it sound so altruistic." Edward squeezed Elinor's shoulder, and I rolled my eyes. They could act as sentimental as they wanted—*I* knew that Elinor and Edward were together because it was practical, not because they were caught up in some whirlwind romance. Love was the one area of Marianne-ness I still had to avoid, no matter how appealing it seemed. "I needed all of you, too."

Gabe turned to me, and the look in his eyes—it didn't feel like pretend. And maybe Gabe was a really great actor. But I didn't think he was. I didn't think I was, either.

Crap.

"And now we have a *new* generation of young lovers!" Mom crowed, clapping her hands together. I did my best to smile, wishing desperately that a giant shark would attack the dining room and put an end to this miserable afternoon. "You two are just adorable."

"Margaret's a great girl." Gabe echoed Edward's shoulder squeeze, and I wanted to wriggle out of his grasp. "I'm lucky to have her."

"Oh, go on, then." Mom waved a hand before taking another sip of her quickly disappearing mimosa. "Give her a kiss!"

The whole world froze.

Gabe's arm tightened around me. Elinor blinked, slow, and even Marianne looked surprised. Edward coughed, choking on his water.

Oh my God.

But what was I supposed to do, say no? With everyone staring at me, Mom grinning, Elinor looking concerned, and Marianne waiting to see what I'd do?

I turned to the side, and Gabe was watching me, waiting for the answer. He'd do it, then. He'd do it to maintain the illusion we'd created. And I should have been grateful for that, but instead I just felt weirdly upset.

Just what you're hoping to feel for your first kiss, right? Which is also in front of your mother and your siblings?

I leaned over, closed the small distance between us, and kissed Gabe quickly on the lips.

It was short. Fast. A brief moment of contact, and then we both leaned back, as Mom hooted with glee and Elinor turned the conversation to something else, probably because she noticed the flush rising over my face. And I wanted to say that I didn't feel anything. That it was barely a kiss, anyway, what was there to feel?

But there had been a touch of a spark. A hint of electricity to come.

I was, all things considered, just about ready to get off the ship here in Miami, walk to the nearest bus stop, and get as far away from everyone here as possible. These people who kept making me feel things, even when I really, *really* didn't want to.

CHAPTER NINETEEN

After we finished our dessert (passion fruit crème brûlée, not quite good enough to make me feel better about how shitty this lunch had been, but it helped), Mom sighed, leaned back in her chair.

"This has been wonderful. Thank you all for making the time." Mom reached out and squeezed Marianne's hand, like she'd been doing all through the meal. "Now. I of *course* need to see the rest of the ship. But why don't we let our love-birds go and get a little alone time?" She looked across at me and Gabe and winked, and my stomach dropped all the way down into my feet. "I see the way you've been looking at each other. I used to look at your father like that."

Kill me.

"Um. Thanks, Mom." I was ready to get out of here, and get Gabe out of here, and if this was how it was going to go down, well, so be it. He probably needed to get to work soon, anyway, just like I needed to die of embarrassment. "Gabe, you good?"

"Yep." He stood up, reaching across to shake my mom's hand. She practically melted, one hand over her heart. Laying it on a little thick there, Gabe, we're not getting married! "Thanks again for having me, Mrs. Dashwood. It was so great to meet you. And you, too, Mr. and Mrs. Ferrars."

"Please. Elinor and Edward," Elinor said, smiling. So, great. Glad she approved of my fake boyfriend. "You'll have to join us for dinner sometime soon."

"Bye, Gabe," Marianne said in a singsong, waggling her fingers, and I made a mental note to find a crab the next time I was on land to hide in her bed.

As soon as the golden double doors of the restaurant slammed behind us, I let out an exasperated sigh before taking off at a sprint across the atrium.

"Where are you going? Why are you *running*?" It sounded like Gabe was keeping up with me, but I didn't bother turning around to check. There was no time for that. I just kept moving, up a few sets of stairs until I got to a lesser-used corridor on deck four. There was a passage between two of the lounges that I'd discovered was almost always empty, probably because the portholes that lined it looked straight into the lifeboats hanging off the side of the ship instead of out to sea. I finally stopped, breathing heavily as I collapsed into one of the curved benches tucked in under the porthole's glass. Gabe skidded to a halt in front of me, his hair wild.

"Want to tell me why you tried to flee the country just there?" he asked, once it became clear I wasn't about to volunteer information. I shook my head, sighed, and looked up at him. Freaking *khakis*. Whoever gave him permission to wear khakis? "You know the *Mab* is, like, enclosed, right? If you run far away enough, you'll just end up where you started again."

"Story of my whole life." I dropped my head in my hands, wishing I could close my eyes and fast-forward through the rest of this cruise, get to college, and start my life over with new people. Gabe just stood there in front of me, arms crossed over his chest, not smiling, the turned-up persona he'd brought out for my family put away. "What a nightmare of a meal."

"Was it?" He smoothed down his hair the best he could, and was only mildly successful. "It seemed like regular family-meeting-a-boyfriend conversation to me."

"You're not my boyfriend." The words shot out fast, my chest suddenly tight.

Gabe grimaced. "I know. But you know what I—they think I'm your boyfriend, Mags, right? That was the whole point. To keep the illusion going."

"The illusion. Right." Because Gabe knew this was all for show. So did I. We both knew exactly what was going on here, so there was no need to freak out. I needed to not freak out. "Still. Once they knew I had you—or whatever—that was suddenly all my mom cared about. Did you notice?" I shook my head, blowing a loose curl out of my eyes. "She didn't mention anything about school, or the fact that I'm moving across the freaking *country* in a few weeks. I bet she thinks now that we're together—or, they think we're together—I won't even go. I'll just give up everything to follow *love*."

"Wow, you say that like it's a disease." Gabe's voice was dry, light, but I bristled at it anyway.

"I told you how I feel about romance, Gabe."

"Yeah, but that was back when you were all, like, Miss Planner USA." That same light tone, as if what we were talking about didn't mean anything. "Opening yourself up to your feelings seems very in line with the whole channel-your-inner-Marianne thing you've got going on now."

"I promise, I'm not going to take things that far." I wished I could have sounded as cool as Gabe. As collected. "It's one thing to let go of my plans, okay? But it's another thing entirely to like— I can't open up to someone like that. I won't."

"So what's the point of all these new experiences, then?" Gabe came over and sat next to me, even though this bench really wasn't big enough for two. Our legs pressed together, thigh to thigh, and it took everything in me not to inhale at the contact. "If you're not connecting with people, you're still just playing tourist."

"I—hey. I connect with people." I didn't look at him. I couldn't look at him when he was this close. If I turned, if I let myself realize how close our faces were to each other . . . "That doesn't have anything to do with romance."

"Doesn't it?" His voice was suddenly sharp. "Sorry, guess I must have looked away when you were being super open with your family back there."

"Not fair." This dress was too tight and too short for the amount of energy bubbling up inside me. It felt like a strait-jacket. "I *can't* be open with my mom. You wouldn't understand. Peter and Luisa are super cool, but, trust me, my mom needs to be kept at an arm's length for both of our sakes."

"Right. Because you're always the grand arbitrator of what's best for people." Gabe didn't move his leg away from mine. I wished he would, but I didn't move mine, either. "You know what's best for Marianne. For Elinor. For your mom. Even for us."

"There *is* no us, Gabe." His leg was like a live wire. "And you can't be mad at me for sticking to that. I didn't promise you anything. You came up with this perfect boyfriend act all on your own."

"Perfect boyfriend act?"

"You know." I deepened my voice. "Oh, I'm Gabe, here's my arm around your shoulder, I care about you, let's kiss in front of everybody just to impress your mother. You don't have to use it again."

"You kissed me, if I remember correctly. And is it so hard to believe I want your family to like me, Margaret?" His voice grew more frustrated. "Why is that such a bad thing?"

"Because we're *not* dating, Gabe." I waved my hand in between us, and if I didn't know better, I'd say that for a second, Gabe looked hurt. But he couldn't have. Because he knew what this was, just like I did. "In case you forgot, I'm not *actually* looking for love out here."

"Yeah, you've made that abundantly clear." Gabe stood up, and I felt the absence of his heat immediately, like something had been carved out of me. "Message received, Margaret. Don't let me bother you anymore."

He strode down the hallway, long steps that made it obvious he wanted to get as far away from me as he could, as quickly as possible.

And screw that. He wasn't the only one who got to storm away.

So even though I liked this hallway, liked my low chance

of running into anyone who would try to hold a conversation with me, I got up and booked it out of there. Because if Gabe turned back when he got to the end of the hall, I needed him to see that I was gone. That I wasn't waiting for him.

I wasn't waiting for anybody.

CHAPTER TWENTY

The library was my best chance at a refuge.

On a changeover day especially, there was hardly anyone in here; most people didn't make a beeline for the library as the first place they *had* to see. It had taken me the better part of a week to discover it myself, tucked away near the stern of the ship between two much more popular lounges, the entrance partially hidden by the large arch that marked the opening to the kids' clubs. In the hallway, the noise from the kids spilled out and threatened to overwhelm you, but somehow, the library blocked it all out, keeping the chaos firmly outside its dark oak door.

And I was relieved that it was empty, because I needed to do some serious sulking, and that would be way harder to achieve if I had to deal with other guests. The library was a tall room, with shelves full of books that went all the way up to the ceiling, like a miniaturized version of Belle's library in *Beauty and the Beast*. The only window was in the far back wall, but it was big enough to keep the room light and airy, despite all of the dark wood. The selection wasn't, like, amazing—mostly a lot of books about boats and/or men being in charge of boats. But there were, though, still a few gems hidden on the shelves, and I pulled down the one I'd been flipping through last time—an illustrated history of cruise travel, so still boat oriented but more up my alley—and settled into one of the high-backed leather chairs in front of the electric fireplace.

I had zero intention of actually reading, but holding the book made me feel better.

What business did Gabe have storming off? It wasn't like I'd said anything revelatory. He knew we weren't anything. We'd settled that the first day we'd met, so it wasn't like he could accuse me of, like, leading him on or something. Not that Gabe would do that. I knew he wasn't angry because he thought I was a tease. But whatever truth I'd been selling, he wasn't interested in it.

Well, fine. I didn't need him.

Except I was starting to worry that I did.

The door creaked open, and I jolted in my seat, sending my book tumbling to the floor. As I scrambled to grab it, I looked up to see Edward, standing in the doorway with a sheepish expression.

"There you are." He nodded toward the chair across from me, a matching high-backed leather number. "We just saw your mother off. Thought I'd see if you wanted some company. Mind if I join you?"

"Uh, sure." I wasn't in any mood to be decent company right now, but I also didn't know how to say no. I was starting to think it was a skill I needed to work on. "How'd you even find me?"

"Just followed the books." Edward walked into the room, slowly and carefully, the way he did everything. Now that Mom was gone, he'd changed out of the khakis and button-down gingham shirt he'd worn to lunch, dressed instead in a worn polo shirt and khaki shorts under a cardigan, since the ship's air-conditioning was working double time today. It wasn't much of a difference, on paper, but it was clear to anyone who knew Edward how much more comfortable he was. The other outfit had felt like old Edward, the one we'd first met, when he was still living with his rich parents and had no idea how to escape them.

I wondered if he'd felt as trapped by his family's expectations as I did by mine.

"Quite a lunch." Edward settled in next to me, one leg crossed over the other, his worn loafer resting on his knee. "Meals with your mom are always an adventure."

"'Adventure' is one word for it," I muttered, then winced. If I'd been with Elinor, or even Marianne, they'd have scolded me for talking about Mom like that. But Edward, while he didn't agree with me, didn't stop me from saying it, either.

I had a sudden memory of a conversation we'd had, near the end of That Year, after Edward had finally gotten up the courage to tell Elinor he was in love with her. (Not *immediately* after that, of course. The immediate aftermath of that was a lot of crying and kissing and hugging.) But the next day, I'd come downstairs early to find Edward already awake, sitting in the breakfast nook of our cottage and steeping a cup of tea.

"Margaret." He'd looked up when he'd seen me, smiled widely, the smile that had barely left his face since he'd told Elinor how he felt. "Sleep well?"

"Not really." I was still in my Marianne phase back then, and so my energy had come out in bursts, overwhelming most people, but Edward had never seemed to mind. "Do you live here now?"

"Oh. Um. No." Edward flushed, which was a common reaction for him. "I slept on the couch. Just for the night. I'm getting an apartment in town." That made sense. Elinor and Marianne still shared a room. I'd gotten my own only because I was willing to take the barely converted attic, with its low ceilings and terrible temperature control. I'd always liked it, though. Having my own space. "I'll keep coming over, though, if you don't mind."

"Obviously not." I grabbed a banana off the counter, held it out for Edward to peel it as I talked. I was still in a cast from the accident, and had mostly adjusted to having one arm out of commission by making people around me assist in basic tasks. "We need a fourth for card games when Mom's busy."

"Edward?" The back door to the kitchen creaked open, and Brandon pushed in with a quiet confidence, the way he always entered a room. He'd had a key ever since the accident and had remained glued to Marianne's side. He was a tall Black man with dark skin and close-cut curls. Marianne had just begun to point out that she thought he looked a lot like Regé-Jean Page from that Bridgerton show everyone was starting to talk about. That was my first clue that she was falling for him, because the resemblance was faint at best. "I thought I saw your car. Does that mean—"

"Yes." Edward had flushed again, ducking his head so that his overgrown hair fell in front of his eyes. "I told her."

"Good." Brandon wasn't one for big, effusive gestures—I liked that about him, liked how he lived in quiet but still loved being around our family—but he reached out a hand and shook Edward's, hard. "Glad to hear it."

"I'm not the only one to be congratulated, from what I've been told," Edward said, and Brandon had laughed, shaking his head.

"It's been—it hasn't been a good month," he corrected himself, glancing over at me, at my cast. *"But it's getting better."*

"And we've got Margaret to help us navigate all the Dashwood chaos, don't we?" Edward said, and I had filled with pride, especially when Brandon nodded and patted my shoulder, which from him was an enormous sign of affection. *"Our girl on the inside."*

It had been a brief glimpse of what I'd hoped our family could be. Marianne falling in love with Brandon, who would fix all of her post-accident broken pieces, Elinor and Brandon's own friendship, Edward coming back to Elinor, Mom fawning over it all, and me in the middle, mixed up in all of it.

Except the intertwined feeling had been one-sided, it seemed, because Brandon had broken up with Marianne even though he'd promised to stand by her. To stand by all of us.

Back in the library, sitting with one brother-in-law where I'd always expected to have two, I sighed.

"Tell me about Gabe," Edward said, once it was clear I wasn't contributing anything else to the topic of Mom. He needed a cup of tea, I thought. Edward always seemed most at home with a cup of tea. "I'm surprised we haven't met him before."

"Yeah, well." I groaned, leaned back against the soft leather headrest. "You and Elinor have been doing your own thing. Marianne needed an occupation."

"But you've been dating?"

"Oh my God. I hate this." Maybe if I closed my eyes, the whole ship would disappear. "We're just—we're friends." I know, I know, I wasn't supposed to tell anyone that Gabe and I weren't *really* together, but I couldn't take all the secrets anymore. "Marianne wanted me to get in on the dating thing, too. So Gabe's helping me out. But you can't tell anyone it's not real. Marianne will flip if she finds out."

Edward nodded. "Got it. Still not interested in finding a paramour?"

"Don't say 'paramour.'" Sometimes, Edward sounded like he'd time traveled from two hundred years ago and was just doing his best to converse like a modern human. "Not like that, anyway. But, no." I tapped my hands against the cover of my book. "I'm not."

Edward's eyes darted back and forth, and he opened his mouth, then hesitated. I waited.

"You know, Margaret," he said finally, "not everyone experiences romantic or sexual attraction to other people. If that's what you're feeling, that's perfectly normal . . ."

"I'm not ace, Edward." How had I ended up here, having a conversation about sexuality with my brother-in-law in a cruise ship library? "It's not that I've never experienced . . . attraction." Oh God, now *I* was the one cringing. Edward didn't say anything, and I looked back toward him, my head cocked to the side. "What kind of church do you work for, anyway? Where you can ask me about sexuality in a fairly normal way?"

"You thought I asked normally?" His voice was hopeful, and I laughed.

"I mean, I still wanted to die, but it could have been worse." I scooted back in the chair, shifting from where I'd slipped down on the smooth leather. Above us, light streamed in through the big round window, bathing Edward in a bright glow. "You know what I mean."

"I work for a church that tries to undo the harm caused by a lot of other churches." Edward sighed, took off his glasses, and polished them on the hem of his cardigan. "We do our best, anyway. That's what I've always wanted to do, even if it's not some tremendous higher purpose. Just to do my best and try to make life a little better for the people around me, if I can."

"So you weren't, like, called by the pope personally to do this?"

"That would have been a surprising call, since I'm not Catholic and I don't know that the pope is allowed to use a cell phone." Edward offered me a small smile. "Excellent subject avoidance, by the way. You're sure you don't want to talk about whatever has you hiding away in the library?"

"I really don't." I sighed, pulling my legs beneath me and curling up in a ball. "I think I just need to sit here for a while. If you don't mind."

"Of course." Edward leaned over to see the book in my lap. "This library has a fascinating collection. Mind if I join you?"

"I—uh—I'm not going to be any fun." It wasn't that I didn't *want* Edward here. But I couldn't have anything expected of me right now. I just couldn't.

"That's all right. I'm rarely fun." Edward pushed himself from the chair, peered toward the shelf closest to him. "It's all very nautical, isn't it?"

"They love a theme."

"Luckily, so do I." He selected a thick volume off the bottom shelf, and it took me a second to realize it was an old Becky Chambers sci-fi epic. "Spaceships count, I suppose. Though if you don't want me here, just say so, and I promise I won't be insulted."

"It's okay." I'd missed Edward over the last couple of weeks. I hadn't realized it.

"Perfect." He settled back down into his chair, cracking the book open to the first page, and immediately turned all of his attention toward it. Edward was a slow, steady reader, the kind who took forever to turn a page, but if you asked him a question about the book, he would be able to recall every single detail.

I opened my book, too, but I didn't read it. Instead, I just stared down at the page, sitting comfortable in the knowledge that Edward was there, too.

CHAPTER TWENTY-ONE

It took about an hour of staring at my book before I realized that I probably owed Gabe an apology.

Because all he'd done, really, was exactly what I'd asked him to. I was mad at him because he'd pretended to be my boyfriend? That would be like getting mad at the captain of the ship for taking us to the Bahamas. Just because I was afraid I'd like it didn't mean I was allowed to be angry at him for it.

Which meant I needed to find him, and I needed to apologize.

Easier said than done.

That night, I went to the theater for the preview show, the one I'd met him at a month ago, and tried to catch him in the booth, but he booked it out of there the second the curtain closed. In fact, it seemed like he didn't *want* me to catch him. If I was going to track him down, I'd need to take matters into my own hands.

Which was why I was currently standing outside the entrance

to the ship's fitness center at six a.m. on a Sunday, attempting to ambush my fake boyfriend.

Okay, "ambush" made it sound worse than it was. Could an apology *be* an ambush? I was just waiting in a place I'd hoped he'd be, ready to jump out at him and stop him in his tracks to force him to listen to my apology.

Yeah, definitely an ambush. But at least I'd brought apology pastries.

And when I finally saw him approaching the gym, bopping his head to whatever was in his AirPods, I took it as my chance to strike.

"Hey!" I leapt forward from where I'd been sitting behind the reception desk, and Gabe staggered backward, eyes going wide as he narrowly avoided tripping over his own feet. It was only once he'd grabbed the nearest table, almost upending a jug of cucumber water, that he managed to regain his balance. So, you know, off to a great start. "I figured you'd be here. I brought pastries."

"Oh my God." Gabe put both hands on his knees, leaning over as he wheezed. "You scared the hell out of me, Margaret."

"Isn't the point of exercise—to get your heart rate up?" I smiled weakly, held the plate up for his perusal. "Sorry. I didn't think you'd be so easily startled."

"Yeah, well, you basically jump-scared me at six in the morning; forgive me for not expecting it." Gabe walked past me without taking a Danish, heading toward one of the treadmills at the back of the gym. The gym was situated near the front of the ship, with windows that took up the entire wall, so you could watch the ocean as you ran. Gabe stepped onto a treadmill near the end of the row, keeping his gaze forward. "You're not just supposed to loiter in here, you know. It's supposed to be for working out."

"Oh, yeah." This apology was clearly not going to be as easy as I'd hoped, but that was fine. I'd just have to improvise. I placed the pastries down and hopped onto the treadmill next to Gabe, pressing the quick start button. "That's what I'm doing. Obviously."

"You're here to work out." Gabe finally looked at me, if only to run his eyes up and down my outfit. Which, yes, fair. I was wearing a sundress and sandals; not exactly treadmill attire.

"This is part of the training my new swim coach sent over." I hopped onto the side of the treadmill, pulling off my sandals and tossing them. Hopefully none of the fitness staff would look too closely in our direction; I was 99 percent sure you weren't supposed to use the treadmills barefoot. "She wants us to practice working out in uncomfortable situations, to simulate the end of a hard meet. I figured running in street clothes next to a guy who definitely doesn't want to spend time with me qualified."

Gabe let out a sort of humph sound that wasn't acceptance but also wasn't a direct order telling me to leave, so I'd take it. Both of us bumped up our speed until we were running at a comfortable pace next to each other.

Well, it would have been more comfortable if I'd been wearing shoes and maybe a sports bra, but beggars couldn't be choosers.

Luckily, after about five minutes, he gave a big sigh, then stopped his treadmill and reached over to pause mine, too.

"What are you doing here, Margaret?"

"Getting my sweat on?" I gestured toward the treadmill. "I think I can beat you."

"I'm serious." Gabe leaned back against the rail, brushing his hair out of his eyes. "Last time I saw you, you made it very clear you didn't want to see me again."

"Right." Okay. Apology time. "It's possible I . . . wasn't in the best mindset, after seeing my mom. And I know we've technically been fake dating this whole time, but that was the first time we had to do anything . . . super fake datey, you know?"

"Kind of." He crossed his arms over his chest. "I wasn't trying to make you uncomfortable."

"Trust me, you're not the one who made me uncomfortable." Other people were starting to come into the gym, which meant that a fitness manager was certainly going to notice my non-gym-appropriate outfit any second now, so I had to make this quick. "Look. I'm sorry I was a jerk. I absolutely still need your help, if you're interested. A little hand-holding and one stupid kiss isn't going to scare me away."

"Stupid, huh?" Gabe raised one of his thick eyebrows at me. "Damn. That's harsh, Mags."

"You know what I mean." I flushed, surprising no one. "It's just . . . God, this is embarrassing." I lowered my voice, so the half dozen other athletic enthusiasts wouldn't hear me. "I've never really kissed anyone before? So the whole experience took me by surprise. That's all. I'm not trying to make things weird."

"Oh." Gabe looked around surreptitiously, like he, too, knew this wasn't a topic I'd want broadcast to the mixture of guests and crew who were working out around us. "That was your first kiss."

"We don't need to assign some big fancy meaning to it." I

glanced behind me, and, crap, there was one of the gym's crew members, walking in my direction with a concerned look on her face. "Listen, I'm going to make my terrible attitude up to you, okay? If you're still off on Wednesday, then when we get to Nighthawk Cay, we can spend the day together. Do whatever you want."

"How can I pass up an offer like that?" Gabe noticed the crew member, too, and reached down to grab my plate of pastries and handed it to me. "It's a deal. Now will you get out of here so that I can actually work out and you don't get permanently banned from the gym?"

"Aye, aye, captain." I gave him a salute and jumped off the treadmill, grabbing my shoes and ducking around the crew member before she could say anything.

And even though I'd been dreading that conversation, dreading having to actually talk to Gabe about anything resembling feelings . . . it hadn't been too bad.

As I emerged from the fitness center onto the pool deck, where the crew was pulling out lounge chairs and refreshing towels, I couldn't help but smile. The wildest part was, I didn't tell Gabe that he could plan the day because I wanted to push my own boundaries of plan setting or go with the flow-ing. I just wanted him to be happy.

The joke was going to be on me when I ended up riding on the back of the shark or something. But that was the price you paid for—

Friendship. *Definitely* friendship.

CHAPTER TWENTY-TWO

It was weird, getting ready to go out onto Nighthawk Cay with just Gabe.

Not, like, bad weird. But Marianne was lying on her bed, flipping through a magazine while she watched me tame back my hair, and it was definitely one of the stranger role reversals we'd had for a while.

"So you have no idea what you two are doing?" she asked, turning the pages in her copy of *Vogue*. "You're just letting him plan it?"

"That's the idea." It was a very Marianne move, I guessed, but with Gabe it didn't feel like it was falling under the *choose your fighter, be exactly like one of your sisters at all times!* umbrella. We were just being ourselves, I guessed. "Pass me those hair ties?"

"You must really like him." Marianne rolled a small zippered pouch in my direction; I grabbed it before it fell onto the floor. "You never let anyone be in charge of anything."

"Well, things change." I guessed she hadn't noticed how I'd

let her be in charge of me for the last month. Marianne was being weird, more subdued than usual, but I didn't have time to delve into it, because I needed to meet Gabe on deck two in five minutes. "I'll see you tonight, okay? Love you, bye!"

Before she could say anything else, I grabbed my backpack and ran out the door, letting it slam closed behind me.

Maybe it was selfish. But I didn't want to think about Marianne today.

⚓

I stopped dead in my tracks when I saw Gabe, waiting for me at the bottom of the steps.

Not because he was, like, so good-looking that he stopped me in place or anything. I mean, he *was* that good-looking: strong and dark in a way that I'd thought I was getting used to and then, bam, it would hit me out of nowhere again. But what surprised me this time?

He was wearing *color*.

Not just dark blue or something, either. Gabe, sound tech Gabe, perpetually-dressed-in-black Gabe, who I had assumed was allergic to color, was dressed in a lime green tank top and white-and-blue floral swim trunks. Lime green wasn't a color I'd ever expect to look good on anyone, but somehow he pulled it off, and, no, I didn't know what hot-guy sorcery he was using to do it.

"Oh my God." I ran down the last few stairs, stopping to stare at Gabe. "Were you in a Crayola factory explosion? Do you think you're entitled to worker's comp? Because back in Barton, there's a lawyer with a *ton* of billboards about this very situation."

"You're funny," Gabe said, not laughing, but I thought his eyes might have crinkled a little at the edges, under his aviators. "You ready to go? Got all your supplies?"

"My friend, I am prepared for anything you throw at me today." I flipped my backpack around in front of me, opened it to let Gabe look inside. "We've got a second swimsuit, we've got water, we've got snacks, we've got sunscreen, we've got four peanut butter sandwiches Elinor insisted I take that definitely got squashed by the sunscreen. I also have five euros that Edward found in the bottom of his suitcase, in case this excursion turns extra international, which is weird because he's never even been to Europe." I may have abandoned a lot of my planner instincts, but I still knew how to pack a day bag. "Did I miss anything?"

"Only one way to find out." He held his hand out toward me, and—I knew what I should have done. I should have brushed past his hand, headed off the ship and onto the gangplank and into the world, alone, just like I'd always meant to.

But this was a day for trying new things.

I grabbed Gabe's hand, and let him lead me into our adventure.

FIFTEEN minutes later, Gabe finally came to a halt in front of a sailboat, probably forty feet long, that was docked at the end of a long pier. It had two hulls (which was, like, the main body of the boat) instead of one, like two snowshoes that the rest of the boat was built on top of. Two huge sails shuddered above the deck, rippling in the wind before me.

It was undeniably beautiful.

"Here she is." *She,* right, I kept forgetting the weird way people gendered ships. He dropped my hand to gesture toward the boat, and I ignored how much I immediately missed the contact. "Do they have catamarans in New Jersey?"

"Is that fancy cruise speak for 'sailboat'?" I asked, then waved at the curly-haired Black woman wearing a polo shirt who stepped off the boat and opened a folder as she approached us. "Because I have seen a sailboat before."

"Not exactly." Gabe reached into his backpack, pulling out two tickets and handing them to the woman. "That's what they call a boat with two hulls. They're super smooth to ride on, and you can also get pretty awesome air when you're going fast enough."

"What is with your constant obsession with getting me as high up in the air as possible?" I joked as we climbed on board, joining a few other couples and families that were already settled. "First the parasailing and now this. You have some sort of height complex."

"Maybe." Gabe shrugged, taking my hand again to hold me steady as he led me toward the front of the boat. Instead of solid floor, this area had thick netting strung between the two hulls, and he stepped down into it, sitting cross-legged and patting the space next to him. "Maybe I think you just deserve the chance to soar." His tone was genuine, caring, even as I groaned, even as my whole chest seemed to squeeze tightly around my heart.

"That was the worst, and I'm embarrassed for you." It took me a second longer than Gabe to settle onto the netting— although I'd gotten used to the gentle rocking of the *Mab* over the last month, I felt the up and down of the ocean way more on this smaller vessel. "I might have to wear a disguise to be seen with you today."

"I think you'll manage somehow." Gabe gave me one of his famous half smiles, our knees pressing together. "Do me a favor and hold on tight. This is going to be the ride of your life."

A shiver went through my whole body, just hearing him say that.

Good lord. I needed to get my shit together.

CHAPTER TWENTY-THREE

The catamaran was, indeed, awesome.

I felt like one of the dolphins that sometimes followed in the wake of the *Queen Mab*, jumping and bouncing in the waves. I didn't know how fast we were going, but it felt like a thousand miles an hour, and with each wave we pushed over, the bow of the boat rose up and crashed back down into the ocean, sea bursting through the netting and instantly soaking us. I was screaming and laughing, all at the same time; and Gabe grinned, the widest I'd ever seen, as the water cut the heat, cut the world, and turned us into a bubble of spray and salt and Gabe and me, caught in a moment I wanted to last forever.

Eventually, the boat slowed down to a more manageable speed, and we approached the southern tip of Nighthawk Cay, where we would drop anchor in a cove to swim and eat lunch.

"I feel like I've already been swimming," I told Gabe as we sat up, both of us laughing at our appearances. We were completely soaked, though the sun kept me from being cold;

I suspected I'd be dry soon, and made a mental note to reapply my sunscreen. "Thanks for that, though. I was looking at some of these sailing excursions, but it's way more fun with someone else."

"Bold words coming from Margaret the Independent." Gabe shook out his hair like a dog, and I yelped as he sprayed me with tiny droplets. "Isn't your whole motto basically that life is better alone?"

"Unattached is different than alone, thanks. Although if I was alone, I wouldn't have to deal with all of your hair spraying me with water." I gave him a small shove and deftly sidestepped the question. That version of me felt a lot further away, sitting out in the middle of the ocean with Gabe. "I don't think it's a bad thing for me to do *some* stuff alone this summer, though. Get used to leaving the family before I head off to school this fall."

"You know they're not just, like, sending you off into a void, right?" Gabe rubbed at the back of his neck. "You guys can still keep in touch. Airplanes have been around for a good hundred years now. It doesn't have to be all-or-nothing."

"My family's big on all-or-nothing, Gabe." I shook my head, feeling the curls that had come loose from my ponytail hit the side of my face. "You either have love, or you're destined to be alone forever. You're either super smart and sensible like Elinor, or you're a romantic mess like Marianne. And I love them, and I love being around them, most of the time, but I don't know." Elinor or Marianne, Elinor or Marianne. I'd spent the whole summer vacillating between one or the other. It was exhausting. "I've spent my entire life being defined by my family. I've never gotten to live life as just *me*."

Gabe nodded, slow. The sun was beating down on both of us now, the water more tempting by the minute. Most everyone else on board had already jumped off the back of the boat, the captain and first mate keeping an eye on the water to make sure everyone was still accounted for. But I didn't make a move to get in, and neither did Gabe.

Then he spoke.

"I—I'm not saying that way of thinking is wrong." Gabe chose his words with care. "But I think it's easy to take a family that loves you for granted when you have one. I've seen you with your sisters this summer, Mags. Your relationship may not be perfect, but you all genuinely seem to care about each other. If you have a problem with the way you're pulled between them, why not talk to them about it?"

"Or I could just ignore the problem and move a thousand miles away." I said it as a joke, but Gabe frowned, and my throat tightened.

"You know how I live with my grandmother, when I'm home?" he asked, and I nodded. "That's because my mom died when I was little. My dad was never in the picture, and my mom raised me on her own, until—it was an accident." I resisted the urge to hug him. "I'd only met my avó a few times, because she split her time between the States and Brazil. But she moved to the States full time after Mom died, and I moved in with her." His voice was monotone, like the best way he knew to tell this story was to keep as much emotion out of it as possible. "Avó loves me, and I'm glad to have her, and to have Tia Luisa and Tio Peter, and everything. It could be a lot worse. But I don't come first for any of them, you know? I'm not their—I'm not their number ones. They do the best they can, but their life isn't built around loving me the way my mom's was."

"I'm sorry, Gabe," I said softly. "That's—you know my dad died. I get it."

"Yeah, but all of that just made me want to cling to everything I have as tight as possible." He shook his head. "That's why I come out here. My avó still likes to go back to Rio during our summers, so if I'm here, at least I'm with my aunt and uncle. And if there was ever a problem with them, I'd want to fix it, not run away."

"I'm not asking you to understand." There was an edge in my voice, because, while I respected Gabe's grief, even related to it, I wasn't about to let him question mine. "You don't have to get it. I do." I didn't say what I was thinking—that I didn't come first for anyone in my family, either, because all I'd ever been was the extra daughter, the extra sister. I had to be like Elinor or Marianne because it never felt like there was *room* to have a Margaret around, too. And I tried not to think about it much, because it made my chest tighten and my breathing quicken, to think that I was headed off to school in a month and I had no idea who I was. Who I was going to be, when I was away from them.

"Fair enough," Gabe said after a second, and I didn't know if he meant it, but I knew he was going to move on for now. "Come on. What do you say we try out the water?"

"Don't have to ask me twice."

We both stood up, heavy with heat and held-back emotion. Luckily, I received an *excellent* distraction when Gabe pulled his shirt over his head, tossing it down by his backpack. Wow. Who knew that running soundboards could keep you so ripped? Because none of the tech guys who went to my high school looked like that. Or maybe they did, because it wasn't like I had watched any of *them* undress—not that I was watching Gabe undress, of course, even though I definitely was—but either way, I never noticed.

With Gabe, I noticed.

I was suddenly glad that I'd gotten a few new bathing suits before the trip, replaced the cruddy old two-piece that had gotten me through last summer. Gabe glanced over at me quickly, and then just as quickly averted his eyes, and I felt a weird sense of accomplishment that he was looking at me just like I was looking at him.

"Come on." As we walked toward the back of the boat, I held out my hand. Gabe took it. His palm was warm and dry, comfortingly assertive in mine. "Count of three."

And as we counted down and jumped in together, neither of us let go.

CHAPTER TWENTY-FOUR

The rest of the afternoon passed in a state of pure bliss. Gabe and I swam around the catamaran, then floated gently off the side, using pool noodles that the first mate tossed us to bob above the water. We chatted about the ship, about our remaining ports of call, about what we thought next week's batch of guests would be like. But we were comfortable in the silence, too, just floating in the sunshine, occasionally bumping into each other and neither of us seeming mad about it.

Eventually it was time to get out of the water and eat a late lunch, a glorious spread of grilled fish and burgers washed down with sickly-sweet sodas out of the coldest cans I'd ever touched. Everything, I was starting to learn, tasted better when you were on a boat. From the way Gabe chuckled as I wolfed down my food, he'd noticed my enthusiasm.

"Good?" he asked, when I went for a second burger. I gave him a thumbs-up, my mouth full, and he gave me one of his half smiles.

If I were designing the rest of our day, I would have made it endless. But unfortunately, we had to head back to the main port at Nighthawk eventually, and this time, I was the first one up on the netting. Gabe settled in beside me, and the thrill that kept coursing through my chest might not, I was realizing, have been entirely about the crashing waves.

I could see the *Queen Mab* docked a little ways away from us, and she looked friendly, comfortable, but I still didn't want to go back. I wanted to stay in this moment forever, sitting up on the bow of the boat, my legs tucked beneath me as I let the now-gentle waves lull me into a sense of absolute calm.

Well, except for the thudding of my heart whenever I thought about Gabe.

It was getting a little chilly up here, though, the ocean breeze cutting through my still-damp bathing suit. I shivered.

"Cold?" Gabe asked.

"A little." I did my best to stop shaking. "So much for the never-ending Bahamian sunshine, right?" The sky had developed some light cloud cover as we sailed back to the dock, blocking out the harshest rays of the sun. "I'll be okay."

"Do you want to . . ." Gabe cocked his head to the side, then, after just a moment of hesitation, reached out his arm and wrapped it around my shoulders, pulling me closer to him. "Is this okay?"

"Yeah. Thanks." One-syllable words were about all I could manage, honestly, the way that my heart was full-on caught in my throat.

I took a deep breath, tried to clear away my nerves as I tucked myself in next to Gabe. I was being stupid. Gabe was my friend. Just because I'd had, overall, very little guy contact in my life (besides Edward, and I guess Brandon, but they didn't count) didn't mean I needed to fall apart just because a guy friend—who happened to be very good-looking—touched me. Besides, I reminded myself sternly, I didn't *do* this. I didn't get all fluttery over guys. I had more important things to worry about.

"This is a friend arm, right?" I asked, the breeze ruffling my hair. "Because I haven't changed my stance on my anti-romance thing."

"I know." Gabe's voice was soft, so close to my ear he didn't need to be any louder. "Strictly a friend arm. I promise."

"Good." After a second, I rested my head on his shoulder, noting how perfectly it fit in the space below his head. "I appreciate that."

"Anytime," Gabe said, and then we didn't say anything for the rest of the ride in.

We managed to dock and get off the boat without incident. The rest of the guests hurried back toward the ship, or to the souvenir shop conveniently positioned right at the entrance to the island, but Gabe hesitated at a fork in the path.

"What is it?" I rubbed my towel against my ponytail, trying to wring water out of it. "Lost already?"

"Not quite." Gabe glanced up at the sun, getting lower in the sky. "We've got a little time before the ship leaves the port, you know."

"Did you figure that out from the *sun*?" I shook my head. "Okay, Boy Scout."

"Don't hate on my sailing skills." Gabe let out a long-suffering sigh. "I was just thinking. We've got enough time to check out the lighthouse . . . if you want."

"Really?" Gabe had talked up this lighthouse for weeks,

but I still hadn't made it over there; I told myself *that* was why I was excited, not just the prospect of extra, uninterrupted Gabe time. "That would be great. You're sure we can make it?"

"Eh, they probably won't leave without us." He started toward a sandy path off to our left that was flanked by low, scrubby bushes. "Come on."

I followed.

It took us about fifteen minutes to reach the lighthouse, and what struck me most about it was how it appeared out of nowhere, the dense trees and bushes that had overtaken us suddenly parting to reveal the beacon. It wasn't a huge structure, probably only five or six stories tall, but it seemed gigantic when it just showed up like that.

"There she is." Gabe nodded, satisfied. "Nowhere better than this on the whole island."

"It's cool, for sure." I didn't want to tell Gabe, but I didn't know if I really . . . got it. It was an interesting building, but the best place on the whole island? "I see why you like it."

Gabe looked over at me for a second, and then laughed.

"Come on." He approached the small black door that stood out from the whitewashed walls, and gave it a push. It opened softly for him, almost like a magic trick. "We're going up." And then he stepped in, disappearing quickly inside the darkness.

Obviously I had to dart in after him.

The interior of the lighthouse was dim, and Gabe pulled out his phone flashlight so we could see better. There was a small landing at the base, where you could maybe fit a couple of rickety chairs, and then a winding spiral staircase that led straight up. Gabe began to climb without a word, and I followed him.

At the very top, another door, this one bolted from the inside. He turned back toward me, his face cloaked in shadows.

"Ready?" he asked, and even though I didn't know why, my pulse jumped.

"For what?" I asked, but before I could get an answer, Gabe unbolted and pushed open the door, stepping out onto a small observation platform that overlooked . . .

The greatest view I'd ever experienced.

You could see everything from up here. The endless sea in one direction, vast and infinite, and on the other side of the island, the small port where the *Queen Mab* was docked, friendly and inviting at this distance, a speck against the ocean. I could see the small buildings that housed the island's shops and grill, the houses where a few crew members lived on the island for maintenance between dockings, and across the densely packed trees, a hotel that guests could stay in between cruises, if they chose. The wind whipped at my hair, bringing the smell of salt even closer.

I shivered, watching the world unfold before me.

"Not bad, right?" Gabe had stepped behind me, his voice a whisper near my ear.

"Not bad." Goose bumps rose on my arms, and I didn't know if it was from the breeze or from how small I felt. Gabe must have noticed, because he stepped closer to me, wrapped his arms around my shoulders as he pulled me back into his chest.

"Still okay?" We weren't that different in height, so his

head was pressed right against my neck. "I don't want you to get hypothermia."

"Yeah." I could barely breathe out the word. Suddenly I couldn't feel the wind, and the breathtaking view of the sea and the island was reduced to a pinpoint, because all I could see, or feel, or experience, was Gabe. Gabe, who held me like a promise. Gabe, who'd opened up to me and opened me up in return, who knew me better in four weeks than anyone else. Gabe, whose skin was hot against mine, and even though we were standing so close, it still felt like an enormous tension, a rubber band pulled taut, a frisson that threatened to snap us together at any moment.

God, I wanted to kiss him. Not a small, barely anything kiss, like we'd had on the ship, in front of my entire family. I wanted a kiss that counted. To spin around in his arms and pull him toward me so there would be no doubt how I felt.

Because, I realized, horrified, I knew exactly how I felt.

I'd fallen a thousand percent in love with Gabe Monteiro, and that was my absolute worst-case scenario.

This was a plan that had gone awry in the most dangerous way. I had learned to manage when itineraries changed, when expectations changed, when people changed. But one thing remained true—the way I felt about Gabe could destroy me.

"We should get back to the ship." I stepped forward, even though it was the last thing I wanted to do. Gabe released me right away—of course he did, he'd constantly asked if things were okay, gotten my consent every step of the way, so it wasn't like I could be mad at him for the way I'd fallen. I'd told him a thousand times that we were just friends. If he'd ever thought of me in a different way, he would have shut those feelings down weeks ago. "It's getting late."

"All aboard isn't for another hour." But Gabe stepped aside anyway, held his arm out toward the open door behind him. "After you."

"Thanks." I gave him the best smile I could manage, tried to hide how much I was freaking out inside. How much I felt every shivering inch of closeness as he followed me down the stairs, as we fell in step together back toward the ship, as he high-fived me goodbye and I told him I'd catch him at one of the shows tomorrow, to figure out our next best steps for Operation: Marianne.

I wanted to scream. I wanted to cry. I wanted Gabe.

And I absolutely, one thousand percent, couldn't have him.

CHAPTER TWENTY-FIVE

When I got back to the stateroom, salty and windswept, I was alternating between floating and panicking.

So, you know, the usual Dashwood combo.

I'd planned on showering and then lying face down in my bunk until I could figure out what to do with my feelings, but that plan quickly changed when I found Marianne sitting at the edge of her bed, wiping away tears.

"What's wrong?" Suddenly I had bigger things to worry about than my own problems, which was honestly a relief. I dropped onto the bed beside my sister, peering over to see her face. "Are you hurt?"

"No, I'm not hurt." She half laughed, still crying, as she wiped at her face. "I'm fine. Don't worry about me." *Literally impossible*, I thought, bumping my shoulder into hers.

"Come on," I said. She was dressed to go out, in a lacy red A-line number that flowed out at the waist, the top cut in a sweetheart neckline. "Talk to me."

"Tomas stood me up, okay?" Shit. "So I ended—whatever

was going on. We were barely dating. I shouldn't be upset. It's not like we were in love."

"That's . . . It's just a speed bump." I needed a plan. No—I needed to chill out. No, I needed— God, I hated all of this. "We'll just have to find you someone else, right? Someone better."

"Margaret." Marianne's voice was sharp. "You don't need to keep throwing guys at me like I won an Oprah giveaway. I just want to relax."

"You're just saying that because you and Tomas didn't work out." If she stopped chasing guys, I'd have nothing to do, and that meant I'd have to spend more time thinking about Gabe, and I wanted to avoid that as much as possible, thanks. "There are plenty more guys on this ship. I'll set something up."

"So I can just keep watching you and Gabe fall all over each other while I go on another date that goes nowhere? You have to get why that doesn't sound appealing." Marianne flopped back on the bed, her curls spread out behind her.

The words spilled out of me before I had a chance to consider their impact.

"Gabe and I broke up, too."

"You did?" Marianne sat up again, so fast I was worried all the blood was going to rush to her head. She did look kind of flushed, but that could have been from the crying. "When?"

"On the—today." *Improvise, Margaret, improvise.* I wished this cabin were a little bigger, so I didn't have to be quite so close to Marianne right now; she didn't need to experience my lying sweats. But, hey, if I wanted to find a middle ground between constant planning and constant spontaneity, maybe this was it. "We did a sailboat ride and it was fun and everything, but he . . . wanted to see other people." Probably shouldn't have thrown Gabe under the bus like that, but it wasn't like Marianne was going to track him down and corroborate my story. "So I need to find someone new, too! It'll be perfect."

"Or we could just, you know, hang out." Marianne glanced back at her pillow, like she wanted nothing more than to lie back down on it. "We've barely gotten any guy-free sister time."

"And miss an opportunity for some perfectly good romance? No way." I shook my head. "We are going to scour this ship until we find new guys for both of us, and I'm not going to rest until we do."

"If that's what you want." Marianne's smile was weak, but I assumed that was because she was still exhausted from such an emotional roller coaster of a day. Personally, I was feeling pleased as anything—this was the perfect excuse to avoid Gabe and my inconvenient feelings for him without having to actually confront them. "Maybe we can wait until tomorrow, though? I'm still pretty exhausted by the whole, you know, kind of breaking up with someone thing. It's been happening a lot more this summer than I'm used to."

"Yeah, of course." I put my arm around my sister, giving her a quick squeeze. I wasn't going to let her spend her last week on board moping around, because even if she said she wanted sister time, I knew what that meant. "Sister time" would involve staring longingly into the sea and wishing she had her old life back. No way. Marianne was getting off this cruise ship happy if it was the last thing I did.

And in the meantime . . . I just had to figure out how to fake break up with Gabe.

IF you were thinking that talking to Gabe about all of this five minutes before a show was absolutely a coward's move, the answer was yes, it was, and also, that was one hundred percent what I was doing.

"And Marianne is just in this really fragile place right now," I continued, standing next to Gabe as we both squinted in the sun on the top deck. Gabe was running sound for one of the kids' pirate parties that the ship was hosting next to the pool, and to my delight, he'd been outfitted with a red-and-white-striped bandana and an eye patch. If anything, this made it a lot easier to fake break up with him. "So I feel like if we can work together to find new guys, just for a couple of days, she'll be able to rally and get her groove back, you know?"

"And that can't happen with you and me fake dating?" Gabe reached for the soundboard and missed the slider entirely; with a curse, he pushed his eye patch on top of his head. "This is the worst uniform decision production has ever made, by the way. Completely messes with my depth perception."

"You need a parrot, to push all the buttons for you." It was a gorgeous day, not too hot, for a change, and if I wasn't in the process of breaking up with my fake boyfriend, this would have been the perfect place to hang out for a couple of hours. But I couldn't risk Marianne seeing me and Gabe together, and I couldn't risk hanging out with Gabe again until my feelings for him died way, way down. "You're sure you're cool with this?" I shouldn't even ask, but I was only human. A human who was unfortunately deeply into the guy she was standing next to. "I don't want to break your heart or anything."

Gabe laughed. "Nothing to be heartbroken about, right? Because we're not really dating."

"Obviously." Why did it feel so shitty to agree to that?

"So it's not a concern." He shrugged, then turned his attention back to the small stage in front of the pool, where a bunch of pirates—I recognized Torden among them, and waved—had gathered. "Just like . . . message me how it goes or whatever."

"Are you mad?" I didn't like his tone. It didn't sound like the Gabe I'd gotten to know. "Because you said—"

"I'm not mad, Margaret." He cut me off. "I just need to work."

So that wasn't my favorite way to end things, but my mission was firmly accomplished. I nodded, gave him a small wave—he didn't return it—and left the pool deck, heading for some shade where I could clear my head.

CHAPTER TWENTY-SIX

I spent the next day desperately racking my brain to figure out how to get Marianne—and me, too, I guessed—another love match. Unfortunately, I was starting to scrape the bottom of the barrel, ideas-wise. And without Gabe to bounce said ideas off, I could tell that they were all lousy. As convenient as it would be, I didn't *really* think that getting a skywriter to advertise Marianne's phone number over the entirety of the Bahamas would yield good results.

So that Saturday night, for lack of a better option, I recruited Elinor.

I know, I know. It was truly a desperate choice. But no matter how much Marianne said she was fine, I knew she needed some distracting. She'd been happy enough with Tomas, I knew it. And until I could get our last guy, Xander, to work out some time in his schedule to hang out with Marianne, I was ready to keep her thoroughly tucked under our sisterly wings.

And, no, Elinor didn't know that this was all part of a

giant scheme. I just told her that Marianne seemed a little down, and she'd sprung into action, so quickly that I almost wished I'd had her on my side the entire time.

Of course, if I'd done that, there'd be no grand payoff where I revealed to her that I had single-handedly cured our sister of heartbreak. But at this point, I was less interested in payoff and more interested in making it through this summer in one piece. Even if that one piece involved, apparently, something called a silent disco.

I'd never had much interest in checking out the silent disco that the *Mab* ran a few times a week, up in the Skylight Lounge. Mostly because I didn't really understand the concept. According to Edward and Elinor, who had gone a couple of times, everyone wore headphones and rocked out to whatever music channel they wanted, but to anyone walking in, it would look like they were dancing to nothing. Which I guessed was funny to watch, but if I wanted to dance to music only I could hear, blasting BTS in my bedroom back home was good enough for me.

But this was how Elinor had declared we would distract Marianne, even though Marianne kept insisting she didn't *need* distracting. When we got up to the top deck late that afternoon, I expected a lot of Edward and Elinor types waltzing in silence, but as we crammed into the multitiered lounge, the room was pulsing with excitement. It also wasn't nearly as silent as I'd expected. Sure, there wasn't any music, but with thirty or forty people already dancing, singing along, jumping up and down . . .

It was deeply chaotic, and a month ago, it would have sent me running in the other direction. But now I kind of loved it.

"There's usually three or four channels," Elinor explained as she passed giant headphones out to me, Marianne, and Edward, who gave them an extra dose of disinfectant wipe before pulling them over his ears. "The headphones light up in different colors, depending which channel you're on, so you can see who's listening to the same music as you."

"Or you can tell if everyone else is on a way *better* channel," Marianne added, carefully adjusting her hair around her headphones. Her eyes were glimmering with excitement, and even though she'd said she didn't need this, I was suddenly immensely grateful to Elinor for insisting on it. Maybe it would even be . . . fun?

After claiming a couple of lounge chairs for our bags, the four of us headed for the edge of the dance floor, switching on the headphones all at the same time.

Immediately, I winced. *Loud.* But a minute of messing with the knobs turned it down to a reasonable volume, and soon I was bopping along to some *Lover*-era Taylor. Marianne was on the same channel as me, her headphones glowing pink, while Elinor and Edward were swinging around the dance floor to what I discovered, when I toggled my channel over to their blue one, was big band music. Edward wasn't bad, either, twirling my sister and even offering her a modest dip.

I giggled, switching back to Taylor as Marianne caught my eye and laughed.

"This *is* kind of fun," I admitted as she took me by the hands and twirled the two of us around, going under a bridge we created with our arms. As I shouted along to lyrics about cruel summers, I watched the guests around us salsa, and headbang, and occasionally all come together to dance along to "Y.M.C.A." or hop their way through "Cotton-Eyed Joe."

And it was awesome.

The rhythm of the music carried through the room like one of the waves that occasionally rocked the ship; I had the strange feeling, not for the first time since I'd stepped on board, that I was a part of an organism I didn't understand. Something bigger than me. It wasn't unlike the way I'd felt, every now and again, when we'd have the whole family together, Mom and my sisters and Brandon and Edward, even though those occasions had been few and far between the last couple of years. It was weird, in a way. Brandon loved being with our family—at least it had always seemed like he did—and even though I didn't expect him to necessarily confide in his much-younger not-quite-sister-in-law, I'd spent enough time with him to know when his enjoyment of something was genuine. He'd lit up, when we were all together. Elinor had told me once that it was because he didn't have much family of his own, not anymore. He'd fallen in love with Marianne, but he'd fallen in love with all of us, too.

I wondered if he was lonely now. Without any of us.

Because in this moment, with my sisters surrounding me, packed into a ship that I'd gotten to know like a second home, I didn't *want* to run away. I wanted to find my own place *within* the two of them, figure out how to be more than just the third Dashwood. Here on the dance floor with my family, I didn't feel like I was bouncing back and forth, trying to be one of them or the other. I just felt like I was being me, or at least was on the way to figuring out who that was.

Gabe would be into this. The thought came into my head

halfway through an Olivia Rodrigo scream-along with Marianne. I grinned at the idea of Gabe here, fist-pumping to Springsteen. I couldn't see him dancing, giving in to his inhibitions like that, but he *would* like the atmosphere. How everyone was lost in sound. How we'd created our own little concerts.

But it didn't matter if he'd be into this, I reminded myself. Gabe and I needed to keep our distance.

I wished we could have gone to this together, though. Before I stopped pretending I could be around him without falling.

An hour into the disco, the crowd had thinned out considerably, as most people headed down toward the dining room for dinner service. Edward was sitting in a lounge chair, surrounded by empty glasses of water and watching Elinor twirl along to something slow in front of him, her eyes closed. In the center of the dance floor, now almost entirely empty, Marianne was trying to convince me to do the *Dirty Dancing* lift with her, raising her arms above her head to show me her form—like *that* was the part I was hesitant about.

"Attention, ladies." A voice cut through the music in my headphones, and I glanced up in surprise to see the DJ waving at our group. He'd hopped over the sound system to make announcements a couple of times before, but it took me by surprise every time. "I have to wrap up soon. Any requests?"

Marianne and I turned to face each other, eyes wide. Then, almost simultaneously, we turned to look at Elinor, who was already shaking her head.

"Oh, no." She held her hands out in front of her, waving them back and forth as Edward watched her with curiosity. "I'm not doing that. I don't even *remember* that."

"You absolutely do." Marianne grinned, then turned back to the DJ. "Do you have 'Super Trouper'? Specifically from the *Mamma Mia!* movie soundtrack?"

"Oh my God." Edward stood up from his chair, quickly toggling his headphones back on. "I forgot about that. When was the last time the three of you did this?"

"Five years ago." I held my hand out toward Elinor. "Come on. You're the best Meryl Streep we've got. We can't do it without you."

Elinor hesitated, and for a second, I was worried that she'd meant it when she'd said no. That she really was too grown-up and partnered to play with her sisters anymore. That keeping her dignity in front of the world mattered more than the three of us together.

But when she took her hair out of her ponytail and shook it down around her shoulders, I knew we had her.

"Yes!" I shouted, and Marianne high-fived Elinor as she made her way in between the two of us, striking our starting pose in the center of the dance floor.

Elinor and Marianne had both been in middle school when the movie version of *Mamma Mia!* came out, and consequently, quickly became obsessed with it. I was only two, way too little to understand the allure of ABBA or Meryl Streep as a singing goddess. But the two of them brought me into their dance routine anyway, probably because it was guaranteed cuteness points at their school talent show when I toddled out in a bell-bottomed, sequined jumpsuit. We'd busted out the routine all the time, one of the biggest constants of my childhood. Even when Dad died and we moved to Barton, it was the first thing we did in the new house, to christen it as ours.

We hadn't done it since the accident.

But I still remembered it, every step and second: the opening pose, where we all held pretend microphones and then burst from our line into dramatic disco back-to-back poses, how Elinor would step forward for her solos and Marianne and I would shimmy and turn around her, oohing and aahing in the background. There was dramatic pointing, there was step-touching, and there were a *whole* lot of hip thrusts as Elinor shouted to Edward about being in the crowd. Edward, for his part, looked delighted, changing his headphones to match our channel as he clapped along and cheered. The other few guests in the lounge joined him, hooting and hollering as we came to our big dramatic finish.

As Elinor grabbed each of our hands, Marianne and I spun in toward her in time to the music, finishing in a massive huddle of chaos and sisterly love just as the final note hit, and Edward—along with the rest of our modest crowd—burst into applause.

And as I looked at my sisters, at Elinor, laughing so much she'd started to cry, and Marianne, squished under Elinor's armpit with her arms twisted all around her as her eyes sparkled with fun, pressed against me like we'd never been apart, I was the happiest I'd been in a long, long time.

"I can't believe how well you hit that step ball change in the third verse, Marianne." I was still babbling half an hour later, when the DJ had high-fived all of us before wrapping up and we'd finally filed out of the lounge. Edward was grabbing us a bunch of pizza from the buffet, and Elinor, Marianne, and I had gone out to the highest observation deck of the ship, where we could catch the orange rays of sunset making their way across the ocean. "Flawless."

"Please. It was, as always, all in service to our magnificent Meryl stand-in." Marianne had procured frozen drinks for the three of us, and handed them out as we all shimmied into one shared hammock, a sister squish. "El, have you been practicing on your own? Who does Edward stand in for? If you say it's me, I'm tossing you out of this hammock."

"You wouldn't dare." Elinor used the one leg she had hanging over the edge to send us rocking, up and down, up and down. "I'll admit, it was nice to let my hair down a little."

"Literally." I sipped at my smoothie, the artificial strawberry flavor coating my tongue. "When was the last time you took out that ponytail holder?"

"Ganging up on me. Just like always." It wasn't an admonishment. "*Now* this feels familiar."

"Only because you excel at taking it," Marianne said, leaning over to plant a big smack of a kiss on Elinor's cheek.

"It's been a good summer," I said, as I watched the sun set slowly over the ocean, sending its rays scattering toward us, like shards of stained glass. And it had been, hadn't it? I was figuring myself out. Having Marianne here had been a challenge at first, but in the end, it felt good to be closer to her again. To embrace that side of myself. Maybe it would help me have more fun in college. And lying here, all squished with my sisters, even things with Gabe didn't seem so bad.

My feelings for him would cool off in a few days, and then we could hang out again. Strictly platonically. Everything was working out.

"It has," Elinor agreed, and then the two of us turned and looked at Marianne together. She laughed, like she didn't have a care in the world.

"And getting better every day." She knocked her glass against mine, plastic tinking against plastic, then closed her eyes as she sipped. "The Dashwoods at sea. Whoever would have thought it?"

"Not me," Elinor said, closing her eyes with a sigh. I nodded. And as the three of us settled into silence, I felt something that I hadn't felt since . . . well. Since Dad died, maybe.

A deep and total sense of contentment.

Maybe I *could* fit somewhere. Right between the two of them.

CHAPTER TWENTY-SEVEN

The next couple of days were some of the best I'd had on the *Mab*. We tried out miniature golf, gave pickleball another go (still terrible), and mixed together ice cream flavors until the soft serve turned a concerning gray color.

I'd been avoiding Gabe, and while I missed hanging out with him, I felt proud of myself, for cutting things off when I had. When push came to shove, I'd still been able to protect my heart.

And, yes, I did have a bunch of messages from him that I was ignoring. But that was just . . . collateral damage. This was for the best, for both of us. Gabe would realize that eventually.

Still, when Elinor asked if I wanted to join her and Edward to watch the sunrise on Nassau on Wednesday, I was happy for a distraction, even though it meant waking up *way* earlier than I wanted to.

"Come on. It'll be worth it to have the beach to ourselves." Elinor prodded me down the gangplank as I yawned, my feet dragging in my flip-flops along the ship's carpeting.

"You can't even *see* the sunrise from the beach." Okay, I was a little grumpier than usual, but Marianne and I had stayed up way too late the night before, giggling and comparing notes on all the guys she'd dated in high school. (I had no idea liking *Lord of the Rings* was such a prevalent personality trait in guys in the early 2000s.) "We're not facing the right direction. I feel misled." Marianne had had the right idea, sleeping in. She'd laughed out loud at Elinor when she'd invited her.

"Don't worry." Edward swung his backpack off his shoulder, reached in, and pulled out a croissant wrapped in a napkin. "I brought along our guaranteed Margaret mood booster."

"Breakfast pastries *are* my love language." I squealed out loud as I reached for it.

Sitting on the beach half an hour later, my mood *was* drastically improved. The ocean sparkled with early morning light, it was warm but not *too* warm, and we had the whole space completely to ourselves. Maybe there was some merit in getting up this early after all.

Or maybe not.

Because as we eventually roused ourselves and left the beach, ready to head back toward the ship and collect Marianne for the rest of the day's activities, I saw the very last person I'd expected to see. A person who, frankly, I didn't think I was ever going to see again.

"Oh my God. Brandon?" Elinor stopped so suddenly that Edward, holding her hand, tripped and nearly fell off the sidewalk. "What are you doing here?"

Because there he was, in the flesh. Brandon. Coming out of the door of a coffee shop, tall and sturdy as ever, like one of the oak trees that grew around Barton. Serious, deep-set eyes, sharp jaw, the hint of stubble he sometimes had. He looked more tired than usual, the bags under his eyes aging him past his early thirties, but otherwise . . . it was just Brandon.

I knew I should hate him, for what he'd done to Marianne and to our family, but also, God, I'd missed him. This was the guy I'd assumed would be my brother, and then he'd been cut out of my life without any closure, so it made sense that those feelings would be hanging around. But I still felt guilt wash over me, because he'd destroyed my sister, and I shouldn't have felt *anything* positive when I saw him.

"Elinor?" Brandon's voice was low and velvet smooth. Marianne always said he had a mouth for poetry, whatever that meant. All I knew was that hearing it now sent a shiver up my spine. "What are you—this isn't the day your ship docks in Nassau."

"The port days got changed around. Weather stuff. What are *you* doing here?" Elinor asked, and I was amazed she could even get words out, because I was speechless. Also, why did he know our ship's schedule?

"I have a work conference at the Atlantis. I really didn't think I was going to see you." He sounded so apologetic. *Good.* As my shock faded, my anger started to surge. Because he *should* be avoiding us! He'd broken Marianne's heart, broken the structure of our whole family. "Marianne's not with you?" Why did he seem so nervous? Coward.

"She's back on the ship." Edward stuttered as he spoke. Even Elinor, the most poised of all of us, now seemed at a loss for words.

"Mornings. Right." Brandon's face flickered with a sad

smile. "That—that makes sense. Good. I wouldn't want her to think . . . anyway." He glanced over his shoulder, back toward the coffee shop, like he could escape. "Perhaps it's a good thing I ran into you. I've tried emailing Marianne about this a few times, but she hasn't responded."

"Why would she respond to you?" The words shot out before I could stop them, sharp and angry. Elinor nudged me, but, whatever, it felt good to stand up for my sister. We may have started this summer apart, but we could be in this together. "After everything that happened?"

"It's not about us." Brandon sounded so tired. He sounded the same way he had after the accident. "Marianne's job has been calling me, something administrative to do with the leave she's taking. And I thought she might want to change her emergency contact to you, now that she's ended things. So that this doesn't keep happening."

Brandon's voice was tight, controlled. So controlled, it took me a second to hear what he'd said.

Elinor realized it first.

"Did you say—Marianne was the one to end things?"

"Uh—yes." He rubbed a hand over the back of his neck, wiped away sweat, even though the heat of the day had barely started to kick in. "You knew that, didn't you? If I spoke out of turn, I didn't mean—"

"You spoke perfectly," I interrupted.

My whole summer. I'd given up my whole summer, what was *supposed* to be the last, perfect, quiet family summer before I left for college. Instead, I'd given that up to take care of my sister. My sister who had gotten her heart broken by the love of her life. And it turned out she'd broken up with *him*?

"I'm sure there's an explanation for this." Edward stepped forward on the sidewalk, using his best Gentle Pastor Voice. "Maybe we misunderstood?"

"I hope we misunderstood." Elinor was angry, too, I realized, from the shaking of her voice, the way her hand gripped the tote bag at her side. "Marianne told us that you broke up with her."

"Why would I— No." Brandon's face twisted in discomfort. I didn't blame him. "Quite the contrary, in fact. I proposed."

"You *proposed*?" I shrieked, and Elinor and Edward winced as several passersby turned to look at us. "Sorry."

"Yes. I thought it would be well received, given our history. But as you can see"—a deep sigh from Brandon—"that wasn't the case."

"Brandon, I'm so sorry." Elinor reached forward, laid a hand on his arm. "If I'd known . . ."

"I'm sure Marianne had her reasons for saying whatever she said." Brandon was looking around the street, and I suspected he was looking for a way out of this conversation. I needed to get out, too, to get back to the ship and demand answers from my sister. "I'm not trying to cause trouble. Elinor, can I just give her office your contact information instead? Just so they have someone still connected to Marianne?"

"That's fine." Elinor let out a long, shuddering sigh. "You don't have to go, you know. We can get—we can get coffee or something."

"I don't want you to do anything that would make Marianne uncomfortable. And I really do have to get back to the hotel." Brandon thrust his hand into his pocket. "Maybe we can talk when you get back to New Jersey. If you think that's appropriate."

"Of course it is. You've been my brother for years, Brandon." Elinor's voice came as close to breaking as I'd ever heard it, and Edward stepped up beside her, put his hand on her shoulder. "Marianne breaking up with you doesn't change that."

"Well . . . thank you." Brandon's face was full of discomfort, as it always was when people around him got emotional. "It was good to see you all. Truly. And give Marianne my best."

And then, with the world's most awkward goodbye—Brandon was never a people person to begin with, and I could tell he just wanted to get out of there—he was gone, and Elinor, Edward, and I were left standing in the middle of an increasingly busy Bahamian street, rewriting everything we'd known about this summer.

"I'm going to kill her." It was the first thing I managed to say. "Who does she think she is? Playing with us all summer?"

"She was still hurting." Edward steered me and Elinor out of the street, walking us briskly back toward the ship. "We shouldn't discount that."

"And you shouldn't discount that she lied to all of us this summer, and joined the whole trip under false pretenses," Elinor said, and I couldn't help but be taken aback by the strength of her reaction. I'd expected peacemaker Elinor, *I can take care of everything* Elinor, not the blazing anger I saw in her eyes. "So as soon as we get back on the ship, we're going to find Marianne, and we're going to see what the hell is going on here."

It was the closest Elinor ever came to cursing. But it made sense, I thought, as we scanned our ship cards and strode back onto the *Mab*, because this whole summer was starting to feel like the closest I'd ever come to a curse.

EXCEPT Marianne wasn't in the stateroom.

It didn't seem like a big deal at first. Annoying, sure, but the *Mab* was only so big, so she had to turn up eventually. Elinor and Edward decided to go out and try to find her, but I said that I'd stay in the cabin, in case she came back. Honestly, I needed some time by myself anyway, after seeing Brandon. Time to reassess my memories of my entire summer.

Also, if I went out to wander the ship, I was worried I'd head straight to Gabe, because he was the person I most wanted to talk to right now, and I needed to stay strong.

If I was going to pace back and forth somewhere, though, anxiously awaiting at least *one* of my sisters, I probably should have chosen somewhere bigger than our shoebox of a stateroom.

After three rounds of pacing, in which I managed to hit my head on the television twice, I gave up and flung myself down on Marianne's bed. Honestly, if she really had broken up with Brandon, I wasn't sure she deserved the big bed, anyway. She could cram herself into the fold-down bunk for once.

Naturally, I was immediately rewarded for my efforts by landing on something hard that jabbed me in the stomach.

"Are you kidding me?" I mumbled, rolling over to the side and feeling around under the covers to see what I'd landed on. This had not been, by any measure, a particularly stellar day.

Served me right for getting up so early in the first place. After a minute of rummaging through the sheets, I discovered the culprit—Marianne's phone, which she must have left in the stateroom by accident.

I lasted about seven seconds before curiosity got the better of me, and I swiped it open using the same passcode she'd had for literal years—Mary Shelley's birthday, whom Marianne had always admired as the *ultimate* drama queen.

I knew, as I was doing it, that it was a bad idea. It was just that, as much as Brandon had *looked* like he was telling the truth back there, I didn't want to believe him. Maybe this whole thing was one big misunderstanding! Maybe if I went into her Notes app, I'd find a dozen half-written love notes to him. Or maybe they'd been texting, and he'd said something that had scared her off, something I could convince her wasn't a big deal, so she'd get back with him and everything would be okay—

I dropped the phone like it was burning hot.

Because he'd been telling the truth. Of course.

CHAPTER TWENTY-EIGHT

This phone was evidence of a broken heart, all right, but it wasn't Marianne's.

Brandon had been texting her all summer. Apologies mixed with pleas mixed with small updates about his life, like Marianne would still care about it. I didn't read them closely, of course. First, because even though Marianne didn't deserve to have her privacy respected after this, Brandon sure did, and second, because if he'd texted her anything gross and I read it by accident, I'd have to claw out my own eyeballs. But I read enough, skimmed enough, to know that Brandon had told the truth.

Marianne was the one who'd broken apart our family, not him.

A wobbly feeling swept through me, a sudden burst of nausea. Brandon had wanted to *marry* her. They'd been together for years, and he'd never been anything but good to her, and then she just, what, decided she was done with him? God, that was exactly the sort of recklessness I'd been trying to avoid.

And then there was the whole matter of her coming on the cruise in the first place. Either my sister was a pa☐ ological liar who had manipulated all of us into taking care of ☐☐r this summer when she was *totally* fine, or she had so little understanding of boundaries and morals that she didn't understand the depth to which what she had done was not okay. And I'd tried to be like her this summer, so it felt like she'd been manipulating *me*, too, when I had a perfectly good life set out for me, following in Elinor's footsteps and playing it safe and not hurting myself or anyone else around me.

But Marianne didn't care about that, did she? She was pure, undiluted selfishness.

It would have been better, probably, if Elinor and Edward had found her first. But they didn't, and when Marianne let herself into the cabin twenty minutes later, it took everything in me not to throttle her. To rage and scream and cry because she'd ruined my summer and, by extension, ruined me.

But I channeled my inner Elinor. Spoke in a calm, clear voice as I tossed the phone down on the bed between us, a glove thrown in challenge.

"Why did you lie about Brandon breaking up with you?"

Marianne froze in the doorway. She'd clearly come from the salon, her hair blown out and gorgeous blond waves falling over her shoulders. But no matter how good she looked, how put together, I could still see her coming undone. The way her shoulders dropped, her eyes closed, and she sighed, long and hard.

"Were you going through my phone, Mags?"

"Right, because that's the part we need to concentrate on right now." I couldn't believe she was trying to deflect. "And not how you lied to us for an entire summer."

"Don't exaggerate." She came into the room the rest of the way, let the door close behind her as she reached down to take off her sandals. "We broke up. The instigating party doesn't matter."

"If it didn't matter, you wouldn't have lied to us about it." Was she really this dense? Or did she think I was really that stupid? "What were you thinking? Brandon was the best thing that ever happened to you."

"Right. Of course he was. Do you know how unhappy I've been, Margaret?" Marianne's words caught me by surprise, and I flinched. She didn't even sound like Marianne. Marianne didn't do frustrated. "Not just this summer. For a while now. Because while everyone around me had their perfect little lives, I've just been *stuck*. Stuck in a life that was completely suffocating me."

I couldn't believe what I was hearing.

"What are you talking about? You had the perfect life. You and Brandon were in love."

"Yeah, and that was, like, the one defining feature of my entire life, right?" Marianne shot back. "Marianne is in love! Finally, she's okay! Get her out of our house, quick, and let her be someone else's problem. And I've never even gotten a chance to see what it's like on my own, without a safety net, because you and Elinor and Mom, you never let me."

I blinked.

"So that's why you ended things?" She didn't even know what I'd sacrificed to make that safety net she apparently hated so much. I'd given up this whole trip, just for her. To make sure she never had to be alone, because I knew that was the thing she hated most in the world. And, what, now she was saying that was what she wanted? "Because you got *bored*?"

Marianne didn't say anything. Just stared at me, the color draining out of her face. And that told me everything I needed to know.

"I can't believe this." I hated how calm Marianne was, how small and vulnerable she seemed. I wanted to be vulnerable, for once. "I didn't want to believe him when he told us, you know. I wanted to believe in you. My sister."

"Why did you even talk to Brandon?" she asked, holding on to the closet door like a lifeline.

"What do you mean, why did we talk to Brandon?" I'd gotten used to the rocking of the ship by now, for the most part, but it was like I could feel every bump and every dip, and I was just hanging on for dear life. "We ran into him in Nassau. He's got a conference. Which you would know about if you hadn't ruined everything by breaking up with him."

"No." Marianne shook her head. "That's—whatever. I knew he had the conference. I didn't remember the dates. I mean *why* did you talk to him. You thought he broke up with me. Why did you even talk to him in the first place?"

"Because." I was getting more and more frustrated. She didn't even care about the right parts of this conversation. The parts where she should be defending herself. "Because he's our family."

"No, he's not." Marianne pulled her hair back into a ponytail, crushing down the blowout, but I guess that didn't matter anymore. "Not the way I am. But ever since he came into our lives, it's been clear that you all respect him way more than you respect me."

"What are you talking about?"

"I'm *talking* about how no one trusted me to handle myself this summer, because I didn't have Brandon by my side to protect me!" Marianne snapped. "I'm talking about how ever since Brandon and I got together, you and Elinor and Mom finally treated me like someone you could *begin* to trust, because I had Brandon in charge of me, right? Brandon, taking care of me, because that's what Brandon does—he swoops in, he makes everything perfect. And do you know how demeaning that is, Margaret? To have everyone in your life think you only have worth because of the person you're with?"

"That's not true." I felt guilty as I said it. It was true. Of course it was true. "And it still wouldn't be an excuse to lie to us." My voice was shaking.

"Oh, and you've been completely truthful, too, right?" She took one step forward toward me, eyes blazing. "Pretending that you were having such a good time hanging out with me, finding dates or whatever, when you really wanted nothing more than to get me, like, immediately hooked up with some guy on the ship so that you could get on with your life without me."

"Only because you got on with your life without me first!" I shouted, and then there was a banging on our door.

"Margaret? Marianne? Is everything okay?"

It was Elinor. I pushed past Marianne and pulled the door open, tilted my head so she'd come inside.

"Oh, great." My voice quavered. "Marianne did break up with Brandon, by the way. Her phone confirmed it before she did. And she doesn't seem to particularly care that he's, you know, heartbroken. What do Brandon's feelings matter compared to Marianne's *whims*?" It was, as blows went, a low one, but I didn't care. I looked over at Marianne, triumphant, and was startled to see that the anger in her face had softened into hurt. Next to me, though, Elinor looked just as angry as she had when we'd run into Brandon.

"I didn't want to believe it."

"You did though, right?" Marianne's expression hardened again. "Because your best friend Brandon told you?"

"That's not fair."

"What's not fair is how my own family cares more about my ex-boyfriend than they do about me," Marianne snapped. "We can't all marry literal ministers, Elinor. Sorry if I didn't stick with the guy you all liked because he kept me out of trouble." With both Elinor and me in the doorway now, Marianne backed up, almost tripping over the corner of the bed. "I get it—I'm not Saint Elinor. I'm a screwup, okay? Just let me be a screwup. Stop trying to make me as perfect as you because, trust me, it's never going to happen."

"So, what, you're just giving up?" Elinor's voice was cold as ice. "Going to run back to Will now?"

Marianne gasped, and I had to admit, I did too.

Will O'Brien was Marianne's last boyfriend, back when she and Brandon were just friends. He'd lived in Barton, and from the moment that they met, it was instant fireworks, exactly the sort of love Marianne had always chased after. The problem with fireworks, though, was that their endings were just as explosive as their beginnings. Will had been the guy Marianne was crying over when she'd crashed her car, me in the passenger seat. It was completely totaled; we both could have died, and she almost did.

Brandon had found us. Tracked down the car and called 911, talked to me through the broken window until the ambulance got there to cut us out. Marianne was unconscious next to me, and I didn't know if she was ever going to wake up, but Brandon had stayed with me the whole time. Kept me from panicking. Made sure that Mom and Elinor met us at the hospital, and stayed with us all night while they operated on Marianne, until we learned that she was going to make it.

My world had been broken after that, but Brandon had, at least, done his best to hold things together. I didn't understand how Marianne could have ever let him go.

"I don't need to explain every aspect of my life to you, Elinor." Marianne matched her tone. "You're not my mother."

"I know I'm not. But you won't even let me be your sister." She broke on the last word. "And you know what? I'm done."

"What do you mean, you're done?"

"Done trying to *help* you, Marianne." Elinor was dressed for a fun day on a tropical island, which was a stark contrast to the least fun day on a tropical island I, personally, had ever had. "I can't spend my whole life pulling you out of old patterns. If you think you need this as some messed-up kind of self-discovery, fine. But I'm not enabling it."

"Elinor, I'm twenty-six years old. I can make my own decisions." Marianne suddenly looked a lot more vulnerable. "I just want you to respect that."

A beat of silence, as Elinor and Marianne stared at each other. I might as well not even have been in the room at all. Finally, Elinor held up her hands.

"Marianne, I love you. And I'm sorry. But I just can't."

And then she left, closing the door behind her.

And for a long moment, Marianne watched me. Not saying anything. Almost challenging me to pick a side, once and for all. Elinor or Marianne. The Dashwood sisters and baby Margaret.

I turned and followed Elinor out the door. She was waiting for me outside.

"Good. I think we should—"

"Stop." I held up my hand toward my sister. "I need to be alone right now."

"What?" Elinor's face fell. "I thought . . ."

"I just need to sort this out. On my own." I hated this. Hated the way Elinor was looking at me. Because even though I'd pulled away from her the last few weeks, I didn't think she'd fully understood the extent to which I had moved out from under her wing. How much I'd come to appreciate the freedom from constant planning and overthinking I'd experienced this summer.

But it was clear now that I didn't want to be like Marianne, either. And without either sister to guide me . . . I didn't know who I was.

"Okay." Elinor nodded, quick. "Be safe."

"Yeah." That's what I was doing, by leaving. Being safe. "Always."

And I was gone.

CHAPTER TWENTY-NINE

I decided to get off the ship, give myself some room to breathe. We were still in Nassau for a couple more hours, and so within a few minutes, I was standing on solid ground again, at the end of the long concrete pier that the *Mab* was docked at. Finally. She'd become suffocating all of a sudden, with her tiny staterooms and narrow passages and claustrophobic families—or maybe that was just mine. Either way, I decided, this would be a much-needed chance at independence. Exploring alone. It was something I needed to get used to, anyway. Being by myself, without any sisterly archetypes to guide me.

The streets of Nassau were just as bright and colorful as ever, crowded with tourists exploring their first tropical island with all the wonder and excitement that it usually brought. They were a pulsing mass, pouring out of stores selling UV-light T-shirts and low-cost diamonds, filing into bars that had brightly colored frozen drinks in their windows and coconuts hanging from their awnings. But I kept walking, past Parliament Square, with its light pink buildings and ornately dressed guards, following East Street until I was at the edge of the hustle and bustle of downtown and finally could hear myself *think*.

I'd never been to the Queen's Staircase before, but I'd heard Edward talk about it. Set on the edge of what felt more like a jungle than a beach paradise were sixty-six steps, chiseled out of limestone and surrounded by lush greenery. It was, Edward had said, a popular tourist spot, and when he'd described it, I couldn't figure out why. I mean, they were *stairs*, right? Stairs were stairs. And as I stood at the base of them (or just off to the side, so that I didn't block anyone trying to go up or down) I still didn't feel that sense of *wow, amazing!* that I kept hoping to feel every time I took an excursion or tried something new. But it was nice here, I guess. Peaceful, compared to downtown.

I wondered what the real Nassau was like. Past the tourist stops and straw markets and the novelty T-shirts. I wondered if I would ever figure out how to see it, or if I was somehow doomed to keep hovering at the edge of the unimaginable. The precipice of the life I was looking for.

I knew I was better off alone. I just wished I was better at being alone.

"Margaret?"

I started at the sound of my name, turned around to see—oh, great—Gabe standing behind me, holding a water bottle, his eyebrows furrowed in confusion.

Crap. I really, *really* didn't want to deal with Gabe right now.

"What are you doing here?" I looked around, half expecting to see him leading a tour group or something. It wasn't part of his job description, but maybe the regular tour leader was sick. "Is there a secret soundboard somewhere?"

"I do, occasionally, get the chance to come out on my own, especially when I'm not being dragged on fake dates by the ship's passengers." Gabe spoke lightly, but guilt pulsed through me all the same. "You made it clear you didn't need me this week. So I'm here. Is that a problem?"

"No. No." Everything felt like a messy blur, from my feelings toward Gabe to Marianne to the way that the air smelled like rain even more than usual. "I was leaving, anyway."

"Hard to avoid me if we're in the same place, right?"

"I'm not avoiding you." An outright lie, but it couldn't be helped. "I'm just ready to go back to the ship."

"Great." Gabe sipped from his water bottle, then dropped it into his backpack. "I'll go with you."

"Gabe . . ."

"You said you're not avoiding me." Gabe raised one eyebrow. He seemed so perfectly at home, here on the edge of the jungle, and I felt like I was still on board the ship on a day when the seas were rough, unable to get my footing. It wasn't fair, part of me screamed, that he could be so nonchalant when I felt like such a disaster. "What's the problem?"

"You're right." Two could play this game. I held my arm out in front of me. "Let's go check out the stairs."

There was a small crowd gathered at the base of the steps, and we waited in silence, looking everywhere but at each other, until it was our turn. Once we started climbing, the only sound was occasional huffing and puffing when the hand-carved stairs turned particularly steep. It was gorgeous here—the entire valley had been carved out of limestone, and trees grew out of and over the rock itself, their roots descending into the valley like they were reaching for the center of the earth—but I couldn't enjoy it, even with Gabe right next to me.

I didn't want to be alone in this. I wanted to share it with him.

Damn him, for making me feel that way.

"Well, there we go, that's the stairs," I said when we made it to the top, moving over to the left to make way for the people coming up behind us. Just below, a small waterfall trickled over the edge. "Time to go our separate ways." I turned, ready to head back toward the port, when he reached out and grabbed my arm.

"Margaret."

"What?" I didn't pull my arm away. Partially because his touch was like an electric storm pulsing through my veins. Partially because the weakest parts of me didn't want to be alone. And partially because I didn't want to give him the satisfaction. "What do you need, Gabe?"

"I just want to talk." Gabe stepped back, (unfortunately) dropping my arm, and gave a hollow laugh, running both hands through his black hair. "Is that a crime now? Because we spent basically every second together for five weeks before you ghosted me, and I'd love to know why."

"I didn't ghost you." If we were in one of the more chaotic areas of town, the straw market or something, I could have just lost Gabe in the crowd. Here, where it was just us and the descending trees, I had nowhere to run. "I told you. I needed to try and find someone else. And now the plan is off entirely, because Marianne and I aren't speaking, possibly ever again, so I *really* don't need your assistance."

"What?" Gabe's eyes went wide. "Why?"

"Turns out she lied to us for basically the entire summer." Maybe if I ran all the way to the beach and jumped into the ocean, I could swim away from this conversation entirely. I was a strong swimmer, after all. Maybe no one would catch me. "Which just proves my point, by the way."

"Which is?"

"That opening your heart can only hurt you." I flung my hand in the direction of the ship. "I'm realizing it's not just romance. Letting *anyone* close is a mistake. Marianne has hurt me so many times." My voice was getting higher, louder. "So I'm shutting myself down. And I'm really sorry, but I have to close off from you most of all. Because every second I spend around you I fall for you more and more, and that means I'm more and more likely to get absolutely destroyed, and I don't want to deal with that, Gabe, okay? I just don't!"

Yeah, I was shouting.

And as soon as I realized what I'd said, I threw my hands over my mouth, horrified. A couple of other tourists looked our way, curious, before walking away quickly, giving us space. Great. Making a scene, a real Marianne move. Across from me, Gabe had frozen, shock-still. Then, slowly, he stepped forward.

"Did you say that you've been falling for me?"

I laughed, but it came out half as a sob.

"Oh, come on, Gabe." I waved my hands in front of me. "You know what you're bringing to the table. And you've just been—you've been so nice, and helpful, and talking to you is, like, my favorite thing in the world, so of course I've fallen completely in love with you, and I absolutely cannot let that happen, because I need to be alone and it's a lot harder to be alone when you feel like this." My voice cracked. "You make the idea of being alone so hard."

Gabe didn't say anything. Just watched me. Stepped toward me again, so we were only a few inches apart, and put his hand on my cheek, wet from tears. The wind was picking up around us, and the clouds were rolling in, a storm was on its way, but the only thing I saw were Gabe's dark eyes, black as midnight, watching me. Knowing me.

And then—kissing me.

This was a real kiss, what I'd been wanting since our barely there peck back in the dining room, since he'd put his arms around me on the catamaran, since I'd run into him on the track and had fallen into him in the sound booth. This was what I'd been waiting for.

His mouth crashed down onto mine, half knocking the wind out of me, and I almost staggered back. I threw my arms around his neck to hold myself steady, even though steady was the furthest from what I felt. His hair tangled in the tips of my fingers, softer than I'd ever imagined, and he held me close, his hands pressed against my waist like he couldn't get enough of me, and I couldn't get enough of him.

I *couldn't* get enough of him. Gabriel Monteiro, the boy I was risking everything for.

Risk. That's what he was, though. A risk. And I had to live my life by guarantees, no matter how good of a kisser the risk was.

Reluctantly, I wrenched myself away, pulled myself back from the softness of his lips and the glow in his eyes.

"Margaret." His voice was low. Intimate. "That was . . ."

"Something that can never happen again." Even as I spoke, my hand went up to my mouth, pressed against my lips like I could still feel him there. Feel his shadow, and the way it moved against me. Visions of what being with Gabe could be like flashed through my head. Holding hands on the observation deck. Kissing in the back of the theater. Taking him to dinner with my family without it being a lie. Figuring out a way to make it work off the ship, when our lives started, building a relationship together . . .

And tying everything I was to him, before he inevitably hurt me. That was what would happen. That was what always happened, when you let passion get in the way of common sense. I needed to end this before it came to that.

"You know my feelings on this," I continued, even as Gabe stepped back from me. Crossed his arms over his chest, over his black T-shirt that was completely impractical for the Bahamian heat but was an integral part of him. "On . . . dating. And stuff." Eloquent, Margaret. "We can't go there."

"You said you were in *love* with me, Margaret." Gabe's voice was racked with frustration. I didn't blame him. "You're seriously throwing that away because of your stupid rules?" A knife, right in my side.

"They're not stupid." I crossed my arms, too, mirroring him. "They're for my own good."

"Come on." He shook his head. "You've turned these rules into a cage. And you think that it's to protect you, but all it's doing is trapping you. You refuse to let yourself live."

"Are you kidding me?" He had no idea. Because I'd had to be nothing *but* brave, ever since Dad died. Then there had been the accident. Then Marianne had basically abandoned me.

Then she'd lied to us all summer. And I was expected to just keep going, like the rug hadn't been yanked out from beneath me again and again. I wasn't building a cage. I was building my armor. "This is the only way I *can* live."

"Sure, Margaret." He scoffed. "Seems like a great plan. But what do I know? I'm just some crew kid you got to play out your tourist fantasies with for a few weeks. So enjoy California." He strode past me, turning to face me as he shot back one last dig. "Be bravely alone or whatever. I won't bother you again."

And then he was gone.

Just like I'd wanted.

And because I *was* brave, no matter what he said, I waited until I got back on the ship before I let myself cry.

CHAPTER THIRTY

I couldn't go to my stateroom, I realized once I reached our deck. Marianne might come back any minute, and she was the last person I wanted to talk to.

Luckily, I had an extra key to Elinor's room, and she had texted me earlier to let me know that she and Edward were headed out on a tour. I had a few hours, at least, before they returned.

So I let myself into their cabin, releasing my breath fully only once the door had closed behind me. I appreciated for the first time how much neater it was than mine and Marianne's, still nearly identical to how it had looked when we boarded the ship for the first time, as opposed to our cabin, which felt more like an H&M dressing room had become violently ill and regurgitated all the outfits it had ever borne witness to. All of their clothes were tucked away, folded or hung up in the room's various hidey-holes, and except for a stack of books on each of their nightstands and their toiletry bags lined up neatly at the edge of their dresser, the room might have been unoccupied.

"Why couldn't I have been like Elinor?" I asked no one, sinking gently onto the small couch. "Why did I have to be another Marianne?"

Because no matter how hard I'd tried, how much I'd convinced myself that I'd become a clone of my oldest sister by sheer force of will, I'd ended up in a totally Marianne situation. I'd gotten hurt over a guy, failed to protect my heart, and paid the price.

"It's not fair." I wiped tears away, but they came even more furiously. Elinor had managed to have a nice, calm partnership with Edward, without any of the passion and drama that invariably ruined relationships. Why couldn't I be satisfied waiting for that? Gabe and I had been good friends, but I'd given in to the frisson running beneath the surface of our relationship, and now I was alone and dying inside. Even the way I loved my sisters—it was too much, too strong, too tight of a hold. I'd thought I could beat it. I'd thought I was strong enough to help them without getting hurt.

But I didn't know how to love by halves, so I had to avoid love altogether. And it *sucked*. It just sucked, and I was so goddamn lonely.

I buried my face in the couch pillow—sorry, Elinor and Edward—and let myself cry. In fact, I gave myself over to it so thoroughly that I didn't realize the door had opened until I heard a soft intake of breath and looked up to see Edward, staring at me in undisguised horror.

"Edward!" I sat up so fast that I got a head rush, wiping my eyes on the pillow held tight against my chest. "Sorry. I thought you were on the tour."

"It was overbooked, so Elinor went ahead and I came back

early. Are you hurt? Should I get Elinor? Or a medical team?" Edward's eyes were wide with bewilderment. I didn't blame him. In all the time we'd known each other, Edward had never seen me like this.

In a perfect world, if I was at my best—or even at my mediumest—I'd have pulled myself together; forced on a smile; and told Edward I was fine, it was nothing, dismiss his concerns thoroughly enough that he would believe me. But I just . . . didn't have it in me today. So instead I said—

"Don't tell Elinor."

And then I pressed my face back into the pillow, because that was the best I could do. With any luck, he'd leave. Let me cry alone in peace.

But when I glanced up, Edward was sitting down, carefully and gently, next to me on the couch.

"Is it anything I can fix?" he asked, his voice quiet.

I let out a deep breath. "It one thousand percent is not."

"All right." Edward nodded. Then, though he did it slowly, hesitantly, as if I might shatter beneath him, he put his arm around my shoulders and gave me a small but reassuring pat.

God. It was such a minor gesture. But you could always feel the care emanating off Edward in waves, and I couldn't handle that right now. I jumped up to my feet, wiping my face and doing my best to laugh.

"I should go." I jerked my head back toward the door. "You probably want to relax after all of this, and after this morning, and everything. Today's been a lot."

"You don't have to run away, Margaret."

"I think it's better if I do." It was too risky to let anyone in at all, even Edward. "I'll see you at . . . I'll see you."

I pulled the door open, fast, and walked as fast as I could out into the hall. Because this was my new normal. Being alone was my reality.

Great.

I didn't really sleep that night.

I didn't go back to either of the cabins, just wandered the ship and occasionally napped for twenty or thirty minutes at a time in a deck chair. Objectively, I knew that was a terrible idea, and that I should go to bed, but I just couldn't bring myself to share a room with Marianne, because of what she'd done, or with Elinor, because of all the ways I'd failed her. This option was just easier, and it was the one I intended to keep choosing.

But I still made a quick visit to Elinor and Edward's room the next morning, to shower and brush my teeth, because, you know, that was important. Edward had already left for the day, but Elinor was sitting up in bed, engrossed in a floppy paperback with her reading glasses sliding down her nose.

"Morning, Mags." Her voice didn't betray any concern, but with Elinor, that didn't mean anything. She was better at hiding her emotions than anyone I'd ever met. "Sleep okay?"

"Not bad," I lied.

"Right." She placed a bookmark in her book, set it beside her. "And where, exactly, did you sleep?"

Damn it.

"I guess I didn't really go to bed." I kicked the toe of my shoe against the carpet. "How did you know?"

"Edward went for a walk this morning and saw you curled

up on one of the loungers." She sighed, laid her reading glasses on top of her book. "You could have stayed in here, you know."

"I know." *Don't ask more, don't ask more,* I willed her, hoping that our sisterly telepathy would kick in and she'd stop pressing. Whether she heard my thoughts or not, she seemed to get the hint, so she just held eye contact for a moment longer than usual before she moved on.

"Right." She gestured to her side, where I noticed my duffel bag on the floor beside her. "I went to your cabin and brought over a couple of things. I suppose it's convenient that you never unpacked, though I still can't believe you've been living out of a suitcase for five weeks. What are you planning on doing when you get to college? Keep all of your clothes in one big trash bin?"

"Funny. Did you . . . you know. Was Marianne . . ." I trailed off, but Elinor must have guessed what I was getting at, because she shook her head.

"I haven't seen her," she said. "We all need some time to cool off."

"That's one way of putting it." It was like saying the Florida heat needed to cool off. Just because it was true didn't mean it would happen anytime soon.

"I know." Elinor let out a small sigh, then pointed me toward the bathroom. "Let's get you ready for the day."

An hour later, once I was showered and (reasonably) put together, a task made much harder by surprisingly rough seas that sent me staggering all over the bathroom, we headed out to get some breakfast. But the scene that greeted us in the atrium wasn't anything like I'd expected.

It was packed with people like it was an embarkation day, all crowding around various crew members stationed throughout the space, holding iPads and speaking to guests in hushed voices with serious expressions. I turned to Elinor.

"What's going on?" There hadn't been any ship-wide announcements, nothing that made it seem like this was different from any other day at sea. "Did something happen?"

"Let's find out." Although her tone was upbeat, the wrinkle that appeared between Elinor's eyebrows gave away her concern. Her gaze darted around the atrium, and she pointed toward the bar. "Look, there's Jono." The cruise director was always a friendly face to see around the ship. "We can ask him."

As good a plan as any. I nodded and followed my sister through the crush of people toward the Australian, who was trying to address three different groups at once. He glanced up when he saw us coming and gave a small wave, but kept talking.

"The captain hasn't made a decision yet. We're still plotting out our navigation, figuring out the safest possible option for all of you, I promise. No decision here is being made lightly." One of the groups threw up their hands en masse and walked away, grumbling, and Elinor and I stepped into the space they'd vacated. Elinor touched Jono's shoulder gently.

"Did we miss something?" she asked. "We didn't hear an announcement."

"No announcement. No announcement!" he repeated louder, as if that would dissuade the people crowding around him. It didn't work, and he closed his eyes for a second before turning back to us. "News spread from the TV weather reports, far as I can tell. But there's a storm brewing off Cuba that changed course unexpectedly early this morning. It was supposed to miss us completely, now it's . . . more complicated." Jono's eyes darted over to the other guests, many of whom looked frankly terrified.

Shit.

"Is there actual cause for concern?" Elinor lowered her voice, mindful of the other guests, and Jono gave another surreptitious glance around before taking Elinor by the elbow and leading us to a little pocket at the far side of the bar.

"Honestly, no one's got any idea yet." Jono's face was riddled with exhaustion; I wondered if he'd been asleep when the news broke among the crew. I also wondered briefly if Gabe was up here somewhere, recruited into guest management, before pushing away the thought. My brain needed to be a Gabe-free zone. "The storm's moving fast and gathering speed, so the captain needs to make a decision—well, now—if we're going to turn around and head back to Nassau or try to outrun the storm or make it to a different port. But they'll make a ship-wide announcement as soon as they know what's going on. At the moment, it's all just wild speculation. I'd head back to the cabin, if I were you." He glanced back toward the atrium. "Guests get strange about storms, sometimes. If they do panic, you don't want to get caught up in it."

Well, that wasn't concerning at all.

"Got it." Elinor nodded at me, the picture of calm, though that eyebrow furrow continued to indicate differently. "Thanks, Jono. Good luck, all right?"

"Thanks." He chuckled lightly. "I'm going to need it."

I watched him walk back into the crowd, where he was

instantly accosted by more guests demanding answers. I turned to Elinor, my heart rate speeding up.

"How bad is this?"

"Come on." She took my wrist, gave me a tug in the direction of the dining room. "Let's get some food, and then we'll figure it out."

This was, I supposed, one way to make my matters of the heart seem less immediately dire.

CHAPTER THIRTY-ONE

By the time the announcement came over the loudspeaker, I was almost bursting out of my skin from adrenaline. Elinor and I had grabbed a quick breakfast and then spent the next few hours in the stateroom, watching the woman on the weather channel repeat phrases like "unprecedented wind" and "the storm twist that no one saw coming." Edward had joined us about halfway through the coverage, and he and Elinor had gone briefly into the hallway to talk in hushed voices, leaving me to starfish on the bed and watch the projections of the storm, a giant spiral of clouds and rain that kept moving closer and closer toward us.

We hadn't seen Marianne, but that didn't surprise me. If I were her, I wouldn't want to show her face in front of us, either.

So when the PA system in the stateroom finally crackled to life late that afternoon, I started violently. I was pretty sure I heard Edward yelp, even if I would never get him to admit it. Elinor shushed both of us as the captain's voice projected through the entire ship.

"Good afternoon, everyone, this is Captain Stafford speaking. We know a lot of you have seen the incoming storm projections for Hurricane Alba. After consulting our charts and tracking the hurricane's current projected path, we've decided that the best course of action is to look for, as they say, the best port in the storm. We'll be headed to our port at Nighthawk Cay, and then evacuating the ship onto our partner hotel on the island. We know this is a disruption to your vacation, and we apologize for any inconvenience, but when Mother Nature speaks, we have to listen. We expect to make port early tomorrow morning—more information will be given to you by the crew over the next hour. They can answer any further questions you have, or you can run down to the atrium and chat with guest services. Thank you again, and we appreciate your cooperation."

The PA cut off, and Edward, Elinor, and I all let out a long, collective breath. Finally we had a decision. And when I turned toward my sister, I saw that it was what she had been waiting for.

"Come on." She sprang into action, jumping up from the couch, grabbing her backpack, and starting to pack. "We're probably not going to be able to take everything off the ship, but we need to have enough supplies for at least a few days."

"Right." Where Elinor looked determined, Edward looked pale, unsure. "I think—I have to report in emergencies like this. If anyone's nervous, they might want to talk to a chaplain about it."

"Who will *you* talk to?" Elinor asked, but she reached out and touched her husband's cheek before turning back to her packing. "I'll take care of your bag. You go."

"Thank you." Edward squeezed her hand, then squared his shoulders, took a deep breath, and walked out of the stateroom, the door closing sharply behind him.

Once he was gone, Elinor turned back to me.

"Can you message your sister, please? I want to make sure she's prepared for this."

"You can message her just as easily as I can." Hurricane or not, I still didn't want to talk to Marianne. I jumped up from the bed, grabbed my own backpack, and began to throw T-shirts into it.

"I need to try and get in touch with Mom. She'll be worried about us. Especially Marianne." Elinor's voice lost some of its bravado, but she had her back to me, so I couldn't see her face. "Just message her. For me."

"Fine," I muttered, grabbing my phone and pulling up the message app. The last message I'd sent, I saw with a pang, was to Gabe. Gabe. He was going to be okay, right? And his aunt and uncle, and everyone else on the ship . . .

No. There wasn't any reason to worry. The captain knew what he was doing, we'd get to Nighthawk Cay in no time, and everyone would be totally and completely fine. I was brave. I was strong. I could do this.

You heard the announcement, right? I messaged Marianne before I lost my nerve. *Elinor says you should pack for a few days.*

The reply came back fast, almost like she'd been watching the phone, waiting.

I got it, she said, and my heart dropped, because this was maybe the only time I'd ever seen a text from Marianne without emojis and exclamation points. Yeah, she hated me. Sure,

I kind of hated her, too, right now. But it still didn't feel good. *I'll be in the room tonight to pack.*

Maybe it was an invitation. Maybe she wanted me to come and see her, while she was packing. Apologize.

Or maybe she wanted to make sure I stayed away.

It didn't matter. I didn't need my sister in order to be brave. I just needed me.

Besides, if there was one thing that having a hurricane of a family *had* to have prepared me for, it was this.

CHAPTER THIRTY-TWO

We hit land around five a.m., and by then total chaos had descended upon the ship.

The crew had handed out printouts listing the *Queen Mab*'s hurricane procedure, a lot of which involved staying calm and sitting in our staterooms. It seemed like most of the ship had taken one look at that, thrown it off their balconies, and proceeded to run screaming up and down the hallways. At least, that was what it sounded like. The crew were doing their best to keep everything under control, but the hurricane had increased in intensity overnight (up to Category 2 now), and so, instead of staying in their rooms, most of the passengers had hunkered down in the atrium, gathered with their families and their bags so they could burst from the ship the very second we hit land.

I knew this because we were in the atrium, too, of course. Elinor had lasted about an hour in the stateroom before declaring that she had to get out of there and dragging me (and all of our packed belongings) into the mayhem that was the rest of the ship, where Edward had eventually joined us. We knocked on Marianne's door on the way out—Elinor had insisted—but she didn't answer.

Now it was finally our turn to get off the ship—they had us deboarding by cabin numbers—and Marianne was still MIA.

"Where the hell is she?" Elinor was standing on one of the atrium's couches, trying to see over the pulsing crowd.

"Could she have gotten off early?" I asked, as Elinor scanned the atrium and Edward wrung his hands together. "Maybe she's already gone." Even as I said it, though, tried to keep my nonchalant façade, it didn't sound right. Marianne wouldn't mess around during something like this. She'd have at least texted, or called, or responded to our texts, or picked up *our* calls, which kept going straight to voicemail. She wouldn't want us to worry.

You haven't acted like you'd worry, a traitorous voice whispered in my head, but I pushed it away. Marianne knew the difference between sister fighting and a real life-and-death scenario.

"Last call for cabin numbers thirty-two hundred to thirty-three hundred!" one of the crew members called into a megaphone, and my chest seized. That was us, and Marianne was nowhere to be seen.

"What do we do? Should we tell someone?" I asked.

"No. You two should go ahead, and I'll stay back and wait for her." Elinor climbed down from the couch but didn't stop scanning the space. "She has to be around here somewhere, and I don't want to take the crew's attention away from their duties."

"What—Elinor, no." This was the worst idea I'd ever heard. Next to me, Edward blanched. "You have to come with us."

"I'll be fine." She gave me what was probably supposed to be a reassuring smile. I was not reassured. "If she got off already, and you find her at the hotel, just call, and I'll head right over. This way, we have our bases covered."

"That's not a good idea, Elinor," Edward said, and I nodded, happy to have a voice of reason here. "Marianne will be fine. You need to make sure you get off the ship safely."

"Edward." Elinor grabbed his hand. "I have to do this. I have to look out for my sister."

And when I saw her face, I knew what she was remembering. Why she had a faraway look in her eyes, even as she hugged me and kissed Edward and told us she'd be along any minute now, we'd barely miss her, Marianne probably got stuck in line for the elevator or went back to the stateroom for something she forgot. I knew what she was remembering, because I was remembering it, too.

The first year or so after the accident, I spent a lot of time wondering if I could have prevented it. If I had realized how upset Marianne was, I could have made her pull over, could have forced her to calm down before we started driving. And I know I was just a kid, but it still haunted me. That I had been there and failed to take care of my sister.

Elinor had the opposite guilt, because she hadn't been there. She hadn't been there to protect either of us.

Through the ship's portholes, I saw rain start to fall. I pictured Marianne somewhere on the ship, scared and alone.

Even if she was surrounded by other guests, she was alone, because she didn't have her family.

And so I understood why Elinor had to stay.

But that didn't mean I liked it.

"I'll see you soon," Elinor reassured us one last time, and Edward grabbed my arm so he wouldn't lose me as we fell into the push of the crowd, shuffling off the ship slow as molasses. We scanned our ship cards, then squeezed down the gang-plank and onto the dock, where a tour bus waited to carry us to the hotel across the island. I didn't look back. I didn't trust myself to.

I kept glancing around, hoping to see Marianne somehow, and be able to run straight back to Elinor and tell her to come with us, but Marianne was nowhere to be found.

I took a few deep breaths, did my best to slow my racing heart once we stepped onto Nighthawk Cay. The place where Gabe and I had that amazing catamaran ride (nope, different memory, don't think about Gabe), where I'd hung out with Elinor (nope, different memory, don't think about Elinor, ei-ther), where I'd . . . I'd always enjoyed myself here, was all. But it was entirely different now, everyone dead serious, no one smiling. Edward and I climbed in the nearer bus, and as I quickly scanned the rows in front of us, my heart just kept sinking. No Marianne.

When we got to the hotel and unloaded into the lobby, though, I was temporarily distracted from my Marianne con-cerns by the discovery of our sleeping arrangements.

"Welcome, everyone! Please proceed down the hall to the ballroom, where we've set up cots for your convenience!" A young woman in a suit was shouting over the crowd, standing on a chair to be seen over everyone's heads. She'd been given a megaphone but, I thought with a wince, she didn't need one. "Thank you for joining us—we're committed to keeping you safe!"

Luckily, I didn't need to worry about finding my own space to sleep, because with Elinor gone, Edward was doing everything he could to channel her energy as an emergency expert extraordinaire. He beelined for the ballroom before the woman even finished her announcement and darted inside, grabbing three beds tucked into a corner before half the guests had even registered the word "cot."

It was like one of Peter and Luisa's magic tricks.

"Wow." I sat down on my cot, which squeaked horribly, watching the rest of the ballroom fill up with people who were way less skilled at bed claiming than Edward. "That was impressive. Did you do espionage in a former life? Because that was some spy-level subterfuge."

"It's good to control something in situations like these." Edward sighed and dropped his backpack, as well as Elinor's, at the foots of two of the cots. "I can take the floor if needed, but this way Marianne can have a bed, once Elinor tracks her down."

"You really think she's going to find her?" I shouldn't have asked, but it slipped out of me before I could help myself.

"Of course. They'll be—they'll be fine." His stutter revealed his nerves, and I gulped. "I should probably make some rounds." Edward wrinkled his nose, appraising the ballroom. "Make sure everyone's coping with the stress all right."

"You'll keep an eye out for Marianne?" My voice sounded small. Edward reached out, squeezed my shoulder.

"Of course, Mags. If I see her, I'll let you and Elinor know right away."

"Maybe I can go look?" I didn't want to just sit here, holding down our corner and doing nothing.

Edward pursed his lips. "I don't know. Elinor would want you to stay with the beds."

"Come on." I picked up my backpack, laid it carefully on my cot. "We've claimed them, right? And you can't search for Marianne *and* do your chaplain thing at the same time. Let me help. If she's here, we need to let Elinor know as soon as possible so she can get off the ship."

"Fine," Edward said with a sigh, and I jumped from the bed. "But we'll check back here in half an hour. If your sister gets back and you're wandering the hotel on your own, she's going to kill me."

"You got it!" I was just happy to have a purpose, I told myself as I took off at a light jog. It wasn't because I regretted how Marianne and I had left things. I just needed something to do.

That was what I told myself, anyway.

EXCEPT I couldn't find her.

It wasn't for lack of trying, either. The hotel had a pretty basic layout, two ballrooms back-to-back taking up most of the first floor, along with an open lobby that led to the guest rooms. I made three laps of the entire space, checking in with Edward twice, tried to call again and again until my phone service cut out from what I assumed was the storm. But even when the buses had stopped unloading, even when everyone had settled in, holding children in their laps and drinking coffee that the hotel staff had passed out, I couldn't find her. Or Elinor, either, who I kept expecting to see coming through the door, dragging Marianne behind her.

On the third lap, as my panic was rising, I heard someone come up behind me, felt a tap on my shoulder. I figured it was a crew member, ready to offer me a cup of weak coffee and redirect me to my cot.

And as it turned out, it was a crew member. But it was the last one I wanted to interact with.

"Hi." Gabe fell into step beside me, and honestly, the first emotion I felt when I realized it was him was relief. Relief that he was here, safely off the ship. Relief that he'd found me. That I'd finally have someone I could talk to about everything that was happening. Someone I didn't have to be strong for.

But you do, I reminded myself. Because vulnerability with Gabe was dangerous. No matter how comfortable he made me feel.

So I said nothing, just kept scanning the rows of cots up and down for Marianne.

"All right." Gabe sighed. Out of the corner of my eye, I saw him run his hand through his hair. "I'm not trying to— Are you okay? We'll be fine here, you know. Luisa and Peter stayed at this hotel during a storm years ago. It's sturdy."

"You don't need to pretend to worry about me." I couldn't afford to feel relieved. To open up. I had other things to worry about right now, like the aforementioned being unable to find either of my sisters. "I'm not changing my mind."

"That's not— Jesus, Margaret." Gabe grabbed me by the shoulder, stopping me in my tracks. Around us, the ballroom was full of noise and chaos, but just like it always did when I was talking to Gabe, it felt like the world was reduced to just the two of us. *It's not, though.* I gave myself a mental slap. *Marianne. Elinor. You have bigger things to worry about.* "There's a hurricane bearing down on us. I just wanted to check in."

"Yeah, well, unless you know where either of my sisters are, I don't think you can help me." My voice was getting higher, my panic harder to disguise. A couple of guests nearby turned to look at us, curious, and I fought to keep myself level. "Marianne wasn't in the atrium when our cabins got called, so Elinor stayed back to look for her, and now *neither* of them are here. And I can't even get service on this stupid island." I pulled out my phone, held it out to show Gabe. "So I think I've earned a little panic, don't you?"

"That's— Okay, I get that that's scary. But you know they're fine, right?" Gabe's calm, steady voice was having the opposite effect on me. "There's probably just been a delay with the last bus run. They'll be here."

"And if they're not?" I couldn't control my volume. Couldn't control my fear, pulsing through me, threatening to overwhelm me. "What then, Gabe?"

"Hey." His grip tightened on my shoulder, and for a second I let it comfort me. Let it help. "They will be."

I shook off his touch. I couldn't do this. I'd closed this door, and I wasn't going to let Gabe open it again.

"I have to keep looking," I muttered, avoiding eye contact. "Sorry."

And I left him standing there, in the middle of the make-shift aisle created by the rows of cots, and I didn't turn back, not even for a second, as I hurried into the other ballroom, where Edward was waiting.

CHAPTER THIRTY-THREE

"She's not here," I said, when I made it back to my brother-in-law. "And the rain is getting worse." I'd seen it from the lobby, the palm trees swaying as they slapped against the windows of the hotel. "What are we going to do?"

Edward didn't say anything, just sat down on the cot, his head in his hands.

Okay. Okay, okay. That was fine. Edward was down for the count. Good thing I'd learned how to handle things, how to not panic, how to take charge in situations like these. I would not allow feelings to weaken me. Not when my sisters were in danger.

"Should we . . ." My voice wavered, emotions sneaking in to betray me. "What should we . . ."

"We'll go ask someone." Edward's voice was muffled, half speaking into his hands, but then he pulled himself up to his feet, nodded toward the lobby. "Come on. They'll know if there's still people on the ship. And if there's not . . ."

"Right." I knew what that meant. That meant *both* of my sisters were missing.

THE news from the lobby wasn't terrible, but it wasn't good, either.

"The ship has been cleared of passengers," Jono told us when we found him, and I felt my heart sink all the way down into my toes. "There's just crew left. But the last bus has been delayed, for some reason—the weather is interfering with our radios, so it's hard to get a signal. We're still in the outer bands of the storm, though. Plenty of time for them to get here safe."

"That's where they must be, right?" I allowed myself some hope. "On that bus."

"Did the bus break down?" Edward took off his glasses, polished them against his shirt. "Can't you send another one out to get them?"

"We've only got the two, and we ended up with a flat tire on the other on the last trip round." Jono clapped his hand on Edward's shoulder, and Edward's knees nearly buckled from the force of it. "We don't have anything else to send out, not on this little island. But the crew with them is well trained to handle emergency situations. They'll be all right."

"Thanks, Jono." I grabbed Edward by the elbow and steered him back toward the ballroom. Jono was great, but of course he was going to reassure us. What was he going to say? *Oh, yeah, they're in gigantic danger, better panic?* His job was to keep us calm, after all.

Edward half sat, half collapsed on a cot, head back in his hands. I didn't blame him.

Jono said everything was going to be just fine.

I wanted so, so badly to believe him.

EVEN in the ballroom, with no windows to the outside world, I could hear the rain lashing down. It was a constant torrent, an unending wail of wind and water swirling together. Once, we heard a tremendous crash, and half of the ballroom burst into screams. Even after a ship's officer came in to tell us everything was fine, that a palm tree had just gone down, the wave of panic never really went away. More officers and crew flooded the ballroom, trying to calm passengers, telling everyone to stay calm, everyone, please, we have to ask you to stay—

And then the power went out.

It was the sort of darkness you see when you first close your eyes, before your vision gets a chance to adjust, except it was so total that there was no adjusting. I grabbed for Edward, and as phone flashlights began to pop on through the space, I could fully make out his expression.

Terror.

"She shouldn't be out there," he said. I'd never seen Edward like this. "I should have—it should be me. It's always her, and it shouldn't be."

"Edward."

"This is what she always does." He shook his head, and I sat still, afraid of more than just the storm. "She thinks the whole world is her responsibility and she pushes too hard and she married someone who can't protect her or take care of her and now look what's happened." Edward let out a ragged breath that sounded more like a sob. "Now she's alone out there. And that's the one thing I promised her she'd never have to be again."

I didn't know what to say. I didn't think there was anything *to* say. Part of me wanted to squeeze him on the shoulder and leave him be. Give him privacy for his feelings. Keep my distance.

I scooted closer to Edward, laid my head on his shoulder. Maybe we could help each other, Edward and me. We were going to have to.

And in the piercing lights of cell phones that illuminated every panicked outline in the ballroom, I began to speak.

"All I ever wanted, since the accident, at least, was to be just like Elinor."

"I know, Mags." Edward's voice vibrated against the top of my head. "You didn't exactly try to hide it. You dressed up as her for Halloween your freshman year."

"I did that ironically. But that's not the point." Elinor had burst out laughing when she saw me, insisted I wear it to visit her at work after school. I pushed the memory down. "I guess I just saw Elinor as, like, this beacon of strength, you know? Marianne and I had always been so alike, and when I saw how much being like Marianne could hurt, I decided I needed a new guidebook. Elinor was the best option available." I did my best to breathe. It wasn't easy. "Marianne feels too much. That's what got us in this whole mess to begin with."

"What do you mean?"

"I mean, if Marianne had just been happy with Brandon . . ." I shrugged. "But she wanted passion. Ordinary life couldn't just be good enough for her."

"Margaret." Edward nudged his shoulder up, dislodging me, and I sat up next to him. "Do you not think Marianne deserves that?"

"What?" Sorry, was *Edward Ferrars* defending passionate love now? "It's not a matter of what she deserves. She deserves the world. But that kind of love isn't healthy. Look at you and Elinor."

"What about me and Elinor?"

"You're just . . ." Oh boy. This wasn't a conversation I'd expected to have today, but I didn't see a way to back out of it now. "You love each other. Obviously. But you don't let it consume you the way Marianne thinks love should. You're . . . you're sensible."

Edward looked at me for a minute, his brow furrowed. Then one side of his mouth quirked up into a smile.

"I suppose Elinor would be—will be," he corrected, as my heart clenched, "will be happy to know that we've been able to present a calm exterior in front of her baby sister. But I assure you, Margaret, Elinor and I feel as . . . as passionately about each other as any two people can." Oh, God, kill me. I didn't want to hear about Edward's *passions.* "I know that we're quiet. But the volume of our affection doesn't correspond to its fervor."

"Okay, stop." I pressed my hands against my burning cheeks. But inside, my mind was whirring. Elinor wasn't a passionate-love kind of person. I'd assumed her and Edward's relationship was just as calmly affectionate on the inside as it appeared to the rest of the world. But if I'd been wrong, that meant my whole worldview was in a tailspin. "I get it, you love each other with the fire of a thousand suns, etc. But you *pursued* that relationship in a calm way, right? When you got together, it was the right time. The circumstances were good."

"Margaret." Edward stared at me like I'd grown a second head. "When I started dating your sister, my family *cut me off*. Does that seem like good circumstances to you?"

I needed to find a new cot. Possibly in Siberia.

"No," I mumbled into my hands. "I guess not."

"I'm not mad," he said quickly. "I just don't want you operating under false information. What Elinor and I have isn't some kind of marriage of convenience. It's real, and it's hard, but we fight for it every day, because it's the thing we choose above all others. As for passion . . . trust me when I say we're very much in love."

"Again, gross, no more details, thank you." In a way, it was good that the power was still out. I didn't need to see Edward's face any better than I already could in the light of our flashlight. And if Elinor, sensible Elinor, whom I'd used as my role model, could have a love as strong as the love I'd always wanted, then why couldn't I?

"Relationships are complicated beasts." Edward sighed, seeming to read my mind as he wrapped his arm around my shoulders and pulled me in toward him again. "Love always is."

"Sounds right." I let my breathing steady, in rhythm with Edward's. Around us, hundreds of other people were talking in low whispers. I wondered how many of them were holding tight to each other, speaking quiet truths. "Is it really worth all of the pain? Loving someone?"

"I don't know, Margaret." The frame of his glasses pressed against the top of my head. "You're always so determined to be on your own. Doesn't that hurt, too?" His voice was quiet.

Sad. "I'll tell you one thing, though. I'm glad we're here to-gether."

We sat like that for a while, neither of us quite crying, nei-ther of us quite not. We were suspended in this bubble, the two of us, the only ones who knew the full extent of what we might lose.

For the last five years, I'd done everything I could to avoid loss. Ran from every relationship, romantic or familial. I'd been close to Elinor, sure, but did I even know her, if I didn't know that she'd had this grand love affair? Or had I worked so hard to be perfect and self-sufficient that I'd isolated myself from her, too? And now I didn't know if I'd ever see her again, or Marianne, and it turned out there was nothing you could do in life to escape losing people. To hold yourself far enough away from them that it didn't hurt. So I wished, right now, that I hadn't bothered trying. That I had opened myself up to the people I loved, or could have loved, because if it was going to hurt anyway, I wished that I'd had joy to accompany it. I'd held myself back, thinking that eventually things would be easier, or safer, that everything would work out perfectly for me to open up. But those hopes had been dashed—not even by my specific circumstances, though those hadn't helped. I was starting to think that life had dashed that plan from the very beginning, that you couldn't ever wait for things to be guaranteed. You just had to be strong enough, brave enough, to try anyway. To jump and reach for love, not knowing whether you'd land safe or not.

I hoped Edward had that. The joy part.

"What do you like best about Elinor?"

"Margaret." His voice held a hint of admonishment, which

I couldn't help but think he'd learned from my sister. "She'll be back. We don't need to write her eulogy."

"I know. I—I've just spent the last five years idolizing her. And now I'm worried there's this whole other part of her I didn't bother to know because I was happy with imitating the surface level." I sat up, turned toward my brother-in-law. "What's she even like, Edward? When she isn't trying to be perfect. When it's just the two of you."

Edward looked at me in the dim light. Then after a moment, he nodded.

"She's softer." His voice was quiet, a little reverent. "Because she knows she doesn't need to be hard. Kind. She anticipates every need you have before you even realize you have it, but you know that." I nodded. "Mostly she's—it's nice to see her relaxed. When it's just us." He smiled. "Sometimes she'll even let me do things for her, though I suspect a part of her hates it. Hates letting anyone else take care of her. I don't know, Margaret." Edward shrugged. "I know her so well that there's no way to describe it. The best part of loving someone, and loving them for a long time, is that you forget where you end and the other person begins. The lines that divide you become blurred and soon you're just . . . Elinor and Edward. You pick up each other's cues and realize how they're feeling before they even feel it, because you've designed your whole life around them, and they've designed theirs around you. It's not that either of us are different, when we're together. It's that we're incomplete when we're not."

As it turned out, even Edward Ferrars still had the ability to surprise me.

I wiped away the tears that rolled down my cheeks, trying

(and failing) to not let him see that I was crying. Holding myself back even now. "I'm not going to lie, Edward. That sounds terrifying."

"Of course it is." To my surprise, he laughed. "Loving someone and letting them love you, too, is the scariest thing a person can do. But I've gotten to know you pretty well over the last five years, Margaret Dashwood, and I know for a fact that you're not a coward."

"I'm not so sure about that." I felt like a coward, holed up here in a ballroom while my sisters were God knew where. "I've gotten pretty good at putting up a front. I barely know who I am, when I'm not trying to be one of my sisters. There may be a big giant coward hiding inside of me."

"No." Edward shook his head. "There's not. Because whether you know yourself or not, I *do* know you. And I see the person you're trying to be. And I know that person is trying to be brave, and to always do the right thing, and to take care of everyone else around her. To keep them safe. It's one of the things I love most about you."

Damn it. Now I was really going to cry.

"Aw, Edward." I tried to sound jokey, but I doubted it came across that way. "You love me."

"Of course I do, Mags." He sounded surprised. "You're my sister."

I swallowed hard, tried to break up the lump in my throat.

I'd never thought of Edward as particularly courageous. But it was possible he was one of the bravest people I knew.

"She's going to be okay." I wasn't my sister, I wasn't the person Edward needed right now, but I could do my best. I could be brave, *actually* brave, for his sake. For Elinor's, and for Marianne's. For mine, too. "She'll find her way back to you."

"To both of us," Edward said, but his voice cracked as he said it. I reached out and hugged him close. Tied us together, just like Elinor had. Because Edward was maybe the person in the world who knew me best. Not the me I pretended to be. The real one. It was time to figure out how to be Margaret.

Finally.

CHAPTER THIRTY-FOUR

I wouldn't say that Edward and I fell asleep, exactly, but we were both drifting in and out of consciousness, trying to nap to make the time go faster, when a huge commotion in the hallway sent both of us jumping to our feet, running as best we could through the packed-in bodies, and flinging open the ballroom door to the lobby to see what was going on. If it was what we hoped.

And it was . . . to an extent.

"Margaret! Edward!" Marianne, wet hair plastered to her forehead, eyeliner smeared down her cheeks, ran toward me and pulled me into a soaking hug. "You're here! Thank God."

"Marianne," I managed to get out, although my face was squished down into her shoulder through the sheer force of her hug. I wrapped my arms around her, too, let myself feel, at least briefly, glad. Just behind her, Torden, of all people, was grimacing and wringing water out of his T-shirt, and even though I barely knew him I was happy to see him, too. I pulled my head back from her shoulder, though it was a bit of a struggle. "What the hell happened? Where were you?"

"Oh my God, it was so stressful." Marianne released me and ran to Edward, whom she hugged tightly before he could protest. "Our bus broke down, like, halfway from the pier, and at first they wanted everyone to stay on the bus, but then they wanted us to walk to the nearest shelter, and then they didn't again. And the crew kept going back and forth until they decided they would try to *fix* the bus, and that took forever, but they finally got it working again and now we're here!" Marianne finally took a breath and looked around, confused. "Where's Elinor? Was she not worried about me? That's typical, isn't it, like some stupid fight matters when I could have died—"

Oh no.

"Elinor stayed back on the ship to look for you, Marianne," I said. Edward let out a sound that was more of a whimper than anything else. I felt my heart rate pick up, fast as the rain outside. "When you didn't come down to the atrium when our cabins were called, she stayed back to find you. She wasn't on the bus?"

"What?" Marianne turned around in a circle, like Elinor was going to be hiding behind her, like we were all going to shout *surprise!* and tell her this was the worst prank in the history of the world. "I ran into Torden when I was heading down to the atrium, and he was freaking out about the storm. Something about his ancestors being on the *Titanic*? So I hung back with him until he calmed down."

I stared daggers at Torden, who shrugged.

"What can I say? I'm a method actor."

"You're a—never mind." I turned my attention back to Marianne. "You really didn't see her?"

"No, I obviously wouldn't lie about something like this. She stayed back for me? Why would she do that?"

"Because she'd do anything for you."

Both Marianne and I turned toward Edward as his voice cut through Marianne's.

"You know that. She'd do anything to make sure you were safe."

I heard Marianne take a sharp intake of breath. Edward was turning around in circles, not stopping until he saw Jono, ushering in the other guests who'd arrived with Marianne.

"Jono." Edward grabbed him by the arm. "Are these the last of the guests?"

"Yes, thank God." Jono blew out his lips, and the world froze around me. "It's getting nasty out there. Glad to be done."

"Elinor's not here, though," I said. "She never made it."

Even in the dim, barely-there glow of our flashlights, I could see all the color drain from Jono's face.

"That's not possible." He looked around frantically. "We cleared the ship. Oi, Jenny!" He waved down a tall woman with broad shoulders in an officer's uniform, soaked to the bone. "You know Edward Ferrars, yeah? The chaplain? His wife never made it to the hotel."

"That's not possible." Thanks, Jenny, real helpful. "All of the guests have tapped out of the ship. I'll have officers check through the ballroom, just in case she came in and no one realized." That was impossible; if Elinor was here, we'd know.

But Jenny was gone before we could say anything, and Jono, too, with just a quick "Hang tight, it'll all work out" to hold us over.

There was no way in hell I was going to *hang tight*. And from the expression on Marianne's face, she was thinking the same thing.

"I'm going to look for her."

Marianne and I both spoke at the same time. Edward's jaw dropped.

"What?" He shook his head, fast. His hair had gotten huge since we'd been evacuated, sticking up from constantly running his hands through it, and between that and his glasses, he looked like a mad scientist. "Marianne, Margaret, no. it's not safe out there."

"And she's out there anyway. Because of me." Marianne's voice was fierce. "We know she's not on the ship, and you said she's not at the hotel, which means she's out in this storm and I'm *not* leaving her there. She would do the same for me—she *did* do the same for me—and if she's hurt, I'm going to find her. Margaret, Edward's right, you absolutely can't come." I opened my mouth to protest the hypocrisy, but Marianne spoke over me. "If I'm not back in a few hours, you should probably tell someone." She glanced down at her sundress, soaked to her skin. "At least I put sneakers on."

It was Marianne like I'd never seen her before. Marianne strong, even though she was on her own.

But she wasn't going to be on her own for long.

"I'm still going with you," I said, even as Marianne and Edward gave me horrified looks. "Gabe showed me around the island before, and it'll be safer with two of us. Easier to search."

"Margaret, it's too dangerous," she protested, but I stopped her.

"If it's not too dangerous for you, it's not too dangerous for me."

Marianne looked at me for a long moment, then nodded. Edward threw up his hands.

"Okay." Marianne stuck her hand out for me to shake. "But if something happens to you, I'm going to make your ghost come back so you can explain to Mom that this was *your* idea."

"Deal." I took her hand, adrenaline rushing through me. I was brave, damn it. I could do this. "Edward, you can wait here in case Elinor comes back, right?"

"*Obviously* not." Edward marched forward, sighing, and grabbed ponchos from a small stack by the front door. "You two. What part of you thought I was going to stay here while you went out to search for my wife?"

Well, when you put it like that.

"I just thought—" Marianne began, but Edward cut her off.

"I realize I may not be the grand romantic hero of your books, Marianne, but I can do what needs to be done to take care of the woman I love. Lord knows she so rarely needs it." His smile was grim, determined, as he stacked an abandoned first aid kit on top of the ponchos. "Besides, the two of you were about to run out into the middle of the storm without any sort of rain protection for yourselves, or medical supplies if she's hurt, and if that's how you're planning to start your search, I certainly don't want to see how you planned to proceed with it. So come on." He held out our hurricane supplies, a determined look in his eyes. "Let's go find my wife."

I was starting to see the appeal of this whole love thing.

CHAPTER THIRTY-FIVE

Here's the thing about hurricanes: they're a lot more than just heavy rainstorms.

Part of me knew that already. Had seen the news coverage for various storms, seen what they did to houses, to cars, to entire cities, to people. I was young when Sandy hit New Jersey, but I still knew people who'd been affected by it. Seen the aftermath. But seeing a hurricane and being in one were two entirely different things.

First of all, it turned out that actually I'd never experienced wind before. That soft, gentle breeze I'd called wind back in New Jersey was nothing. This wind was trying to turn me inside out, to rip off my skin and pull off my hair, to wreck me against the nearest hard surface and skewer my skin with sand. It was like walking into a brick wall, this wind. At the best of times, it felt impossible to move forward. At the worst of times, it actually was.

And that was before we even got to the rain. Growing up, I'd always liked rainstorms—the way the water sounded, pitter-pattering against my window, watching it drown the outside while I was safe and dry inside; the way that no matter how bad the storm looked, it always cleared up. It always passed through. But with this rain, there was no passing through. There was only the endless, relentless pounding, over and over and over again, the way that the whole world was reduced to water. Each drop, if you could even begin to divide them up that way, was a razor-sharp needle stabbed into my face. I didn't know rain could *hurt* so much. Could take up so much of the air that it felt like I was more underwater than not. Could try so hard to destroy me.

A hurricane isn't a sentient thing. But this storm felt evil.

"Margaret?" Marianne called back to me from the front of our line—her leading the charge, me behind her, Edward behind me. It hurt to even open my mouth, but we'd taken up this call and response as we ventured into the storm, a reassurance that we were still together.

"Here!" The wind swallowed up the word, but I reached forward to squeeze Marianne's outstretched hand.

She nodded. "Edward?"

"Here." My brother-in-law, when I glanced back at him, showed no signs of distress, only determination, and I felt a rush of affection for him.

We'd planned out our rescue mission the best we could before leaving the hotel, sneaking out a side exit to avoid being stopped by the crew and the hotel staff. Edward's best guess was that Elinor would have tried to walk from the ship to the resort, so we'd stick to the main road and immediate surrounding areas, hoping to find her sooner rather than later.

It had seemed like a great plan back in the lobby, but we'd

been out here for what felt like at least an hour with no sign of Elinor. We'd been going as slowly as we could, watching the ground and moving in a zigzag pattern to minimize the chances of missing her if she'd fallen, but with each labored step, I was getting more and more scared for my sister.

Marianne must have been feeling the same way. She stopped walking, drew the three of us into a huddle, heads pressed together, a temporary shelter from the worst of the storm.

"This isn't working!" She had to shout to be heard over the roaring wind. "We're almost to the pier—she would have crossed paths with the bus before now if she'd stayed on the main roads. We need a new plan. Edward, any ideas?"

"She might have tried to look for somewhere to take shelter?" he offered. "I don't know. I don't think she would have stopped moving until she found you, Marianne."

"We could try down by the beach? Maybe in one of the activities huts, or a guest cabana?" Marianne suggested, shielding her face against the rain. God, I hoped Elinor wasn't there. Whenever we'd ventured too close to the shoreline, we'd felt the harsh sting of sand against our skin, scraping into our eyes and choking out our breath. No, Elinor wouldn't have gone down there. If she'd taken shelter, it would be somewhere high and dry. Or at least, the highest and driest place she could find.

Just beyond us, I heard a tremendous cracking, and Marianne screamed as another palm tree, mere feet from where we were standing, fell, blocking off part of the path. Edward pulled the two of us into him, and all the anxiety I'd felt this entire summer billowed up inside of me, threatening to overwhelm me, to drown me like the storm wanted to.

I buried myself into Marianne and Edward, closed my eyes against the raging winds, and did my best to think.

Where had we gone when we were on the island together? There had to be something she'd remember, somewhere she'd think to go. I knew my sister, didn't I? We were the three people who knew her better than anyone else in the world. One person who had chosen her and two people who hadn't needed to. We should have been able to find her. If I was in her shoes, if I was looking for Marianne . . .

The thought hit me like a flash.

"The lighthouse!" I shouted, startling Marianne and Edward. "I told her about Gabe and— I told her about it. That you could see the whole island from it. If she couldn't find Marianne, or if she was lost, it's definitely easier to find than the hotel. And it would be the safest place to get to—that lighthouse has stood through a hundred storms."

Marianne and Edward looked at each other across our little circle. Then Edward squeezed my shoulder.

"Margaret, you're brilliant." He stood up, cursing as he staggered back in the wind. "Lead the way."

"Okay." Marianne nodded, then pushed me to the front of the line. I just needed to find the light. Find the light, find Elinor. I hoped, at least. And hope was all that any of us had. "Let's go."

EDWARD saw her first.

Tucked just inside the door of the lighthouse, Elinor had dragged herself out of the worst of the wind and the rain and then seemingly collapsed there, at the base of the stairs. My sister looked terrible: bruised and battered, clothes torn, her arm lying at a weird angle that made me immediately nauseous.

But when she saw the three of us, her eyes lit up like everything was right in the world.

"Edward! Margaret! Marianne!" Her voice was hoarse, battered by the wind, as we all pushed inside and Marianne gave the heavy door a thorough pull closed behind us. "How did you—"

Then she didn't say anything else, because Edward was there, dropping to the ground beside her. He pulled her up into him and hugged her, keeping her injured arm clear but holding her more tightly than I'd ever seen. And then he was crying, sobs that shook his entire body as he pulled my sister into a kiss worthy of a movie star.

"You're okay," he kept repeating, his voice shaking. "You're okay."

"Yeah." Elinor's voice was soft, her hand in her husband's hair. "I am."

After a minute, Edward leaned back, laughing softly to himself as he wiped his face, and Elinor turned toward Marianne and me. When I glanced over at Marianne, I saw that she was crying, too.

"I'm sorry," Marianne started to say, and then she joined Edward on the ground next to Elinor, and they were hugging, and before I knew it Marianne had reached back and pulled me down, too, into the embrace, into the family, and soon Edward was absorbed and even though we were still, all things considered, in a pretty terrible situation, I had the thorough and indescribable feeling that we were going to be all right, the Dashwood family. Somehow, just somehow, everything was going to be okay.

CHAPTER THIRTY-SIX

Over the next few hours, the four of us listened to the storm rage, protected inside the lighthouse, the front door heavily bolted behind us as we settled in, staggered up and down the stairs. Though I suspected nobody was going to get a *good* night's sleep, we took turns closing our eyes, and the rest of the time, Elinor filled us in on what had happened.

"I was looking all over the ship for Marianne," she began, as Marianne stared down at the ground, "and when I heard them call for the last bus, I was on the opposite side of the ship. I made it down to the atrium and the crew member in charge of the deboarding checked me out and told me to hustle, but when I made it to the end of the pier, the bus was pulling away and didn't see me." Her back was pressed against the smooth white surface of the lighthouse's interior walls, and she was cradling her arm in her lap. It was definitely broken, and Edward had fashioned a sling out of the supplies he'd found in the first aid kit until we could get actual medical attention. "The rain wasn't too bad yet, so I thought I could just follow the main road to the hotel. It's only a mile or two. But the storm got worse, and I must have gotten turned around. After I got knocked around by some debris"—she indicated her arm—"I knew I needed to find shelter, fast. That's when I remembered Mags telling me about the lighthouse." She bumped her shoulder into mine, ever so gently. "Luckily I could still see the light, even with the storm."

"Lucky you didn't get yourself killed," Marianne said, brushing her hand over Elinor's messy hair. Her voice held no admonishment. "We could have lost you."

"Yes, well, I wasn't going to let you go again." Elinor sighed, closing her eyes briefly, and Marianne leaned her head on Elinor's shoulder. I squeezed in closer, too.

"Do you think maybe next time, we can stop getting ourselves into these life-and-death situations?" I asked, and Elinor laughed. "Because technically it's my turn next and I'd rather just . . . not, if it's okay with you. I'd prefer if we just stick together."

"I mean, so would I," Marianne said. "You two are the ones who pulled away from me."

"What?" Elinor asked, surprised. "No, we didn't. You're the one who moved."

"Sure, but whenever I came back, or called, it was always the two of you joined together." Marianne sighed. "You didn't need me anymore."

"Of course we do!" Elinor said. I stayed quiet. It wasn't like Marianne was wrong, but I didn't know if I was up for admitting that yet.

But if I was going to try being vulnerable with the people who loved me, maybe I needed to start here.

"I maybe pulled away a little." I raised my hand in the air, like I was in a classroom. "Sorry."

"A little?" Marianne snorted.

"Okay, maybe a lot," I admitted. "But I was just trying to get my life back under control after all the chaos of That Year."

"We could have done that together," Marianne said. "You didn't need to push me away."

"Sure, but I'd spent so long basically being your clone, Marianne, and then I was trying to be Elinor instead, and so I thought that if I spent too much time with you I'd just, like, snap back into old habits." From the way Elinor and Marianne were looking at me, I knew I wasn't making any sense. "Sorry. But you guys have to have known that, right? That I was just copying everything you were doing?"

"I mean, I guess a little," Elinor said, looking to Marianne for confirmation. She nodded. "But that's what little sisters do."

"Sure, but it was *all* I did. And why would I want to be anything else? If I tried to figure out who I was, I'd just get slotted back into being baby Margaret. The littlest and least important of the Dashwood girls."

"That's not true." Elinor shook her head. "You're a lot more than that."

"Am I?" I asked. "I don't think I am. I went straight from being just like Marianne to being just like Elinor, because I thought the world shone down on you two, and there wasn't room to be anything else. That's what people always asked me, you know that? Growing up. *Is this one sensible like Elinor or a romantic like Marianne?* I got, like, shoved into these archetypal ideas of who the two of you were, and I couldn't find my way out. And then in my head, I reduced both of you to what the world thought you were like, too, and I didn't know how to break through and find the real people underneath. And so after the accident, since everyone was pulling away anyway, I figured, fine." I took a deep breath. "Just be like Elinor. Being like Marianne only gets you hurt." I glanced sideways at my sister. "Sorry again. It's just that you're—"

"Obsessed with love. I get it." Marianne's voice was hollow, and I felt an ache in my own chest, but I didn't take the words back. It was too late. "Look, I guess I don't mind that you used my life as a *do not attempt* template. But avoiding love completely isn't the answer either. That's how I ended up in my current shitty situation, you know."

"What do you mean?"

"Mags, I didn't break up with Brandon because I didn't love him anymore." She sighed. "I broke up with him because I loved him too much."

Silence overtook the tower. Across from me, Edward closed his eyes, then opened them again.

Finally, Elinor spoke. "That doesn't seem like a good reason to break up with somebody."

"Thanks, Elinor, I hadn't thought of that." Marianne's voice was sharp, but then she sighed. "Sorry. I've had a lot of time to think about this the last couple of months."

"Why don't you start at the beginning," Edward said, giving Marianne his best encouraging-pastor smile. I didn't know if she bought it, but it at least made the whole thing seem more normal. "Tell us what happened."

"I don't know." Marianne bit her bottom lip. "Look, the accident affected me, too, okay? I'm—I'm really, really ashamed that I let a guy get to me like that. To hurt me to the point that I hurt myself. And you, too, Margaret." She reached over, touched me gently on the arm that had broken in the crash. "And I'll admit, Brandon felt like a safer choice. He's a lot more . . . steady than the guys I usually go for."

"But?" Elinor prompted.

"But I fell for him so hard." Marianne flapped her hands in the air in front of her. "And then I started to realize I still had no idea who I even was without the context of a guy."

"So you broke up with him," I said.

"Yeah, I did. I don't think that's what he expected when he proposed." Marianne's laugh was shaky. "I just thought—what am I doing? Am I even with him because I love him, or because it's safe? Like, I thought I loved him, obviously, but what if it *was* just that I loved love so much I'd do anything to have it? Or that Brandon was just the safest version of love I could find? I had no idea what I wanted to do, or what I liked. It felt like I'd lost my entire life to love. So, yeah, I ended it." She shrugged. "It was the worst day of my entire life. Worse than anything that happened with the accident. But it had to be done."

I didn't know if that was true. But Elinor caught my eye, shook her head at me. I got what she was saying: let Marianne figure that out on her own.

"Anyway." She sighed. "I figured the cruise would take my mind off things. Get some guy-free time while I hung out with my sisters and figured out who I was, without a guy to define me."

"Ah." I'd made a huge mistake. "So me forcing you into dating . . ."

"Was basically the opposite of how I wanted to spend my summer," she finished with a smile. "But I also saw how worried you were about me. You weren't going to ever relax with me just, like, wandering the ship unattached. I figured if I dragged you into these dates, too, we'd at least get to hang out."

"I'm an idiot." I shook my head, sending drops of water splashing. "I'm sorry, Marianne." I probably needed, while we were getting things off our chest, to admit what I'd *actually* done this summer. "While we're coming clean, I should tell you . . . I also may have hand-selected all your dates in an elaborate audition process."

"*What?*" Elinor, Edward, and Marianne all said it at the same time, which would have been funny if it had happened to anyone but me.

"I just wanted to make sure the guys were decent!" This was not how I'd expected my first hurricane to go, that was for sure. "Because I . . . didn't exactly trust that you'd pick out anyone good."

"Wow. Harsh, but fair." Marianne settled her head back against the lighthouse wall. "What about Gabe, then? Where'd you find him?"

"He kind of helped me organize it." God, I didn't want to talk about Gabe right now. "We're just friends, though. Or we were, anyway. We're not exactly talking right now. But, yeah, he was just another ruse to avoid getting hurt that failed miserably. Much like the rest of my plans for the summer. Sorry."

"Don't be. You were just trying to help." Marianne wrung out her ponytail, water dripping onto the ground beneath her. "We weren't thinking that differently, in the end. I didn't want to depend on guys for the rest of my life, and you didn't want me to depend on the wrong ones." She shrugged. "I'm not meant for happily ever after, I think. The two of us can just live vicariously through Elinor and Edward."

"Marianne . . ." Elinor started, but Marianne stopped her.

"Elinor. I'm the reason we're in this mess in the first place. In *most* of our messes in the first place. If I hadn't broken up with Brandon, we wouldn't have fought. I would have just evacuated with the rest of you, and we wouldn't be trapped in a lighthouse with your bones sticking out of your arm."

"A little graphic, thanks," Elinor murmured, putting her hand over her sling protectively.

"I'm just saying you're probably right, Margaret," Marianne sighed, leaning back against the lighthouse wall. "Whether you figure out who you are on your own or not, you should probably run as far as you can to avoid being like me."

"Can I say something?"

All three of us started at the sound of Edward's voice, piping up across the stairs. His expression was anxious but determined.

"The way that you all love people . . . it isn't a bad thing." He pushed himself up, adjusting his posture. "It's not some curse, to love boldly. It's your greatest strength. The way that the three of you care for one another, and the people in your lives, that's the best thing about you. Why do you think I've always liked being around your family so much?" He gave a small smile. "My family isn't like that, as you know, and I'll admit they're a rather extreme counterexample. But a *lot* of families aren't like that. A lot of *people* aren't like that. It's why you draw people to you. Why people want to be around you." He reached over and took Elinor's (non-broken) hand. "I'd rather be stuck in this lighthouse with the three of you than safe in the hotel with anyone else."

"I kind of wish we were all just safe in the hotel," Marianne murmured, and Edward laughed.

But I still had questions. "Okay, maybe that's all true. But then why do we all keep pushing people away?" I looked pointedly at my sisters. "Marianne broke up with Brandon. I did . . . my whole thing. Even Elinor hardly ever talked to Marianne after That Year. If love is so great, why do all of our instincts keep telling us to run?"

"You ask just as many questions as you did when you were a kid—do you know that?" Elinor sighed, but her smile was fond. "The thing about growing up is that very little of the world exists in black-and-white, right-and-wrong dimensions. Things can be terrifying *and* good for us. On the other hand, sometimes they're terrifying because they're bad for us. The trick is learning to distinguish between the two."

"That sounds . . . impossible."

"Which is why none of us should be doing it alone," Edward chimed in, and Elinor laughed.

"Thanks, Pastor Ferrars. Margaret, everything that happened five years ago . . . it was hard. Incredibly hard. And I wanted to keep you safe after that. So if it seemed like I didn't trust you, it was just because I was trying to take care of you." She looked over at him, recognition dawning in her eyes. "Which, I'm realizing, is exactly what you were trying to do with Marianne, oh, God." She started to bury her face in her hands, yelping when she jostled her arm. "Am I the worst example of a sister in the world?"

"I can give you a run for your money," Marianne muttered. I shook my head frantically.

"Guys." I scooted forward slightly, so I could address them both. "I promise. I'm not just like . . . a combination of your influences. Or maybe I am, I don't know, but they got all mixed up in my head into new and exciting ways to experience trauma, so it's not like a straight line from what you did to the way I turned out, okay? That's why it hasn't worked, when I just try to be like the two of you." It dawned on me all at once. "I'm my own person. I made my decisions on my own. But what happened with Dad and everything afterward, that happened to all of us. And we all just did what we could to get through it. Together and apart." I shrugged. "I don't blame either of you for that."

We all fell quiet for a minute, with just the wind and rain whipping down around all of us.

Finally, Edward spoke up again. "Elinor has a rule that I'm not allowed to preach when I'm not standing directly behind a pulpit." He smiled, and Elinor snorted. "But I think all of you could use a little forgiveness, and a little grace. Not just for one another but for yourselves. I was there, too, for at least part of what happened. And it was a truly terrible thing for all of you to go through, losing your father, losing everything, almost losing Marianne. It's okay to operate in survival mode, when you go through something like that. But you've all survived, haven't you? Even this, you all survived. And I think that the way you all survive best is when you have one another." His smile passed over each of us, unendingly fond. "I don't think it's a bad thing that you operate best as one family organism. When you get the Dashwoods together, when the three of you are all crammed together like you're meant to be . . . it's like triptychs, you know? The ones that are three separate pieces that make up one picture? They're good on their own, they function independently of each other, but when you put them together, it's something like magic."

All of us stared at Edward long enough that he flushed.

"Wow, Edward." Marianne let out a laugh, and that broke the tension, at least a little. "And here I always thought you would be a terribly dry preacher."

"I've gotten better." Edward shrugged. "I watch a lot of TED Talks."

"Edward's right." Elinor nodded. "We're best when the three of us are together."

"We can still fix that, though," Marianne said. "I know none of us is going to be in the same place next year, but we can visit, right? You guys can come to New Orleans. Ooh, or Elinor and I can come to California! Disneyland, surfing, sourdough in San Francisco . . ."

"I'm starting to think you have zero concept of the geography of California," I said, but Marianne waved me off.

"We can have a whole new set of adventures there, you know? The Dashwood girls on the road. Elinor will drive, obviously, I'll be in charge of the snacks and the tunes and the stops, and Margaret . . ." She grinned at me. "Margaret will do her own thing. We'll figure out what it is. But I'm sure she's going to crush it."

A thrill filled me, a thrill I hadn't experienced since—well, Gabe had thrilled me like that. Before I'd ruined everything with him. "I guess that could be pretty cool."

"We'll visit lots," Elinor added. "I could stand to be warm somewhere that *doesn't* have hurricanes. Or at least, not as many hurricanes."

"Amen," Edward said solemnly, and we all laughed, and despite the horrible situation we still found ourselves in, I felt lighter than I had in . . . forever.

I wanted my sisters to feel like that, too.

I turned to Marianne.

"Elinor doesn't want me to say this," I began, and across from me, Elinor rolled her eyes. "Because I think she wants you to figure it out on your own. But I think that's a terrible idea when we could figure things out together. And, Marianne, you breaking up with Brandon? That was another terrible idea."

"I appreciate where you're coming from, Mags." Marianne sighed. "But I don't think it was."

"You just said you were scared, too," I pointed out. "But earlier, Edward told me what it's like, when he and Elinor are together." I smiled, though across from me, Elinor looked briefly horrified. "Oh my God, not like that." Edward turned bright red. "But like . . . what your relationship was like." I turned my attention back to my middle sister. "He said that the best part of it was the way they changed and grew together. I don't think that's dependence. Or at least, not an unhealthy amount of it. I feel like that's just being in love. Were you happy when you were with Brandon?"

"Of course." Marianne's voice came out in a whisper. "Everything's better with him."

"Because you love him!" I tossed my hands in the air. "Come on, Marianne! You're the bravest of all of us, because you already took this gigantic step to find out who you are. But who you are is *perfect* for Brandon. This is the last thing you have to be brave about. Let yourself be in love with him."

In the barely there illumination of the lighthouse's interior, with light peeking in only through the top windows, I could hardly make out Marianne's face. But I could still see when she started to cry.

"Oh, God." She dropped her head on Elinor's shoulder. "What if it's too late?"

"You and Brandon will find your way to each other." To my surprise, it was Edward who reached out, patted Marianne on the ankle. "You always do."

"And we'll help you." Elinor moved like she wanted to put her arm around Marianne, then thought better of it. She glanced at me meaningfully, and I quickly scurried up a few more steps, until Marianne was in between both of us, and wrapped my arms around her. "But we'll figure it out. I promise."

"Okay," Marianne mumbled through the tears that were welling up, and I hugged her as tight as I could. And all I could think was that maybe it wasn't too late for me, either. I didn't know if I'd discovered the kind of great love, yet, that Elinor and Marianne had. But I was starting to suspect that being brave, that not being afraid of love, of connection, meant that

I owed it to myself to find out. That I owed it to *Gabe* to find out. And if I got hurt . . . I got hurt. That was the cost of being human. Of having these experiences in the first place.

And so I hugged my sister as the wind raged on, and I started to formulate a plan.

CHAPTER THIRTY-SEVEN

It was midmorning when the storm finally broke. There'd been a brief pause in the night when the eye passed over, but Edward had warned us not to be lulled into a false sense of security. Sure enough, the storm had come raging back with a vengeance; and even though I'd felt a shiver of fear, I hadn't let it overpower me. Told myself that I was as safe as I could be, that there was nothing I could do but be with my family and hope for the best.

And then the sun was shining, and Elinor was stirring from her sleep while Marianne complained about a crick in her neck, and as Edward opened the door with care, we stepped out into what was—somehow—one of the most glorious days I'd seen all summer.

Of course, the sun also did its part to illuminate the damage to the island. Huge palm trees had fallen across the road, blocking any car access, and we had to pick our way across them with care as we moved slowly back toward the hotel. I did my best not to look around at our surroundings, but it was nearly impossible to avoid seeing the destruction that the island, which had felt like such a refuge, had endured.

"There's the hotel!" Marianne cried, and even though I had spent approximately six hours in that hotel before abandoning it for the hurricane-stricken island, it felt like coming home to a long-lost friend. I let out a whoop of excitement, Elinor and Edward cheered, and after another fifteen minutes of working our way around debris, we were back in the warm embrace of the hotel lobby, surrounded by crew members and hotel staff who were horrified we had left at all.

"What were you thinking?" Jono appeared at our side, his eyes wide and frantic. Apparently his accent only got stronger when he was freaking out. "What were you doing out in the storm? You could have died!"

"Didn't, though." Marianne shrugged, flashing her most charming smile at the Australian. "Come on, Jono. Elinor was just trying to help me. And then we were just trying to help Elinor. Can you really blame us for going out there?"

Jono, as so often happened with men, seemed to find himself powerless in the face of Marianne's charms.

"Er . . . well . . . don't do it again," he finished, blinking fast as he followed the medical team that was pulling Elinor away to be treated, Edward right by her side. I turned to Marianne, grinning.

"What?" She shrugged, all innocence. "I didn't spend an entire summer working on my flirty eyes just to let them go to waste."

"Jono seems nice." I said it as a peace offering. "And probably single. You could ask him out. Have some fun for however long they keep us out here."

"Right." Marianne's smile faltered. "I think I might be done with our dating experiment for the summer. Possibly because I never wanted to do it in the first place."

"Ha." I ducked out of her way. "So are you going to get back together with Brandon, then?"

"I don't know." Marianne sighed. "I don't know that it's entirely up to me."

"But you still love him?"

"Oh, Mags." She shook her head. "Of course I do. I always will."

"Marianne?"

Oh my God.

I turned toward the front door a split second after Marianne, because while I knew that voice, had known that voice for five years, I didn't know it as well as Marianne did.

Brandon. Bursting through the spinning door of the lobby, soaked in rain and exhaustion, dressed head to toe in foul-weather gear and wearing an emergency responder vest. He stopped dead in his tracks when he saw Marianne, and she froze when she saw him, both of them locked in place, staring each other down across the lobby like they'd both seen a ghost. Objectively, I knew Marianne looked terrible—for once—her hair a disaster, her dress ripped and stained with mud, sand coating her legs. But Brandon looked at her like she was the world.

"Brandon," Marianne breathed, and then they were running to each other, and Brandon caught Marianne up in his arms, pulling her to him and burying his face in her shoulder.

"I'm so glad you're here," Marianne was saying, and, "I'm so glad you're okay," Brandon was saying, and they were kissing and hugging and Brandon was swirling her around like she was as insubstantial as air, but in that moment I knew she was the most substantial thing he had ever seen.

"I'm sorry I pushed you," he said when he finally put her down, when they managed to put a few inches between them and take deep breaths in between their tears. I didn't think they even realized they had an audience, that me and half the crew and staff and passengers in the lobby were all watching their reunion with bated breath. "I'm so sorry. We don't need to do anything you're not ready for."

"Brandon—"

"As soon as I heard about the storm, I volunteered with the first emergency services group I could find and came out here." This was the most I'd ever heard Brandon speak in front of a crowd at once, but seeing Marianne must have unlocked something in him. "I needed to know that you were all right. And if we never speak again, I understand, but—"

"Brandon." Marianne interrupted him again, smiling. And then she backed up a few feet, grinned up at him, and dropped to one knee.

I wasn't the only one who gasped.

"Marry me," she said, as Brandon blinked away tears. "I was scared before. But I'm not now."

Brandon's response was a whisper in her ear as he dropped to his knees in front of my sister, but from the way they embraced, I knew what he'd said.

Now *that* was being brave.

For a summer that had started off with so much going wrong, everything was almost right again. Almost. There was one thing that needled at the back of my mind, one thing

I knew I needed to do, as I slipped back into the ballroom to grab a change of clothes out of my backpack and find a shower somewhere. To be brave about, like Marianne had been brave. Like Elinor had been brave.

Everything was almost right. And I could make it right, completely right, if I could just talk to Gabe.

AFTER I'd cleaned up to a more appropriate seeing-someone-you-liked level (Marianne may have reunited with Brandon at her absolute dirtiest, but Gabe and I didn't know each other *that* well), I'd scoured both ballrooms of the hotel, hoping to find Gabe before they started dividing everyone up to get them home. The *Queen Mab* would be staying in port for a few days to make sure she hadn't been damaged in the storm, and everybody who wanted to be flown home was arranging for transport to Nassau, which had sustained minimal damage. I didn't know if Gabe and his aunt and uncle would be hanging around, so I needed to find him fast.

I should have known to look for a stage.

Behind the hotel, near the debris-filled pool, a few of the crew members had set up a small platform with some of the kids' club staff performing on it, doing dance routines and puppet shows for the children who had been on board. Standing off to the side, talking in a low voice to Peter and Luisa, was Gabe, and my whole chest warmed to see him. Which, of course, made me feel immediately terrible, because it was just a physical reminder that I was absolutely in love with this guy, and he'd liked me, too, and I'd done everything possible to hurt him, to hurt both of us, just to *avoid* getting hurt. And if he never wanted to speak to me again, well, I'd understand. But I had to at least let him know I was sorry. I owed both of us that.

Squaring my shoulders and trying to channel the courage of both of my sisters, I walked up behind him and tapped him on the shoulder. His eyes widened as he turned around, shocked.

But it was Luisa who spoke first. "Margaret!" She swept me into a hug. "Thank goodness you're all right. That was a scary one, wasn't it? And I heard that a few guests actually left the hotel and wandered out into the storm. Can you even imagine what they were thinking?"

"Yeah, they sound like troublemakers. You're all—you're okay?"

"We're okay," Peter answered, because Gabe was still staring at me like I'd risen from the dead. Which I guess I had, because I'd probably been dead to him. "The ship got pretty knocked around in the wind, so we'll have to repair a few of our props, but we can manage that easily once we get back home."

"You're leaving, then?" I was asking Peter, but I was looking at Gabe. As handsome as the first time I'd seen him, in perfect control of the show, giving everyone their light. Giving me my light.

"The line is sending us home to Atlanta," Luisa confirmed, her hand on her nephew's shoulder. "It'll be a bit of a skeleton crew for the trip back to Florida, so it's easier for us to just head out from here. We've got a ferry over to Nassau tonight, and then an early flight back to the States. What about you and your family?"

"I—I don't know." Tonight. That was so much sooner than I'd expected. I'd hoped selfishly to have the rest of the week to apologize to Gabe, to ease him back into being my friend, and maybe into being something more. But it didn't seem like I was going to have the luxury of that much time. That was fine, I told myself; all I needed to do was apologize, and I shouldn't expect anything else. "I was wondering if I could talk to Gabe for a minute, though? If you could spare him?"

Gabe still hadn't said anything, and I was starting to worry that wasn't just, like, because he was surprised to see me. It was possible that it was because he didn't have anything he wanted to say to me.

Courage, Margaret. Courage. Just . . . be yourself.

"Of course." Luisa gave her nephew a little push, and he looked back over his shoulder at her with an expression I could only call concern. "We can figure out our cues on our own for this one, Gabriel. Go."

Luisa, at least, didn't hate me. Probably because Gabe hadn't told her what happened. Still.

I led us away from the stage and the clamoring children, around the side of the hotel to a small garden. A lot of the shrubbery had been torn up and tossed around by the storm, but the heavy concrete benches hadn't moved, so I sat down at the edge of one of them and Gabe, after a second of hesitation, sat down at the other edge. The farthest possible edge.

Not exactly a good sign.

Unable to take the suspense anymore, I jumped to my feet and launched into the minimal semblance of a speech I'd prepared.

"I was an idiot."

That, at least, got Gabe to turn his face up toward me, one eyebrow raised.

"The whole thing I was trying to do, to keep my emotions disconnected from my relationships . . . it was stupid at best and psychopathic at worst. That's not how being a person works. I see that now." I took a deep breath, the humid, sticky air coating my throat. "It was incredibly unfair of me to ask you to try and do the same thing. If you like someone, you shouldn't be afraid of liking someone. You know? That's not, like, smart or evolved or whatever. It's just cowardly. Does that make any sense?"

"Um." Gabe, to his credit, hadn't run for the metaphorical hills at my rambling, but he didn't look like he fully got what I was saying, either. "A little?"

"What I mean is that my whole life philosophy was completely screwed up." I kept talking, fast, trying to get all the words out before Gabe inevitably gave up on me and left. "I was so worried about getting hurt that I hurt myself by holding everyone at arm's length. And that's ridiculous, because even when I tried not to care about people, just because I thought I wasn't supposed to, I inevitably did. And that meant that when they left me, or I left them, I got hurt anyway. So all I was doing was denying myself the parts of relationships—romantic or otherwise," I added hastily, "that make life worth living. That makes being a person . . . being a person."

"Spoken like a true philosopher."

"I'm trying to say I'm sorry." The words burst out of me, louder than I intended. "And when I told you I was in love with you . . . I meant it. Okay?" That got his attention. I kept pushing. "I've spent my whole life trying to be like my sisters. But now I'm trying out being Margaret, and I don't know a lot about her yet, but I *do* know that she's absolutely head over heels in love with one Gabriel Monteiro. And I'm not saying that because I expect you to, like, fall to your knees and declare your love for me, too. Because I fully acknowledge how much I hurt you, and I know you can't always come back from that. I probably shouldn't get to come back from that. But I also know that I'm done running scared from every feeling I ever had. And if that means telling you how I feel, so be it." I took a deep breath. "So there it is. And if we never see each other again, I'm glad I told you. I'm still glad you know."

"Margaret." Gabe came to his feet slowly, watching me with those chocolate-pool eyes the entire time.

I kept rambling. "If you hate me, could you not, like, lay into me too much, though?" I asked, brushing a frizzy piece of hair—the hurricane had wreaked havoc on my curls, and the hotel gym shower I'd taken hadn't helped—out of my face. "I don't want to deny you your cathartic experience, or anything. It's just been kind of a long day."

"Margaret." Gabe didn't say my name, I realized, like an admonishment or an interruption. He said it like a discovery. A wonder. A joy. "Are you serious with all this?"

"Um. Yeah." I flushed. "Trust me, I'm as surprised as anyone. I thought I'd kept all my capacity to love locked way, way up. You did a pretty good job unlocking it this summer, though, with all your romantic hideaways and secret not-dates and telling me all your deep inner workings."

"You thought the hideaways were romantic?"

"Oh, come on." I rolled my eyes. "You can pretend all

you want that we were just hanging out. But I know what you were doing. You were trying to win me over. And it worked, so you can't blame anyone but yourself for that." Something clicked, and I looked up sharply at Gabe, who was still moving slowly toward me. "Wait. Do you not—do you not hate me?"

"Margaret." Gabe's voice was slower, and his mouth was getting closer. "I one hundred percent, absolutely certified, certainly positively do not hate you."

And then there was no more distance between us as he pressed his lips to mine.

The last time we'd kissed, it had been angry, harsh, full of passion and promises I wasn't prepared to keep. But this kiss was as tender as the sweetest embrace, as soft as the sky looked after a terrible rain. I wrapped my hands around Gabe's neck, pulled him closer, and he met the pressure with his hands on my waist. As he breathed against me, his kiss was filled with something I couldn't quite recognize. Something, though, that I was starting to suspect was love.

Love. Me! Margaret Dashwood! In love and actually happy about it!

Gabe pulled back, his forehead pressed to mine, his grin bigger than I'd ever seen it.

"I'm in love with you, too, Margaret Dashwood," he said, and in that moment I knew why people risked everything for this. Why they threw caution to the wind and jumped into the unknown, because in that moment, I'd have done anything to keep this feeling. And that didn't feel like a curse. It felt like the best gift I'd ever gotten. "Just to keep things fair. So what now?"

"What, now you're the one who needs a super-specific plan?" I shrugged, rubbed my thumb against the back of his neck, and he laughed. "No idea. I'll be in California soon. You can visit. We can FaceTime. We'll figure it out."

"I like the sound of that," he said, kissing the side of my neck. "Figuring it out with you."

And then we didn't say anything for a long time after that.

CHAPTER THIRTY-EIGHT

As it turned out, we didn't need to figure anything out *too* immediately, because while I was gone, Marianne and Brandon had done a lot of figuring out on their own.

"We're getting married tomorrow!" she squealed when I returned to the ballroom at last, Gabe in hand, to find her, Elinor, Brandon, and Edward locked firmly in conference, Elinor's arm being checked on again by one of the emergency medics. Elinor and Marianne broke apart to let me in, pulling me down between them, and I couldn't stop smiling, even in the face of such absurd news. "We figured, why wait, right? It'll be a few days before we can get home. Why not have a party?"

"But—what about Mom?" My head was spinning, partially from all the kissing and partially from this momentous news. "If she's not at your wedding, she might literally die."

"She's coming in tomorrow morning with one of the supply helicopters," Brandon explained. His arm was wrapped around Marianne's shoulders, and I suspected he didn't plan on separating from her ever again. "I had to call in a few favors, and she's going to have to unload some boxes, but she seemed surprisingly excited about the prospect when we talked to her on the radio. Something about wanting to meet a firefighter."

I caught Marianne's eye, and we both giggled.

"Edward can do the ceremony," Marianne continued, reaching across and squeezing Edward's hand. "And then we'll just file the paperwork when we get back to Miami. It'll be low-key, obvs. But everyone that matters will be there. And what can I say?" Her eyes lit up as she turned to her fiancé. "I'm sick and tired of not being married to this man."

Why the hell not, right?

"Okay." I grinned, letting go of Gabe just long enough to hug Marianne and Brandon in turn. Brandon gave a small oof of surprise at the contact, but he was going to have to get used to it. I was overflowing with love these days. "Let's have a wedding. But can I make a suggestion for the entertainment?" I turned to Gabe, who was watching this whole exchange with barely concealed amusement. "What do you think, Gabe? Could you and your aunt and uncle stick around for a couple more days?"

"I'll see what I can do," Gabe said, but from the way his eyes twinkled, I wasn't worried about him making it happen. He leaned forward, kissed me hard and fast, and then jogged off to find his aunt and uncle.

I needed to get him out to California *stat*.

"Um, Margaret?" Elinor's voice snapped me out of my reverie. "Any chance you want to tell us what *that* was?"

Okay, it was possible that I had some explaining to do of my own.

I grinned, caught Marianne's eye, and winked.

"Just figuring my own stuff out. We can talk about it later." I pulled Elinor up by her good arm, then reached for Marianne. "We've got a wedding to plan!"

MARIANNE and Brandon's wedding day was as perfect as they both deserved.

Mom got in early, screaming the whole time the helicopter was landing but stumbling off merrily with a crate of medical supplies in her hands. She promptly dropped said crate at the feet of one of the other volunteers and ran for Marianne, openly sobbing as she hugged her and pulled Brandon in as well. Once we were able to untangle them, Elinor swept Mom away to the bridal suite we'd concocted (it was still our same corner of the ballroom, but Edward had done his best to get all the mud and sand off the floor).

While she spent the morning "freshening up" and exclaiming over last-minute details that Elinor made sure to take care of immediately, I worked with Edward and a few of the other crew members to turn the hotel lobby into a wedding venue. We didn't have much—mostly, we used felled palm fronds to create a half arch by the doors—and honestly, it looked pretty terrible. But Marianne, when she poked her head in to see how it was going, just laughed and shook her head, so I took that as success enough.

Gabe had taken charge of refreshments, getting one of his

crew buddies to run him back to the ship to grab as much prepared food as he could carry in a few duffel bags and a golf cart, and I'd even glimpsed his aunt and uncle practicing a routine that they'd chased me away from as soon as they'd seen me watching. As for Marianne and Brandon, they'd been excused from all responsibilities, and had, according to Elinor, spent the morning walking around the island, helping with cleanup efforts and talking, talking, talking.

I half believed her about the *just talking, Mags!* part.

And then lunchtime arrived, the time we'd set for the ceremony because the power still hadn't come back on in the hotel and doing the whole thing in the dark, while potentially romantic, didn't actually seem that practical. Right before I ducked into the ballroom to meet with Marianne and Elinor, Gabe appeared from the kitchen and grabbed my hand.

"Hi," he whispered, and I grinned, returning his greeting with a kiss. None of us had anything formal to wear, obviously, but Gabe had ended up in a hotel staff polo shirt and a pair of khaki shorts, and somehow, he seemed hotter than ever. (Well, a halfway unbuttoned white shirt and a pair of breeches still would have been an improvement, but I needed *something* to look forward to when he came to visit in the fall.) "You look great."

"You do, too." I, like my sisters, had raided the hotel gift shop for my outfit, and a bathing suit coverup was the most formal thing I could find. It was pretty, though, a flowy halter dress covered with tropical flowers. If it wasn't for the fact that the flowers were printed all over with the hotel's logo, I might have actually gotten away with it as formal wear. But it still felt like me, whoever that me was turning out to be.

"Thanks for everything you've done for this. It's going to be a good day, isn't it?"

"With you, Margaret?" He kissed me again, turning me into a dip as I squealed. "Every day is a good day."

When I made my way to Marianne and Elinor, they were sitting quietly, just the two of them, holding hands, Marianne's head on Elinor's shoulder. For a moment, I almost backed away, but then Marianne beckoned for me to join them. The Dashwood girls, three sisters who had fought through a storm and come out the other side, who had gotten the prizes of love they deserved, because even when the world tried to beat them down, they stayed together and they stayed strong. And with Edward, and now Brandon, the circle of love we shared had grown a little wider, a little stronger. Just like I'd let Gabe into my circle, and who knew? Maybe one day, he'd be a Dashwood, too. And even if he wasn't, we'd both be better for having loved each other. Because I was made up of all the love I had in my life, and I would keep growing from all the love yet to come.

It was a perfect day for a wedding. Brandon cried, and so did Marianne, and somehow, Mom didn't, just looked on with the proudest eyes and the widest smile. And afterward, we all watched in amazement as Peter and Luisa performed a gorgeous series of tricks and dances that they dedicated to Brandon and Marianne, all longing glances and meaningful embraces. Then we danced, all of us, to tinny music from one of the battery-operated radios Gabe had tracked down. Brandon and Marianne, of course, and Elinor and Edward and Gabe and me, but I danced with Brandon, too, swung around the floor with Edward, performed a complicated and entirely made-up routine to "Dancing Queen" with my mom and my sisters. And when "Super Trouper" came on, this time Edward shared the spotlight with Elinor as our Meryl, and he absolutely crushed it.

By the end of the evening, as the sun started to lower, and we'd all munched on pretzels and chips and peanut butter sandwiches, I was exhausted but so, so happy. Gabe and I swayed in each other's arms, and I was surrounded by love, encompassed by love, buoyed by love.

Sure, there were times that love could hurt you. But I knew, undeniably, that it was worth it for this. That anything was worth it for this.

"I love you, Margaret," Gabe whispered in my ear as the sun set behind us, and I said it back, knowing that for the rest of my life, no matter what happened, I'd be better for having loved Gabe Monteiro. For having loved my family. For not being afraid of connection.

Gabe and I danced, and my family surrounded me, and I knew I could do anything. *Be* anything.

I just had to be myself first.

ACKNOWLEDGMENTS

Here we are again! It's hard to believe this is my third book to come out into the world. Playing with Jane Austen's characters is always an immense joy and privilege, and to take them on a tropical vacation is even more of a delight. As a full-on ocean-loving beach girl, getting to spend time on the *Queen Mab* was so much fun—but just like every ship needs a crew, this book wouldn't have been possible without the help of my amazing team.

First off, thanks to Moe Ferrara and everyone at Book-Ends, for your continued support of my fast-talking girls and all of the shenanigans they get into.

To Sarah Grill, editor to the stars, who held my hand through draft after draft and never ran out of boat puns. It's always the suite life with you.

To the entire team at Wednesday Books—Rivka Holler, Zoë Miller, Eric Meyer, Diane Dilluvio, Cassie Gutman, Kelly Too—thank you for your love and support of both me and this book. And to Olga Grlic, for your amazing cover design—you blew me away with this one, and it really is the beach read vibes of my dreams.

To my critique partner and great friend, Ann Fraistat, who is always down to brainstorm the most chaotic scenarios and will always tell me when I forget to describe a scene. I couldn't do this without you.

To the other amazing authors who've offered me support, friendship, and guidance along the way—Ashley Schumacher, Tiffany Schmidt, Stephanie Kate Strohm, Jenny Howe, JC Peterson, Emma Lord, and Andrea Tang, among others— thank you for everything.

I grew up cruising, a benefit of living in Florida, but also because of my grandparents, Frank and Janet Wockenfuss, who showed me how much fun ocean-based adventures with the whole family can be. I'm raising a souvenir refillable cup in your honor. I'd also like to thank Jen Lefforge and Kelly and Joe Young, whose YouTube cruise videos were just the inspiration I needed while working on this book.

To bookstores and libraries everywhere, and especially to the booksellers and librarians inside them, who have gotten my books into the hands of people who need them—you really are the music makers and the dreamers of dreams, and the world would be a much smaller and sadder place without you. A special shout-out, of course, to my family at One More Page Books in Arlington, Virginia, home of the world's best boss, Eileen McGervey, in addition to the best staff ever. Much love, too, to the group chat that spawned out of it— Lelia, Rebecca, Anna, Rosie, and Lauren—who are some of the most supportive friends a girl can ask for.

And to my other friends, from D.C. to Pittsburgh and everywhere else we've landed, thank you for your endless support, encouragement, and preorders. I don't know what I did to deserve all of you, but I'm sure glad you're here. Special thanks to Carly, who is always down to hear me blabber on about my books with literally no context. I promise you can read it now!

To my amazing extended family—how did I get so lucky to be related to the coolest people on the planet? I don't know, but I'll take it. Special shout-out to Lucy, who, as of this writing, is the latest member of the Quain family—can't wait to read you a lifetime of stories, kiddo.

Did I mention I have a great family? Because my in-laws are the absolute coolest. Love to Virginia, Randy, Erica, Ben, Avery, and Cooper, who never cease to make me glad we're now related. I hope you enjoy the Brazilian touches in this book—they're in your honor.

And to my amazing parents, Bill and Jeanne, and my sister, Kathleen—I've said it before, and I'll say it again, I keep writing books about families because mine is the best one out there. Thank you for your constant support of my dreams, and, Kathleen, thanks for letting me drag you around on our "research cruise." You are truly a dancing queen.

I will continue to thank my cat, Jenny, in every acknowledgments that I write, even though she can't read, because if she ever figures it out I want her to have a written record of how much I love her. Jenny, thank you for forcing me to take breaks whenever you decide it's time to crawl onto my lap and push my laptop away. You're the best girl.

And finally, to Dustin, the light of my life and the best partner I could ever ask for. In the spirit of being competitive, I'm putting it in writing so that it counts as an official win: I really, truly, love you most.